FRACTURED MATES

A MYSTICS AND MAYHEM NOVEL

USA TODAY BESTSELLING AUTHOR

HEATHER RENEE

Contents

Chapter One

Sophie

I've always thought of that time I murdered my mate as the greatest day of my life, but maybe I've been wrong. As I sit in this old diner, huddled in a corner booth all by my lonesome and relishing in the most savory meal I've ever tasted, I start to question what should hold the title of "Best Day Ever."

Staring at the meaty burger topped with an Anaheim pepper, pepper jack cheese, and bacon, all drizzled in barbeque sauce, I try to convince myself that a kickass foodie day has to be better than anything else. Especially anything to do with the man I wish I'd never met.

Yet, the animal in me won't ever agree to that.

Killing Thane changed everything for us and you know it, my wolf says compellingly. *He would have caged us, and that would have only ended one way.*

I know she's right, but as sauce dribbles down my chin and my chest rumbles in satisfaction, I can't find the will to agree. All I can appreciate in this moment is the delicious meal and the Oreo shake it came with.

It's been over ten years since I fled my pack and was relocated to Texas. While the pack there had been everything the protectors who found me had promised, I hadn't stayed long.

The need to be on the go, doing as I please, and watching my own back is too strong for me to stay in one place for long. The alphas Cait and Roman have allowed me my freedom, insisting their pack is still my home, but their words only serve as a safeguard for me.

When I'm asked where I'm from and say East Texas, people don't screw with me as much. Well, as long as I don't stick around long enough for them to get suspicious.

Though, from the sounds of it, Cait and Roman are ready to "retire," so the pack will soon be in the hands of Dawsyn and her dragon mate Cillian. I'm not sure if my wanderer arrangement will continue working out, but I'm going to take advantage as long as I can.

"You look like you need a few more napkins, hon," the waitress says with a knowing smirk as she sets a stack next to my plate. "Can I get you a refill on your shake?"

I nod with my mouth full, then force myself to swallow. "Thanks. This is the best burger I've ever tasted."

She winks at me, a spark of confidence shining in her hazel eyes. "Of course it is." She glances back toward the kitchen and sighs. "My Henry knows what he's doing back there."

The longing in not only her voice but her gaze sends a twinge of pain through my chest, one I resent with every fiber of my being.

Being human, this woman doesn't know the connection of a fated mate bond, but I do.

I know how all-encompassing it can feel, how in one moment you can feel so lost, then start to believe that everything in the world is finally right. Yet, I also know how wrong those feelings can be. How everything you've been told suddenly becomes the biggest lie to ever exist.

A shudder runs through me, and I close my eyes until the waitress speaks again. I hadn't even realized she was still standing next to the table.

"Are you cold?" she asks. "We can move you farther from the vent.

Grabbing one of the napkins, I wipe my face and shake my head as I force a smile to my lips. "I'm good. Thank you."

She pats the tabletop and returns my grin. "Well, all right, then. You just holler if you need anything at all and I'll have a refill right up."

If only all humans could be this nice...

I stare back down at my burger, but my normal, ravenous appetite has faded away. Thinking about Thane typically does that to me.

He's the only son of a bitch who has that kind of power over me, and he doesn't even exist any longer.

I buried him in the ground twelve years ago, but he still finds a way to fuck with me. I thought once he was dead that I wouldn't miss the mate bond. Yet, no matter how much I hate him and am glad he's dead, there's a part of me that can't stop caring about him. That alone pisses me off more than anything else, knowing that he still has some sort of hold on me, even from the grave.

Taking a deep breath, I calm my rising rage and close my eyes. I picture the river back in East Texas and the rock I used to sleep against when being around the pack became too much.

Their sympathetic looks were a constant reminder of what I'd been forced to do.

And we had every right to kill him, my wolf says, as she always does. *He would have raped us, caged us, and eventually killed us, one way or another. It was him or us. How do you not see that after all this time?*

I do *see it, but knowing something and believing it are two different things. I know that shifting and allowing you to rip Thane's heart from his human chest was the right thing to do, because he truly was a monster. Yet...I became a murderer and lost my fated mate all in the same moment.*

We did that, *she corrects.* Plus, he was a shitty person and deserved what he got.

And I'm not, I reply. Which means I still have guilt, no matter how happy I am to be on our own.

My wolf becomes quiet, and I take that time to pick a bit more at my burger, then thank the waitress for my refill before drinking half the shake in just a couple of gulps.

I stare at the other patrons in the diner. They're smiling

and laughing, enjoying their simple life in this backroad, country town in southern Colorado. Nobody here is alone like I am, and while I tell myself I prefer it this way, I've been thinking about the past way more than usual and have been heading in the direction of East Texas for weeks now.

There's nothing wrong with having a pack, my wolf says, listening in on my thoughts.

I know she'd be happy about that. As much fun as we have on the road, doing as we please, deep down, pack is life. They're family and safety and home. I've known that since the first time I ran away—right after initially meeting Thane—and felt truly alone.

Thane's parents had moved to our pack in South Carolina and were instant celebrities with their deep pockets and powerful wolves. So much so that even my parents took their side when I told them I wasn't ready to be a mate.

I had no idea why the fates would do that to me at only sixteen, especially since Thane had been twenty-three, but I learned quickly that I was the only person I could count on.

Thane didn't like that I had my own opinions. He wanted me to cower before him, to do whatever he commanded, but that isn't who I've ever been. I wanted to be his mate, but I wasn't ready to let him fuck me or believe he owned me.

Maybe I would have been if he'd shown me even an ounce of respect, but he'd never even called me by name. He'd merely referred to me as *his* mate in a way that made it clear I would be his *property*. I couldn't fathom letting that happen.

Though, it wasn't just the future with a fated mate that I lost back then. I lost my home and my family, including a little sister who had only been five at the time. I ran from them, and nobody objected. To say that left me with a few additional issues would be an understatement.

Since then, I've avoided pretty much everyone I can. But as the years tick by, I wonder if I've made a mistake.

Not in killing Thane—that fucker deserved what he got, regardless of my lingering guilt—but by running away from my problems and never turning back.

You know what we need to do, my wolf says, voice filled with compassion.

She's not wrong. Neither of us has said the words out loud, but we've both known for weeks now.

It's time to go home. Our first home.

Before we can go back to South Carolina, though, we need to see Cait and Roman. They've done more for me than anyone else would have ever considered—even my own parents. They deserve to know what my plans are, and I'm going to give them that respect. Right before I tell them I want to be relinquished from their pack, allowing me to rejoin my old one, should that be an option.

I gave myself twelve years to heal, and I've done what I can to move on. The rest will need to be done where it all went wrong. I know the only way to truly get past what happened is to face it head on. At least I know enough about myself to know that's what I need.

Time clearly hasn't done shit for me.

We're stronger than we were back then, my wolf says. *We can handle whatever waits for us there. Remind them that leaving didn't make us weak.*

No, it didn't. Not many wolves could have done what I had, nor could they have survived the soul-deep loneliness that came with not only leaving our home, but with severing ties to our fated mate.

I don't know that I would have survived without my wolf, and she's been the only companion I've needed in my life...until now. Though, it's not necessarily companionship I'm seeking by going home. Closure and a fresh start where I should have always been feels more accurate.

If Thane hadn't shown up, I'm certain I never would have left my pack. But I wouldn't be the person I am now if he hadn't, so who the hell knows what might have been.

With a sharp shake of my head, I reach into my back pocket and toss a hundred-dollar bill on the table. It's more than quadruple the amount to cover my bill, but well-deserved for how damned tasty everything was and the excellent service.

I pluck a few more fries from the plate and give the quarter of leftover burger a longing glance when I stand from the booth.

Food can be my mate, I think to myself and chuckle.

I've entered into a very committed relationship with all things food, and I have no complaints whatsoever.

Especially fudge brownies with ice cream. That's my kryptonite. I'll eat every crumb, even when I'm certain I'll be sick.

If only the carbs you love could service *more than your stomach,* my wolf complains with snark.

It's not as if we've been celibate, you little hussy, I retort. *It's only been…*

Eleven weeks and four days, she finishes when I take too long to sort out the timeline in my head.

Yes, I was lucky enough to be paired with a badass wolf, but she also has needs I never anticipated. Not to say that I don't enjoy sex. It's just…not all that great.

Because you're doing it wrong.

I'm halfway out the diner door when her words make me stumble. I'm not sure if I should be entertained or insulted.

Both, she answers for me, all too smugly.

Damn wolf.

That's enough from you, I reply, my irritation back in full force. It doesn't last long, though. *We're going to East Texas, and then maybe we'll stop in New Orleans to see Matt.*

She sighs. *I guess he'll do. His wolf is only mildly annoying.*

I chuckle as I get into my car. Strong, horny, and picky. That's my wolf.

Glancing back at the diner, I'm already having regrets about not taking my leftovers, but I don't dwell for long.

I've made up my mind. We're going to show Cait and Roman the respect they deserve, and then we're going to make our way back to South Carolina.

I have no clue if I'll be welcomed. Especially after having killed a pack member. While I know it was in self-defense and the protectors promised me that I was safe from retribution, that doesn't mean his family hasn't held a grudge or even my parents for the ramifications I'm sure they dealt with from my leaving.

I haven't spoken to them in years—really, only my mother—but at the same time, this isn't about them. It's about me. Nothing is going to stop me from getting the closure I seek.

Returning to my pack will either give me back the home I've been running from for far too long, or it will give me the absolution from the guilt I've been holding on to.

Either way, I'll get what I need. I'm done waiting.

Chapter Two

Sophie

Driving up the tree-lined road toward the pack house in East Texas, I'm consumed with feelings I don't bother to sort out. I'm here for one reason and one reason only. I might have preferred to be on my own for the most part over the years, but I still respect the hierarchy.

Nobody greets me when I park my car in front of the two-story white house. Then again, nobody is expecting me. I take in the pristine siding and admire the two turrets, only one of which I've been in to speak with Roman.

I spent most of my time here avoiding the pack house. I thought that was just because I'm not much of a people person, but staring out the window, I can admit that trying to be part of their pack only served as a reminder of what I'd lost.

Sure, I'm the one who ran away, but thanks to Thane and his pompous family, not once did my parents ask me to come back once they'd learned what I'd done. I can assume all the reasons for that as I've done many times in the past, but I'm not doing that any longer.

Gods, this is possibly the dumbest thing I've ever done or the smartest. Either way, I'm not backing down. I can't live with *what ifs* any longer. I refuse.

No more wondering what might have been if Thane had never shown his smug face in my pack. No more wondering what my life would be like if he hadn't been the world's biggest douchebag.

Just no more.

I catch my reflection in the rearview mirror before I open the car door. My light-green eyes look tired from all the driving I've been doing, but my sleek, chestnut hair shines, thanks to the shower in the hotel last night.

A small, white scar at my hairline glints under the sunlight filtering through the window. One of two physical reminders that Thane was ever part of my life. I close my eyes, turn away from the mirror, and get out of the car.

If I'm going to move on, I need to get that fucker out of my thoughts and keep him out.

As I step onto the first stair, the front door opens and there stands Dawsyn. I expected Cait, but seeing her daughter is no hardship. She's just as kind as her mother and equally as understanding, especially when it comes to me wanting to be on my own. At least, she had been. Becoming the official alpha might change that.

"Sophie," she says with a friendly grin. "You're the last person I expected to see today."

I shrug and continue up the steps to shake her hand. "I was in the area."

"Bullshit." She chuckles. "Now, get in here and tell me what's going on."

My brows raise at her command, and I toss a curious glance her way. "Tell *you*? Not your parents?"

The way her head rises, strands of dark-brunette hair framing her round face and golden eyes briefly glowing, tells me my answer, but it's the pride in her voice that makes me happiest.

"I'm handling all alpha duties for the pack now."

Before she's even finished the sentence, I clasp her shoulder and match the smile on her face. "It's about damn time."

She doesn't boast. Instead, once we're inside the pack house, she leads the way toward the stairs on the right. "How about we chat in my office?"

I nod and follow behind, noticing tension building in her shoulders.

She's nervous, my wolf says.

Yeah, I'm seeing that, too. Though, there's no way she could know why I'm here. Suddenly, I'm even more glad I decided to stop at the pack first.

We climb the steep stairwell through the turret and arrive at the small landing that leads only to what used to be Roman's office. Dawsyn pushes open the door, and I blink several times.

The walls have gone from darker tan to a light, cream color. The dark wooden desk I remember from before has been replaced with a sleek, metal one, and the previous hardwood floors are covered in a plush, grey carpet that feels soft, even under my boots.

On the wall are colorful abstract paintings, along with a few family photos that I don't linger on long. "I like what you've done with the place."

She sits in the white, leather chair behind her desk and smiles. "Take a seat, Sophie."

When I do, I set my sights on her. "You weren't expecting me today, but you have something to tell me."

Her head shakes lightly, and there's a glint of approval in her bright eyes. "Always so insightful."

"What happened?" I ask, wondering if it has anything to do with why she's in the office and I was never notified. Just because I haven't been in the pack doesn't mean I'm not still tied to this place and these people.

In fact, I should have felt the change of power, but I don't have an increased connection to Dawsyn. Not like I felt being around Roman before I left.

"Is your father dead?" My question is cold and direct and has her flinching back.

"No. Why would you think that?" she replies, face paling.

My hand gestures toward her. "You're not my alpha."

Her shoulders drop ever so slightly. "Well, not officially, but I am in charge, as I said before. We're waiting on the next new moon before the transfer of power goes from Roman to me."

"Then I think I do need to speak with Cait and Roman," I say. Dawsyn won't be able to release me from the pack. Not yet and I'm not waiting another two weeks.

She folds her hands over her desk and leans forward. "Listen, Sophie—"

I shake my head. "I came here because I respect your family. I didn't come here for permission to do what I want."

"You can't go back to South Carolina," she says pointedly.

"And who says that's where I'm headed?" I counter, not having the slightest interest in revealing the truth.

Her lips thin, and she stares intently at me, but I don't break. "Fine. Keep your secrets, but you need to listen to me and know I'm not just saying this because you're here. You were on my list of people to call today."

She slides a piece of paper across her desk toward me. Sure enough, it's a to-do list with my name second on the list.

"Why?" is all I ask.

She shifts back in her seat and swallows. "Your old pack. The alpha is missing, and the beta has been killed."

"Your uncle—"

Dawsyn shakes her head. "He moved on just over a year ago. He and Kelly decided to retire on a beach, minimizing their responsibilities."

"Then, who?" I ask, fingers curling around the navy-blue, suede material of the chair beneath me.

"York Graves took over for him," she says. "Now, he's been named interim alpha, but things are tense there. Your pack isn't the same place you might remember,

Sophie. I need you to stay away from there. At least until things have been...settled."

She could just be referring to the new alpha placement. With bigger packs, a change in leader can sometimes lead to a death challenge. I hope that's something Dawsyn is prepared for, but I'm more concerned about what's happening in my old pack at the moment.

Yet, the way she said "settled" makes me believe something else is going on.

"Who was the alpha before he went missing?" I ask next, because if it's Thane's father Astor, then the alpha isn't missing. He's strategically fucking with my pack.

"A man named Joseph Lane," she replies coolly. "Do you know him?"

I shake my head, but I knew *of* him. He was friends with my father, but not close enough that he came around the house. I'd just heard the name in passing conversations between my parents.

"So, why would you need to call me about this?" I ask. "My pack has been East Texas for over a decade now."

There's no way Dawsyn could have known the decision I made less than twenty-four hours ago, but I want to know what she thinks I have to do with this before I say anything more.

"Because I've been specifically told to keep you safe." Her words are like a bucket of ice being thrown over my head.

I blink twice. "No."

"No, what?" Her lips purse, as if she's more than intrigued by my response.

"You're not keeping me prisoner here, Dawsyn," I say with a growl. "I will fight until my death before I allow that to happen."

She holds her hands up innocently. "Calm down. That isn't and wasn't my plan. I was going to call you back here, tell you what I just have, and advise you to stay with the pack, but you're a grown-ass woman. You're going to do what you want."

This feels like some screwed-up reverse psychology, and I'm not going to fall for it.

"Good," I say, then stand from my chair. "I appreciate the information about my old pack, but that isn't important to me. I came here for a reason, and it seems I need your father."

Dawsyn doesn't bother to stand as she stares intently at me. "You want to be released from the pack."

"I do."

"Why?" she asks. "After all these years, why now? Why still, after what I've just told you? And why haven't you asked me about your family and more about what's happening there now?"

She's going to make one hell of an alpha, but she isn't mine. She can't force me to answer those questions, but I will tell her something.

"It's not my problem," I say. "I don't care that the alpha is missing or that the beta is dead. Just like none of them cared when I left."

At least, that's what I've assumed all this time after

years of silence from them. What she's told me has changed my thoughts. I'm not returning to South Carolina to find my home. I thought I could have both that and closure, but that's only wishful thinking. I only need to see my family. However they greet me will dictate my subsequent actions. Including asking my parents and younger sister to flee whatever fucked-up situation the pack has gotten themselves into.

"Right." Dawsyn finally rises from her chair and moves around her desk to stand toe-to-toe with me. "My father isn't here. He and my mother are on a little vacation. They won't be back for a week. You're welcome to stay or—"

"I'll be back, then," I say. "Maybe I'll even watch you officially get your new title."

Not that Dawsyn and I were ever close or even friends, given our age difference, which is only seven years. As adults now, it doesn't feel like such a stretch, but when I was only sixteen and she was twenty-three, it seemed like a lot. Even still, she's always shown me respect.

When I arrived here as a messed-up teenager with a chip on my shoulder, she never treated me like the child I still was. Instead, she made sure I had access to the resources I needed to become an adult who wouldn't completely fuck up her life just because she'd become a murderer at the ripe age of sixteen.

"Astor Crowe has inserted himself as acting beta," Dawsyn adds, and the words have me tensing, something I'm certain she doesn't miss.

"I. Don't. Care." The words are forced from between my gritted teeth.

Her eyes bore into me, and her mouth forms into a tight line. "Sophie. Don't do this."

I'm torn between lying to her and telling her I don't give a shit what she says. The truth is that I do care, but more than I respect Dawsyn and her family, I need to do what I've already decided.

Neither my wolf nor I will be able to rest until we have this closure. Sure, it's not convenient that the pack is falling apart and the family I despise most is partly in charge, but I'm twenty-eight. Still young in supernatural years, but old enough that I need to move on. I don't know another way to do so besides going back.

Except I don't believe Dawsyn will just let me go if I tell her the truth. As much as I hate lying to her, I don't stop the words as they leave my mouth. Though they're not exactly a lie. Just an omission of what I intend to do afterward.

"I'm going to head to New Orleans," I say, relaxing my shoulders and softening my face. "I have a...special friend there that I need to see."

She glowers at me but can't hold back her smile for long. "*Special*, huh?"

I shrug and return her grin. "I mean, not that special, but my wolf... She's needy and he's, well, easy."

That has her laughing so loudly that sound echoes through the office and has me chuckling as well.

"All right, Sophie," she finally says. "You go have your

fun, and I expect you back here before the new moon. Got it?"

"Yes, Alpha." I wink at her and turn toward the door, thinking I'm making a clean escape, but as soon as my fingers wrap around the metal handle, Dawsyn calls my name, giving me pause.

When I turn my gaze back toward her, I'm pinned in place by golden eyes full of compassion that have my guilt rising even more as she says, "I know you think you want to be relinquished from our pack, but maybe my dad not being here isn't a coincidence. Maybe whatever brought you here isn't, either. Just remember that you're not alone anymore. You have people in this world who care about you right here."

I force a smile to my face and nod once. "Yeah, maybe."

Making a swift exit, I'm out the door and closing it behind me before she can say anything else.

Most wolf shifters are big believers in fate, and I used to be one of them. Until twelve years ago. So, I don't agree with everything she's just said, but maybe I will once I'm done with what I know I can no longer avoid.

Going home and facing my demons.

Chapter Three

Kyler

Wind blows all around me, and waves crash roughly along the sandy beach just two hundred feet below the balcony I stand on. The sky has transitioned from a bright blue to a dismal grey, and as raindrops start to pelt against my skin, I wonder if this is the fates rubbing salt in my still-open wounds.

I shove my hands roughly into my pockets and turn around to head inside the small cottage I've rented for the couple of weeks I have off.

It's been mission after mission lately, and while I need this time, I've only just arrived and already regretting my choice to spend the entirety of my vacation here.

Fourteen years have passed since my mate was taken from me. Though, "taken" is too nice a word. Cara was ripped from this world, her light snuffed out, never to be seen again.

I let the door slam behind me as I enter the house and see the flowers I've left on the table. Every year during this week, I've come here and mourned all over again, wallowing in the misery that has become my life, knowing that the best part of my soul will never smile up at me or laugh at my anger over the little things.

My chest is hollow, as if someone has been slowly carving the center out with a spoon over the years. Still, I grab the bouquet and head toward the front door, intent to stop procrastinating. A new emotion to the grief. Each anniversary is different. Some years, I can't keep my eyes dry for even an hour; others, I don't shed a single tear. There's always a certain level of rage simmering, though.

Even with the hesitation to visit Cara's gravesite, I still sense the unwavering fury that has lived within my heart since she was killed. Yet as I walk out the front door, I can't deny it's not as severe as usual. Maybe I'm finally starting to heal.

Climbing into my truck, I set the flowers on the seat next to me and turn the engine over. The rumble of the exhaust mixes with the pinging of raindrops landing on the roof of the truck, but none of it drowns out the ache growing inside me.

My wolf stirs in my mind, not saying anything, but I can tell he doesn't agree with my thoughts. I don't bother to ask him what, exactly, is bothering him or why.

He's barely spoken to me since our mate died. We still work together just fine, but it's a quiet relationship that we've settled into.

As I drive toward the cemetery, I allow my thoughts

to drift away and only focus on the pain inside me. My wolf stays present but still silent, and I begin to wonder what I might be missing, what he's not saying.

It wasn't until I arrived in Virginia that I realized how off I felt, but for the first time, it's not in a bad way. The darkness I've been drowning in since losing Cara isn't as bleak as I expect. There's a softness to the grief, almost like it's slipping away. As if I'm letting her go, but the tighter I try to grasp the pain, the further it seems to float away, like it's her pulling away. Not me.

My wolf growls quietly in my mind, and I know I've just figured out his displeasure.

It's not as if I want to, I say to him, even though he should already know my true feelings.

Still, he doesn't respond.

We get to the cemetery, and I reach for the flowers beside me before getting out. The rain hasn't made it this far inland yet, so I take advantage, jogging toward the headstones.

This place is mostly filled with human graves, but Cara's family was a little unique in that they preferred to live amongst the humans. That was how they were laid to rest as well.

Considering I had no idea where I was going to live or what I was going to do when she died, I did what I hoped was the right thing. I had her buried with her parents.

But before I can get to their corner of this depressing place, I make a stop in the middle. It took me years to stop hating this man, but I learned that forgiving him for something he couldn't control was something I needed to do for me.

Arnold Franklin Morsey. He lived for seventy-three years before having a heart attack while driving a small pickup truck with a few two-by-fours in the back.

When he crashed into my Cara... I squeeze my eyes closed, attempting to block out the image of that horrid day.

It shouldn't have been possible. She shouldn't have died like that—not with her wolf shifter genes—but she did, and there had been nothing I could do to save her.

When I'd heard her cries through our bond, I had never been so terrified in my life. I felt her pain, but more than that, I felt her fear, which nearly paralyzed me. Even still, the horror of what I might find hadn't stopped me from going to her. Not even as my soul had literally felt as if it were shattering into more and more pieces as I got closer to her.

I place a few of the flowers at the base of Arnold's headstone and remove the ones I last left. I've never seen signs of anyone else here, which added to the reasons for me to turn soft toward the old man.

My hand pats the top of the concrete slab before I stand and nod. The only words I've ever spoken to the man were "I forgive you." He didn't mean to rip my life apart, but it was nice to have someone to blame for a few years.

Making my way toward Cara, I ignore the wind that starts to pick up, just like it had at the house. I'm sure the rain won't be far behind, but nothing will rush me today.

Once I'm standing in front of her grave, there's a warmth that moves through me. It could all be in my head, but I still smile.

"Hello, Mate," I say softly then kneel, replacing the flowers in the metal vase secured next to her marble headstone.

My fingers brush over her name—Cara Samantha Havens. She was only twenty years old when she was taken from this world, and she was mine.

A shiver runs down my spine. I close my eyes, remembering her love and kindness and the light that followed her wherever she went.

Even when I'd shown up at the accident site before she took her final breaths, she smiled for me. Told me that everything would be okay and that I wouldn't always feel so alone. She cared more about me in those final moments than she did for herself.

Tears sting at my eyes and I squeeze them closed, taking a shuddering breath. Without something to focus my gaze on, all I can see is the two-by-four that pierced through the windshield of Cara's car and went right through my mate's stomach.

There was nothing her wolf healing could do. She'd lost too much blood by the time I'd arrived, only seconds before the ambulance. Even if I'd removed the obstruction, we both knew.

I shake my head, demanding the memory to leave my thoughts. Instead, I focus on her blonde hair, light-blue eyes, and olive skin, remembering her wide smile and the dimples on her cheeks that were almost always present.

I recall her laugh and the way it warmed my heart unlike anything else on this Earth ever has. The way her touch branded me until I no longer belonged to myself but to her.

My wolf makes a rumbling noise that feels a lot like acceptance. He doesn't want us to move on. He wants to live in the memory of Cara.

For a long time, that was all I wanted, too. I never wished to be without her, but it's been fourteen years of being on the run from life. Yes, I've been living, but I haven't truly been alive.

I spend my days and nights protecting others or hunting down those who wish to do harm. I have no home. No pack. No family. Hell, I barely even have a wolf.

While my co-workers have been a decent substitute for a pack, it's not the same and never will be. Speaking of work...

My phone vibrates in my pocket, and I groan. The only times it ever rings are when I'm being summoned for another job, but they know I'm supposed to be off the clock right now. Whatever this is, it's important.

With reluctance, I answer. "Yeah?"

"Kyler, it's Maciah."

Well, shit. He rarely calls himself anymore. This must be more than important.

"What can I do for you, Maciah?" I ask, my eyes focused on my mate's name as I await his answer, surprisingly excited about the prospect of another job.

There's a brief pause before he speaks again. "Listen,

I know you're blocked out for personal time right now, and I understand how important these days are to you. I wouldn't call if it weren't important."

This is why I've been one of the protectors for as long as I have. Yes, we work long hours and put ourselves at risk every time we go out, but the people behind us care. Maciah isn't my alpha—he's not even a wolf shifter—but he's possibly as close as I'll ever get to one again.

"It's okay," I say. "What do you need?"

"We have a situation with a pack in South Carolina," he replies sharply. "The alpha is missing, and the beta has been found murdered. The family trying to take over is one we've had our eye on for a while now and, well, it's complicated to the point I can't fully explain, but we need more help."

"So, you need me and some others to go in and neutralize the situation?" I ask. He isn't really saying what he needs, which has my curiosity piqued even more.

"Not exactly." He's quiet again before continuing. "We need you to go in by yourself, extract one particular wolf shifter, get her to safety, and then return with a group of other protectors, depending on what we learn between now and then."

My fingers tap over the back of the phone. I want to ask who this wolf shifter is and why she's special enough to be pulled out alone, but I know it's not my job to ask questions. I trust Maciah with my life and do what he asks, simple as that. Yet, I can't help but think I'm missing something crucial.

"What do I need to know about the shifter?" I ask,

hoping that's the best way to get him to elaborate without me being intrusive.

"Her name is Sophie," he begins. "She doesn't belong in South Carolina any longer, but it's where she's from. She was warned to stay away, but we have reason to believe she didn't listen and is nearly to the pack now. You're the closest protector we have in the area, and we need you to intercept her before she blows everything up."

"How can one girl do that?" I can't help myself. I need to know more.

He chuckles, and the sound doesn't bode well for me. "She's not just 'one girl.' Sophie has been fighting for her life since she was sixteen. Don't underestimate her. The family taking over the pack would like to see her dead, and Dawsyn from East Texas will start a war if that happens."

"Am I safe to assume Sophie is one of their wolves?" Though if that's the case, I'm not sure why Roman didn't just force her to stay. I know that pack well and they're not to be messed with, even on their worst days.

"Technically," he says, then adds, "It's complicated. How soon can you get to the pack down there and stop her from showing her face?"

I glance at Cara's headstone and frown. Normally, I'm here for hours, but oddly enough, I'm ready to go and hate myself for admitting that.

Considering the growl I get from my wolf, so does he.

"I can be there within a few hours," I answer, my

decision made. "Send me her information and I'll update you as soon as I find her."

"Thanks, Kyler," he says. "I knew I could trust you with this. I promise not to make a habit out of disrupting your time off in the future."

He hangs up and I stand, pressing my fingers to my lips before resting them on the headstone. "I'll see you, Mate."

It's never been goodbye with us. I know I'll eventually find her again. In the next lifetime or three after that. Her death didn't mark the end of our story.

More than that, as I've begun to allow myself to heal instead of living in her memory, I know this isn't the end of mine, either. I wasn't left behind to spend my life grieving and protecting others. Even if that's all I've allowed myself to do for over a decade.

That's something my wolf will need to eventually figure out as well. We can still love Cara and respect her memory while moving forward with our lives. I won't ever forget her, but I don't need to live in grief to honor her.

I hope for something from my wolf. A rumble or even rising anger, but unsurprisingly, I get nothing from him as I turn away from the grave and head back to my truck.

It's time to pack up my shit and get to work. I'll have to sort out these new thoughts another day.

Chapter Four

Sophie

New Orleans was a bust. Much to my wolf's dismay, Matt wasn't around the couple of places we looked, and he didn't answer his phone. Since I have no patience, I refused to wait around for a hookup. Though, I did take a detour to stock up on snacks and grab myself some jambalaya and beignets for the road.

Now, we're arriving in South Carolina within two days rather than the three or four it would have taken if we'd been otherwise...occupied.

We could have found someone else, she quips.

And that would have taken time we don't have.

She knows I'm right. She won't admit it, but she also didn't fight me on wanting to get back to our old pack as quickly as possible.

Between my gut feeling of needing to return and the weird vibes we were getting from Dawsyn, I know we need to be here. I don't know why and I don't know what we're going to find, but I'm not backing down or running away.

Not any longer.

It's nearly dusk when I park my car in a dirt area at the start of a hiking trail. Humans frequent these woods and I'm still about ten miles from the pack, but I know I can't just drive right up to their front door. Not like I did in East Texas.

The protectors might have made sure nobody ever came after me, but that doesn't mean I'll be safe just showing up. That's what I need my family to tell me.

My plan is to get far enough on the trail where I won't likely be seen before shifting. I can run the rest of the way and check things out from a distance before stopping by my old home.

Even though it's been well over five years since I've heard my mother's voice and even longer for my father and sister, I could have reached out over the years as well. At least, that's what I keep telling myself, so I don't show up filled with resentment. *That* won't get me my closure.

If they want nothing to do with me when I arrive, well, maybe Dawsyn was right and I don't belong here. But that's something I need to sort out for myself. Not for anyone else to tell me.

After locking my car, I leave my bag behind and start the trek toward the dense and humid woods. The air is wet and the ground soft beneath my boots, as if it just rained. Everything is green with thriving foliage. There's a chill pressing in, but for October, this feels warm to my wolf shifter skin. As long as the bugs I hear rattling within the trees don't come at me, I'm fine with anything else.

A shifter afraid of some cicadas, my wolf says with feigned disappointment. *Honestly, could you get any more lame?*

Shut your mouth, I retort, not at all ashamed that I don't like six-legged creatures crawling on my skin.

With only my keys and phone in hand, I shove them into my back pockets—where they'll be safe even when I shift, thanks to the bit of magic wolves have—and jog toward the forest. Listening with my enhanced hearing, I don't sense anyone near, just more wildlife, but I still wait another five minutes before shifting.

One more cursory check around us to confirm we're alone and I start to let the energy of my wolf push forward.

Her presence begins to take control, and my skin vibrates with a power that has my bones shifting and reforming from human to animal within seconds. Coarse hair pushes through my skin as it basically shreds apart but then snaps back together, thanks to my wolf genes.

I land on four paws, and we shake out our fur as my wolf looks around. We might be two separate minds, but in this form, I consider us one while also allowing myself to take a back seat as she does her thing.

Her nose sniffs the air, checking once again for unwanted guests, and then she claws at the ground before running. We head north, which is actually farther away from the pack, but circling around is the better way to sneak up on anyone who might be out there on guard.

Thankfully, my childhood home is rather far from any other houses, so my hope is that there isn't anyone around to see me slip inside. But I won't be holding my breath on that.

If we were that lucky, we would have gotten *lucky last night*, my wolf huffs, making me chuckle.

Seriously, this beast has a one-track mind. Some days, I'm not sure what to do with her, even if she's rather entertaining.

She continues running through the trees, the wind whipping past us and everything becoming a blur except the path we've already chosen to take. I've never clocked our exact speed, but I know there aren't many wolf shifters who can outrun us.

Maybe that's because we've always been running, but I like to think it's our strength and wit that have us always ahead.

We continue to move strategically through the wooded area, leaving behind the public trails. Soon, we're far enough out that we *shouldn't* see any humans but where the wolves typically steer clear of, just in case.

The pack boundary line is just a mile ahead, I remind my wolf.

I know. She veers left instead of right like I was expecting.

Where are you going?

She's quiet for a beat. *Someone is following us.*

Shit. That was quick. Almost too quick, like they're expecting me, but I don't know how that could be.

How many? I ask since her senses are stronger than mine at the moment.

Just one.

I scoff. *What's the problem, then?*

She doesn't answer me. Instead, she stops behind a tree and looks around. *He's shifted back to human form.*

Then let's tear his throat out.

She tsks at me. *Or let's see what we can learn from him. Shift back.*

She makes a point, so I don't hesitate to draw my wolf shifter magic back, picturing my human form, standing on two feet, fully dressed as I do. Within seconds, the tingle returns, once again breaking bones as the energy moves through my body. This used to hurt like hell, but now, there's almost a euphoria that slithers through me when shifting.

I'm back in control and can scent the man getting closer. He smells of sandalwood, strong and dark. I reach down for the knife I always keep tucked into my boot and hold the hilt tightly within my palm.

He's almost here and not slowing down. I don't know if he expects me to back down or doesn't care that he's given himself away, but either way, he's about to learn I'm not someone to be fucked with.

Using the overgrown magnolia tree nearest to me, I climb up the twisty branches and use the height to my advantage, waiting for this wolf to show his face.

One minute, then two, passes and I can still scent him, but I can't hear his movements any longer. Maybe he's not as stupid as I was just thinking.

Still, I stay put. He'll have to come closer eventually. Or he'll leave, and then I can chase him. Either way, I'm not giving him the opportunity to sneak up on me.

Finally, I hear the crunch of a stick on the ground to my right. My head snaps in that direction. There he is. Standing as still as a statue and looking as if he were carved from stone like one.

His jaw is tight, covered by dark stubble. I don't even see his broad chest move as he seems to wait to see what I'll do now that he's given himself away.

A black T-shirt covers his torso, showing off muscles beneath the short sleeves with black ink tattoos covering the exposed skin of his arm. His jean-clad thighs are thick, and his feet are positioned to run. By the time I make my way back up to his face, his steely-grey eyes are on me and there's a deep crease between brows.

Neither of us says a word as he watches me, and I don't like the way his gaze pierces through my mind, causing an ache in my chest, as if he can read every thought circling through my mind.

Just because he's hot doesn't mean we can't torture him, my wolf reminds me.

Oh, how right she is.

In more than one way, she adds seductively, making my head shake as I leap from fifteen or so feet in the air and land with a light *thud* onto the forest floor.

Once I'm on the ground, my feet don't stay planted. I'm running again with my knife still in hand. Before Mr. Dark and Broody can move, I'm standing behind him with the blade pressing against his heart and my other hand wrapped around his neck. "Who are you?" I demand.

He tries to shake his head, but I tighten my hold until he makes a light, choking sound. "I don't like repeating myself," I say through gritted teeth.

The heat from his body seeps into mine, and I'm having serious regrets about not trying harder to find a replacement for Matt back in New Orleans.

It's been a long time since I've missed the touch of a man, but damn, this one is making me wish he weren't my enemy right now.

"I was sent here to stop you—"

I cut him off and shove him to the ground. "Nobody is stopping me from doing anything."

He's back on his feet and reaching for me before I even finish speaking, but I duck out of his hold, circling around behind him again.

My wolf was right before. We can use him to get the information Dawsyn didn't know about my old pack, or at least didn't want to tell me. Which means I need to be careful with my moves so that I don't *accidentally* kill this guy. A little pain isn't out of the question, though.

He spins back toward me, and my instincts have my fist punching at his throat, but he dodges my hit, rolling away from me without trying to fight back.

Leaping toward him, I wrap my arms around his shoulders and circle my legs around his waist, clinging to his back. My knife is positioned over his neck this time, but before I can speak, he shocks the hell out of me by easily grabbing both my forearms and flipping me over his head as if I weigh nothing.

"Stop, Sophie," he demands, but I don't listen. Not even when it throws me off that he somehow knows my name. Whoever this guy is, he's not going to get in my way. Though, if I'm some sort of target for him, keeping him alive may no longer be an option.

I charge forward again, this time allowing my wolf to push through, turning my nails into claws as I partially shift.

My hand swipes out at his stomach, hoping to see his guts spilling to the ground, but he once again evades me.

I expect retaliation, but he instead sidesteps me, moving just far enough to be out of reach.

"Sophie—"

He says my name again, almost as if he knows me, but I don't wait to hear him say anything more, not even if he wants to tell me how he knows who I am.

"Stay the fuck out of my way or die," I threaten, pointing the knife at him. "I don't much care."

He sighs at me like I'm nothing more than an annoyance to him, which has me seeing red in a split second.

With a snarl, I attack him once more. This time, he can't get out of my way. I sheathe the blade and shove him against a tree, using my claws to cut through his shirt and lightly into his skin.

Blood trickles down his chest, and I reach for his throat, but before I can choke him like I intend, he somehow swaps our positions and has my arms pinned to my sides.

"If you'd fucking *listen*—" he starts, but again, I don't let him finish.

"If you'd just fucking *die*." I get one arm free from his hold and punch his chiseled face, enjoying it when I hear something crack. Could be a bone or a tooth. I don't care. I just know I want to hear the sound again and again until he's no longer standing.

Being on my own for most of my life might have made me a little bloodthirsty, but I have no shame in my darker side. It's what has made me a survivor instead of a victim since the moment Thane Crowe showed up at my pack and decided I was a piece of property to be claimed instead of a mate to be cherished.

Except, before I can hit this sexy stranger again, he's pressing my back against the bark of the tree behind me, his body flush against mine. Frustration fills me...for more than one reason.

"I said, *stop*." His voice is low and grumbly, the deep tenor being absorbed by my entire body.

When I try to get out of his hold again, his grip on my forearms increases and the hard lines of his front side seem to meld with mine.

"No. You won't kill me," I practically spit in his face.

A *ding* sounds from my phone that's still tucked into my back pocket. When he loosens his position, I think he's going to stupidly let me go so I can check it, but instead, he puts his palm over my chest, forcing me to stay pinned to the tree. His hand plucks my phone from my jeans, and he shoves the screen in my face.

"I'm not here to kill you, Sophie," he seethes as I read the screen.

Dawsyn: I know what you're doing. If you won't heed my warnings, at least accept the help I've sent. A protector named Kyler Murphy should find you soon. Listen to him and play nice. There's more at play than can be discussed yet.

Son of a bitch.

"Are you done now?" he asks with a light smirk on his face that I want to smack away.

I give him a solid shove and shake my head before stepping forward and stealing my phone back. "Not even close. Don't follow me."

Friend or foe, hot or not, I don't need this man's help. This is my family, and I'm handling this my way.

I shift and take off for my old home. This guy can kiss my ass.

Chapter Five

Kyler

I watch as she shifts into her honey-colored wolf and darts away from me. I could have easily caught her before she got too far but decide it's better to let her go. Likely not the choice Maciah would want me to make, but I've learned over the years of doing this job that plans sometimes change.

Ten seconds pass before I call my own wolf forward. He's quick to transform and seems almost eager to run. I don't know if it's the distraction of the job or something else, but I don't bother to ask, knowing I won't get a reply.

He gives chase, and we easily pick up her scent. She's moving strategically, staying quiet as she goes, but there's no denying her sweet smell. It's stark amongst the woodsy smell of the forest and has me yearning for something I haven't in much too long.

It's not as if I've been celibate since my mate died, but I've never *craved* another woman in my bed. Merely taken the opportunity when it fit my mood, knowing that denying my wolf even a surface-level connection could be the very thing that makes us snap.

I sense his agreement, surprised when there's no layer of annoyance mixed in with his emotions. Even more, I find myself intrigued by how focused he seems to be on the task at hand. Considering he didn't seem to want to leave Cara's grave, he sure is hellbent on chasing this wolf.

We spot Sophie again, and all other thoughts leave my mind. She's shifted back to her human form, but I stay as my wolf. If she's about to be attacked, I'd rather be prepared to rip heads off.

She stops at the tree line, staring at a house tucked in the forest. It's a moderate-sized home with green-painted wood siding, a few windows, and a couple of wildflower patches. There aren't any lights on, and I don't hear anything, but I smell others. The place hasn't been empty for long, if it even is.

Something feels off. I don't like it. I'd been fine letting her go ahead, but the longer I watch, the more I'm thinking that's a mistake.

I start to creep ahead, but before I can catch up to Sophie, she's running toward the house and hunkering down beneath a window. Well, at least she's being cautious.

As much as I want to follow her, I don't want to alert anyone to my presence until I know if this is a trap. I can't fuck this up, regardless of how stubborn this she-wolf seems. My job is all I have. Even if I'd just been thinking that I want more, I don't want to lose the only thing I have in my life to get me out of bed.

My eyes stay trained on Sophie, taking in her straight, dark-brown hair that falls down to her mid-back and the muscled curves that line her body, reminding me of how it felt to be flush with her as I pressed her against that tree.

I give my head a solid shake. No. She's a job. Nothing more. I've never mixed business with pleasure, and I'm not going to start now.

Not even for a green-eyed beauty who just might be capable of taking care of herself, despite what her pack seems to think. I feel confident about that, considering she cracked my jawbone, which is still trying to heal but with shifting back and forth, even my wolf healing isn't working as quickly as I hope.

Sophie stands and slides the window open. I listen for any movement, but there's nothing other than wind.

Sophie climbs through and disappears into the dark house. When I don't hear any fighting, I decide to shift back and call Maciah.

I don't remove my gaze from the house as I call my boss. It seems my wolf's attention is content to be locked on the situation as well.

"Did you find her?" Maciah says when he answers.

"I did, but she fought me," I reply. "I'm outside of a house that she's just entered."

He cuts in before I can tell him anything else. "Alone?"

"From what I can tell, yes," I say, keeping my voice low. "Everything is quiet, even now."

"Get in there with her, find out what she wants inside that house, and get the both of you out of there," Maciah says. "You need to convince her to stay away from that pack without telling her anything."

"Why?" I ask, then I immediately regret the question. Maciah might not be my alpha, but I respect him like one.

"Because we need to make sure we have everything we need before we...act," he says, and I get the feeling he knows more and isn't going to tell me. Not even if I outright ask.

"I'm happy to do so, but shouldn't I know the risk I'm taking?" I ask, unable to help myself.

He's silent, and I don't think he's going to answer me, but I won't break first.

Finally, he says, "With the alpha missing and beta dead, they've put York Graves in charge since he has the alpha gene, but Astor Crowe seems to be calling the shots. I've had eyes on him for a while now, but I can't seem to catch him with his hands dirty. We need to see how this plays out before we shut it down."

He hasn't said what "it" is, and I have a feeling he isn't going to. Though, I don't miss the point he seems to be trying to make.

"You want the whole snake and not just the tail," I say.

"Yes, and Sophie has history with the Crowes," he adds. "She can't know any of this. Tell her whatever lies you need to, but don't let her think she can get involved in taking them down."

That feels challenging if I'm supposed to get her to come with me willingly, and I say as much to Maciah.

"Find another way to gain her trust, Kyler," he demands. "This is important. Astor has been linked to killing off other packs and selling wolves to humans. Something I expect you to keep to yourself."

Well, shit. I didn't actually expect him to tell me anything. And the fact that he did doesn't make me feel any better. That just tells me this is more important than I realized before. Plus, he's right. Sophie doesn't need to know everything. Not if she's potentially emotionally involved in the situation. Regardless of how strong she is, I'll find another way to earn her trust, even if I have to let her stab me first.

I hear glass break, and my wolf tries to surge forward.

"I gotta go," I say to Maciah. "I'll check in soon."

I'm not even sure if I get the full sentence out before I'm hanging up and shifting. No longer am I concerned with being conspicuous. My wolf charges forward, a dark shadow amongst the green of the forest.

We cross the backyard and are leaping through the window in seconds. My wolf stops, and we hear more fighting coming from the front of the house. Without needing to tell him, my wolf runs that way, but before we can do anything, we're stopped in our tracks.

Sophie is standing over another man, her hand dripping in blood and his heart within her palm.

Holy shit.

I suddenly have a feeling that Maciah and Dawsyn have no clue just who this woman is.

She glances over at me, lets the heart drop to the ground next to the dead shifter, and shrugs. "He tried to kill me first."

"Right," is all I say, since I'm at a loss for words. Until I hear my wolf speak.

More are coming, he says gruffly. *Get her out of here.*

Easier said than done. Considering our previous encounter, I act without bothering to ask for her permission. My wolf's warning means more to me than however pissed she's about to be.

I charge forward and grab Sophie around the waist, lifting her over my shoulder and holding tightly to her legs as she attempts to get away.

"What the fuck do you think you're doing?" she screeches, and I nearly smack her ass to shut her up but manage to refrain at the last second.

"More wolves are coming," I say gruffly as I head for the bedroom window that we both came through. "You're getting out of this house."

Her fists pound against my back, and she reaches back toward her boot, but I keep my palm secure over where I can feel her knife. In no scenario am I letting this she-wolf get a weapon. At least not yet. Her hands are already dangerous enough, as I've just witnessed.

I nearly have her out the window when she digs her claws into my skin. "Put me down or I'll rip out your spine."

My head shakes. "You asked for it."

I throw her out the window. Hard.

Not only does she hit her head on the way through, but she lands with her legs and arms twisted together. Before she can untangle her body, I have her in my arms again, this time cradled in front of me, and I'm running back to the tree line as fast as possible.

The sound of wolves getting closer is clear, even over my pounding heart while the adrenaline surges through me, but before any of them can make it to the back side of the house, we're out of sight. Though, that doesn't mean they're not capable of following our scent.

Sophie tries to hit me, but I have her body boxed in on itself. When she realizes she can't move, she resorts to trying to bite me, but one sharp growl from me, telling her to look back, has her finally acting like a normal adult.

Her eyes glance over my shoulder and back toward the house, then her body rumbles within my grasp. "What the hell are they doing?"

The words are spoken quietly and filled with menace.

"I don't know," I say honestly since I haven't bothered to look back. "But you need to let me get you out of here."

She flinches against me, fighting my hold again. "I'm not going anywhere with you. I need to find my family."

"And if they're already dead and you're next?" I say harshly. "What then, Sophie? You're strong, but you can't beat all those men on your own. Not even for family."

She glares at me. "Put me down."

"Give me your word that you won't run," I counter, even as her nails begin to turn into claws again.

Her lips form into a hard line. "Fine."

"Your word, Sophie," I repeat. "If you're the wolf shifter I think you are, then that means something to you." At least I assume she's honorable if she's been welcome with the East Texas pack all these years.

The rumble that leaves her chest vibrates through her whole body and right into mine, causing me to hold her tighter, but not because I'm worried that she's going to escape.

"I give you my word that I won't run from you," she concedes with a glare that seems permanently etched into her face.

I let her down and glance back at the house. "They're going to sense us soon if they haven't already. We need to shift and get the hell out of here. If you're going to honor your word, then you'll follow me."

"I said I wouldn't run from you. I didn't promise to *stay* with you," she says, crossing her arms and leveling her hard stare on me.

"Sophie, I just saved your life." I sigh. "Don't be fucking difficult."

That has her smirking, and dread fills me as she pats my chest. "Oh, you haven't seen *difficult* yet. I promise you that."

Unfortunately, I believe her.

Chapter Six

Sophie

I walk away from Kyler. Not because I want to, but because I have to. He's been in my presence for mere minutes, and he already has me flustered.

The way he handled me—like, really fucking *handled* me—awakened a part of me I didn't even know existed.

I've been trying to tell you, my wolf says dryly. *You haven't truly been living.*

My eyes roll. Hard. *And attraction doesn't equal living, Wolf.*

Maybe not, but the high you get from it sure makes life more enjoyable.

A growl lightly rumbles in my chest. My annoyance increases, because she makes a point. It's a point I'm not fond of, but I don't make a habit of lying to myself.

It might not be him, I say, hoping that another scenario might make my erratic thoughts and the desire pooling at my core make more sense. That was the first time we've been home in over a decade.

That place isn't our home, she snaps back.

My wolf is right—again—but that doesn't mean being in that house after all this time hasn't brought back memories from my childhood.

I catch Kyler walking in front of me, but he doesn't say anything. I decide to follow him so that he doesn't attempt to trap me in his arms for the third time. Overbearing bastard. I also don't stare at his ass or notice the way his muscles shift beneath his shirt as he moves. Not even the way his dark strands brush over his neck.

While definitely not noticing all that, I keep a decent distance between us and try to figure out why those men would have been watching the house. The window I went through was my little sister's room. Nothing had really changed there. White bedding, white walls, and wooden accents. Simple yet pristine. That seemed to be the family motto growing up.

In the hallways, I tried not to notice that none of the pictures on the wall contained my face. Not a single one. In the living room, everything was pristine, as if the place is just a model home on display. I know better, though. My mother is just a controlling neat freak. At least, she *was*...

I didn't get to inspect the cabinets to see if there was any fresh food, because as soon as I'd entered the kitchen, another shifter threw a glass at my head, then attacked.

My instincts had kicked in—kill or die. That wasn't the first time I've had to fight for my life, and I know it won't be the last. Yet having Kyler walk in and see me with a man's heart in my hand gives me conflicting feelings.

Mixed with the attraction that I undoubtedly felt when pressed against his body, I start to wonder what someone thinks of me for the first time ever. What *he* thinks of me after seeing what I'd done.

It's been years since I've given a single shit over anyone else's opinion. But his, I'm curious about. Especially because he hasn't said a thing about my bloody hands and clothes. Hell, there's even splatter on my face that I can feel drying.

All that aside...I don't trust him. Call me crazy, because I have no reason to have decided this yet, but something about him puts me off.

The fact that he makes you feel *is a really stupid reason, if you ask me,* my wolf says with extra snark.

Good thing I'm not asking.

Sometimes I wish the fates had gifted wolf shifters with mute buttons for our inner beasts.

Kyler is too insistent about being here and stopping me. He doesn't know me. He shouldn't give a shit about what I do.

It's his job, my wolf chimes in again. *Don't you think that he maybe just doesn't want to get fired? Not that he has an ulterior motive?*

I cross my arms and stare at his back as we travel the woods. It's getting dark out, but that doesn't mean my eyes stop staring and enjoying what they're seeing.

My nails dig into my forearms. No. This attraction is fleeting. Whether I can't trust him for reasons unknown or he's only doing his job, he's still not here for me. Plus, I don't mix business and pleasure. Hell, I don't even mix personal with pleasure.

Whatever images I've conjured of him since he had me against that tree...like us being naked instead of clothed and breaking everything in our path as we devour each other... None of it matters.

None. Of. It. Matters.

Plus, that asshole threw me out a window.

He deserves a little payback for that, which I plan to dish out very well. At some point.

"Where are we going?" I consider suggesting we should shift, but I don't trust my hussy of a wolf alone with this man. Something tells me she'd gladly roll over for him.

Or maybe he'd enjoy being on bottom, she quips. *You never know.*

I choke on air, imagining this particular specimen on his back for any woman.

As I get my breathing back under control, Kyler glances back at me, a crease between his brows. "A cabin just another mile or so ahead."

"Do you really think that's far enough?" I press, knowing this pack better than he does. "They're going to know it was me."

He stops and waits for me to get closer. "How do you figure?"

"It's my family house, and from what you so impolitely pointed out earlier, they seemed to be waiting for me." Yeah, that's a whole other shit sandwich I need to sort out.

My stomach grumbles louder than it ever has at the mere thought of food.

Kyler raises a brow and glances down before looking back at my face. "When was the last time you ate?"

I glance at my phone and shrug. "About two hours ago."

Both eyebrows go halfway up his forehead this time. "Right. Well, the cabin has food. We'll be fine there for the night."

His mere insistence that he just *knows* things is another reason that I don't want to trust him. He isn't from here. He doesn't know my pack.

They're not yours and you don't know them, either, my wolf reminds me, more gently than her earlier words.

I know, but—

No buts, *Sophie*, she says as we keep walking farther into the woods and away from the pack. *This isn't our home. I agreed with coming back because you need closure, but that doesn't mean I want to risk our lives for it.*

As she says the words, I want to agree with her. Yet I know there's still a small part of me that hoped we'd return and my parents would tell me how sorry they were for letting me go and how much they missed me all these years. That my little sister would still be five years old and things could somehow pick up where they left off before Thane ruined everything.

Stupid. I'm a grown-ass woman. I don't need my parents' approval. I should have never come here.

Yes, you should have, my wolf says. *You need to believe the words you're saying, and you don't. Until you see that you're not the problem here, that you didn't run away to make things easier on everyone else, you're never going to figure out who you truly are.*

A tightness forms in my chest, and my throat burns with emotions I don't like. Or possibly just don't understand.

"We're almost there," Kyler says, allowing me a distraction that I gladly take.

"How do you know about this place?" I ask, making sure to keep an appropriate distance between us.

'Appropriate' would be stripped naked and letting him take us against one of these trees.

I gladly ignore my wolf's crude thought as Kyler answers, looking over at me with his steely gaze.

"It's my job to know."

His response is clipped. I'm more than confused, because just a few moments ago, he was intrigued by my ravenous appetite. Now, his stare is fixed ahead and he doesn't seem keen on continuing with small talk.

I told you we can't trust him, I say to my wolf.

His wolf might sense something, and he doesn't want to be distracted with something not worth his while.

Wow. Way to give me a confidence boost.

As if you need it.

Again, she's not wrong. I might have family issues, but I know my worth. At least on my own. I'm a wolf shifter who isn't to be fucked with. I wouldn't have survived mostly by myself for as long as I have otherwise, even while being able to say I belong to the East Texas pack.

I scratch an itch on my forehead, then grimace when I feel something sticky. After wiping my skin, I remember there's blood from that shifter at the house on my face.

"Is there a shower at this cabin?" I ask, preferring a steaming, hot one over a cold dip in the stream.

"Yeah, you can wash up while I sort out the food," he says, and I have to hold back a scoff.

Like I'm going to eat anything he makes me. He'll probably try to poison me.

Because he saved you from those other wolves just so he could have the pleasure of killing you himself. Makes total sense.

Fuck. You.

I'm not normally that abrasive with my wolf, but my annoyance with her seems to be rising by the second, and I can't help myself. Especially when she's laughing at my expense inside my own head.

We walk the rest of the way in silence. When we arrive at the building, it's exactly what I picture when I think of the word *cabin*. A small structure made from wooden logs with one front door and no windows to be able to see out of.

There's a stone chimney at the top and moss on the roof. Overgrown foliage surrounds the small porch and around the side of the house, showing no signs of a used path anywhere around.

"Watch your step," he says. "We don't want to leave tracks."

"Because our scent won't be a big enough attraction on its own," I say dryly, more than a little shocked we haven't heard or sensed anyone chasing after us.

He doesn't respond as he opens the front door with a key from his pocket. When he steps aside for me to enter ahead of him, I give him a side eye but don't question the action.

If this is a trap, I'm ready for it.

Except when I cross the threshold, I know I'm either already fucked or somehow completely safe.

Kyler closes the door and smirks. "Still worried about being found?"

Magic presses in around me, blocking out the world beyond these four walls. My skin tingles with the foreign energy, but none of my senses tell me I'm in danger. "How did you know about a cabin with a cloaking spell so close to the pack?"

"I didn't," he answers, moving past me toward the small kitchen area. "I'm a protector. It's our job to be prepared with things like cloaking spells. I scouted the area before you showed up."

Huh. I don't want to be impressed, but I am.

He nods toward the first door past the kitchen. "Bathroom is there. I'll see what's edible in here."

I grin. I have a feeling I'd be much better at that than him, but the desire to remove the blood from my body outweighs my need for food. I can be quick cleaning up when the occasion requires it.

There's an unlit fireplace on my right and a couch centered in front of it. Books and board games fill two bookshelves on the wall next to the fireplace, and the head of a stuffed deer is mounted above it.

Great. A hunter's cabin. Just where a pair of wolves should be hiding out.

I step into the bathroom and find a small, single shower stall and a toilet without a handle to flush. When I lift the lid, I swiftly slam it back down. I don't need to pee that bad. Apparently, having some sort of sewer system wasn't as important as running water to these humans.

In seconds, I'm naked and standing under the hot water. I get soap in my hair and start to lather the rest of my body when the bathroom door is kicked in.

"What the hell?" I peek around the curtain to see Kyler grabbing my clothes and a towel. He wraps the cotton material around me and once again holds me in his arms, almost as if he believes I belong there.

"We're leaving." He growls. "You were right."

Of course I fucking was.

"Let me down," I demand. "I'll shift."

"No time." He runs us toward the bedroom, and there's a window there that I couldn't have seen from the outside.

"If you throw me through another window, I will rip your balls off and shove them down your throat."

My threat gives him a brief pause as he smirks. "I actually think you'd do that."

"Maybe you're not as stupid as I thought."

That has him moving back into action. He manages to open the tall window with me still in his arms. He holds me with only one hand, his fingers digging into my thigh as I hold on to his neck.

I could easily get away, but now that the window is open, I can hear the others. They're at the front shouting at us. If we don't get the hell out of there, we're about to be severely outnumbered.

Kyler sits me down gently in front of him, his eyes casting quickly over my very naked body as the towel and clothes drop to the ground between us. "You're going to have to shift and leave your stuff behind."

"The hell I do," I mutter, shoving my feet into my boots first. I take a few steps back, then call my wolf forward. This isn't the first time we've made a quick escape.

She grabs my stuff with her mouth, and we glance at Kyler. He hasn't shifted yet, but the moment I hear someone shout, "They're back here," he finally moves into action.

We don't bother to wait for him. If he's as good as he seems to think, then he'll keep up.

Thankfully, my wolf agrees.

She sprints through the forest, making our way back to the car. The jeans in her mouth are the only thing I really care about. It has the keys we'll need to get the hell out of this area.

If we don't, these wolves won't stop hunting us.

I knew they were after me. I should have trusted my gut and not stopped running until we were far enough away from the pack to properly regroup.

I'm sorry, my wolf says, but it's not necessary.

She trusted Kyler, and he messed up. What's done is done. At least we know now. Though, I am curious how the pack seems to have broken through the cloaking spell.

Kyler is close and gaining on the lead we have. I can hear the other wolves behind him, their heavy pants and the pounding of their paws against the forest floor. We'll only have a few seconds to get in the car and speed away. Kyler better hope he's in that passenger seat when I start the engine if he wants to come with me. I won't be waiting even a second for his ass.

Not even when I know the way my skin pebbled under his scrutiny just moments ago had nothing to do with the cool, evening weather.

Chapter Seven

Kyler

I've never had a cloaking spell fail. Yes, I knew we'd left scent behind by just walking, but it should have faded enough to throw anyone off our trail by the time we got to the cabin. One that should have looked abandoned to those wolves. Instead, they knew exactly where we were.

Sophie had been right, and I hate to admit it after I asked her to trust me. Still, there's no time to dwell on that.

Wolves are gaining on me, and if I don't hurry, I have a feeling Sophie is going to disappear and I'll have to hunt her down.

That thought has my wolf reacting, but I can't make sense of his emotions. He's both annoyed and bloodthirsty, which is good since we're not going to be able to keep running for long.

The group behind us is fast, and the race could go on for hours. It's better to just end them now.

With a snarl, my wolf seems to agree. He whips around, skidding to a stop. There are three wolves who stop and two more who keep going, assumingly after Sophie.

Normally, I'd be concerned for the person I'm supposed to be protecting, but after seeing a bleeding heart in her palm earlier, not so much this time.

My wolf takes full control, and the rage we normally keep firmly under lock and key finally gets to unleash itself. Our teeth snap, and saliva drips from our jowls as a loud, warning growl echoes from deep within.

None of the three wolves back down. They dig their claws into the forest floor and charge forward. A brown one leaps over my back and bites at my spine while an ebony one aims his teeth for my neck and the lighter grey wolf goes for my legs.

The ebony one sinks his teeth into us, but we're quick to act, ignoring the two trying to get us on our back. My wolf's claws extend and rip across the ebony wolf's face, taking out at least one eye.

He releases his bite on our neck and backs up just as I suspected he would, but I don't for one second believe he's down for the count.

We move our attention momentarily to the grey wolf closer to our front. Using razor-sharp teeth, we grab hold of his neck. Canines break through skin and blood trickles into our mouth, but my wolf refuses to relent.

His bite increases until we hear bones snap and the wolf goes limp beneath us.

Killing isn't usually our first choice, but it's one

we've made many times before and I have a feeling today won't be the last time I take a life.

The brown wolf who's done a fine job of bloodying my back with his teeth and claws while I've been otherwise distracted spots his fallen friend and takes off like a bat out of hell before I can attack him.

We should give chase, but I'm bleeding more than I'd like to admit, and the one whose eye I ripped out is still standing.

He's foaming at the mouth and stalking toward us. While I'm injured, he's definitely worse off with blood dripping from the open wounds on his face. Still, he doesn't back down.

The opposing wolf lunges forward and mine smacks him across the face with an open paw. It's an even bigger insult to the other shifter considering a practically gentle hit has him falling back to the ground.

If we just take him out, it would feel more like murder to me. He can't win, and he isn't going to hurt me or Sophie. Not in the state he's in now.

Yet he attempts to attack again, and I can't *not* fight back.

When his mouth widens, going for our throat, we dart out of the way and go around the wolf's side, pinning him to the ground with ease. With all the crimson coating his head, I doubt that he can even see at the moment.

Our teeth grip his neck, but not in a way that we intend to kill him. If he submits, he can walk away and live to see another day. One spent owning up to his crimes.

My wolf growls another warning at him, and he finally relaxes beneath our hold, letting out a light whimper.

When we back up, our eyes stay locked on the wolf until I hear another one coming from behind.

Shit. That better be Sophie. With all the blood around me, I can't identify the scent coming closer, but whoever it is, they aren't slowing down.

A dark tan wolf leaps over mine and lands on the ebony one I'm ready to arrest, as I so often do. We might be called protectors, but that's only half of our job for the supernatural communities.

Sophie and the other wolf are fighting fiercely, which confuses the hell out of me, considering he could barely stand just seconds ago.

He was playing with us, my wolf snarls as he looks for an opening to jump in, but before we can find one, Sophie's wolf has already done what I'm realizing too late that we should have.

She immediately shifts back to her naked human form and points a finger at me, a deep glare on her face. "You're either an idiot or a traitor. I can't tell which, and that's not good for you."

Her words cut deeply. Idiot and traitor. Two things I've never in my life been accused of. Maybe today wasn't the day I should have accepted a job. Is my grief messing with my ability to make the right choices? I don't know, but I do know that Sophie's anger isn't misplaced.

It's her, my wolf says with another growl. *You need to walk away.*

The pain in his voice isn't only something I can hear but can feel. My own heart aches with what he's not saying.

Sophie isn't our mate, but she's the first wolf in fourteen years to make us feel something.

But I don't know that he's right. As much as I've hated the fates over the years for only allowing me a brief time with my mate, I'd already decided it was time to move forward with my life before I even set eyes on Sophie.

I'm not walking away, I tell him. Once again, he goes back to giving me the silent treatment.

Sophie's naked ass stalks past me and when I try to get a closer look, my wolf jerks his head in the opposite direction.

Well, this is going to be interesting.

I force him to release control and shift back to my human form. I'm not bleeding any longer, but that doesn't mean the injuries my wolf received haven't carried over.

My back burns with every move I make, and my left calf has an open wound. Nothing that I don't believe won't heal within a few hours, but still not convenient.

Pushing through the aches, I jog to catch up with Sophie. Night has fully set in, but with my enhanced vision, I can make out every curve on her body, the white scar that travels over her ribs, and I see the way her dark hair sways over her spine.

Today is the anniversary of Cara's death, my wolf says with undisguised loathing. *How dare you look at another?*

Because it's been fourteen years, Wolf, I reply sternly. *Cara is and always will be my mate, but she never would have wanted me to be alone like I've been. It's taken me too long to accept that, and you're only furious because you feel something for this new wolf, too.*

I would never, he practically shouts in my head, but he can't hide the truth from me. Just as I can't do the same with him.

Would I have rather it been any other day that I met Sophie? Absolutely. But it wasn't, and this is where we are. With a woman who won't hesitate to kill, actually seems to hate me, yet still intrigues the hell out of me.

"I should have fucking left him behind like I said I would," I hear her mutter just a few feet ahead of me.

"You were going to leave me?" I ask, butting into a conversation I know full well she doesn't want me part of.

She swivels around and the deep line between her brows along with the narrowing of her darkening green eyes tells me just how furious she is before she even speaks.

"Of course I was." She huffs, crossing her arms over her breasts, covering them most of the way up. "You made a stupid choice, and it nearly got us killed."

"So, why didn't you?" I press, forcing my lips to stay in a flat line instead of allowing them to rise like they want to.

Her head lightly shakes, and her eyes roll. "Because I

stayed with you, basically agreeing to your stupidity, which made me feel responsible for making sure you didn't die. Something that was about to happen right before I finished off that wolf. Did you let the rest of them go, too?"

The judgment in her tone no longer makes me feel ashamed. Instead, I find amusement in her words. I've heard that there's a fine line between hate and love. While I'm under no assumption that love has anything to do with this situation, attraction does. I'm starting to wonder if she and my wolf are more alike than either of them realizes.

"You must have been so hellbent on murder that you missed the other dead wolf back there," I say dryly. "But yes, another one did get away. Not because I let him go. I made the choice to stay and fight the ebony one instead of chasing after one who was no longer a threat. Maybe that was a mistake, but excuse me for wanting to be done with them so I could find you."

She barks out a harsh laugh. "I will never need you to come to my rescue."

With that, she turns again and heads toward a manmade trail up ahead. I gladly follow and another minute later, there's a parking area with only one car in it. But that's not what catches my attention first. It's the blood splatter and two dead wolves lying in front of the vehicle that give me pause.

There are claw marks everywhere. On the shifters, in the dirt, and even on the hood of her car.

Still naked, she picks up one of the wolves and

catches me watching. "Are you just going to stand there like the idiot I already think you are, or are you going to help?"

While the first time she called me that hurt, this time it's more annoying than anything else. "Are people not allowed to make mistakes in your presence, princess?"

I pick up the second wolf, careful not to get blood all over my clothes as I carry the corpse back into the woods. There's already enough from where she stuck her claws in my chest.

She doesn't respond to my question, though I don't expect her to. We don't go too far before we drop the bodies and head back to the car. I'll have to text Maciah, asking for someone to clean this mess up before any humans stumble upon it in the morning.

Sophie is still naked but doesn't seem to give a damn, even when she's facing me. I take in her full, round breasts before noticing that the scar on her ribs reaches almost to her belly button.

Any rising attraction is halted, and I'm tempted to ask what happened, but something tells me we're a long way from swapping war stories.

When she stands back next to her car, she leans down and picks up her shirt, finally putting it on. When I raise a brow, she shrugs. "I didn't want to get my clothes bloody."

Makes sense.

I open the passenger's door, but she stops me. "I don't think so. I saved your life. You're driving."

"I could have killed that wolf on my own," I reply,

even though I'm already walking around the front of the car to get in the driver's seat.

"Then maybe you should have," she taunts, passing me by, now also covered by her jeans. "We'll drive for at least two hours, find a big city, grab supplies, and get a hotel."

She says the plan as if this is a normal Tuesday night for her.

"Done this a few times, huh?" I ask as she buckles up and I start the car.

Her brow raises as she opens the glove box. "And you haven't?"

She's still judging me, but I let it go, too curious about the items she's reaching for. There's a bag of chips, two chocolate candy bars, some gummy worms, and a few other things I don't catch.

In the next second, she opens the chips and one of the candy bars, eating a bite of each, one after another.

I watch in fascination as she inhales the food like it's the best thing she's ever consumed. After a minute of witnessing...whatever this is, she finally catches me staring.

"What?" she snaps, mouth full and chocolate on her cheek.

"You seem to have quite the appetite," I muse, openly staring at her.

"I'm in a committed relationship with food," she says, almost sounding proud. "Do you have a problem with that?"

I shake my head, then put the car in reverse. "Nope. Not at all."

Sophie is an enigma, and much to my wolf's dismay, I'm actually intrigued by the idea of earning her trust and figuring out just who this murdering, food-obsessed woman really is.

I'm minutes from withering away and turning to dust. My stash of food in the car has done nothing to subdue my hunger, and I find myself wondering how desperate I am to get the soap out of my hair that's now itching my scalp. That or the bits of dried blood from fighting off the chasing wolves in that forest.

Kyler, on the other hand, decided to be a typical guy and use a water bottle to clean himself without asking if I wanted to do the same before the water was all gone.

The man currently at the top of my shit list gives me a onceover as if mocking my thoughts. "You might want to wait in the car while I get us a room key."

I hold my fingers up. "Two keys."

His head tilts as if he doesn't understand English. What the hell am I supposed to do with this pain in the ass?

Fuck him while we have the chance, my wolf quips

with a dark chuckle, and her words do exactly what I assume she was going for.

I choke a little before I explain in layman terms what I mean.

"Two keys, Kyler," I say slower. Okay, maybe I'm overreacting a little here, but given my current state and mood, I don't back off. "Two keys. Two rooms. Just because you've already seen me naked doesn't mean I'm going to share a bed with you or even a room."

His face pales so briefly that it might have just been a trick of the moonlight, then he grins. "You know, Sophie, the fact that you brought that up all on your own tells me that you were already imagining doing just that."

I open my mouth to tell him some not-so-nice things, but he's already up and out of the car, closing the door behind him.

That son of a bitch, I complain more to myself, except my wolf decides to chime in. Of course.

He's quite perfect, actually.

Oh, no, I say to her, shaking my head. *Don't get any ideas. Not this wolf. Not this situation. It's too complicated already.*

To that, she has no reply and her silence worries me, but when my stomach rumbles loudly, I find myself more distracted with locating food. The seedy motel isn't going to have room service, but there should at least be vending machines around here.

Opening my center console, I dig out some crumpled dollar bills and flatten them over my jeans. My clothes are clean, at least. It's just the soap in my hair and blood lightly splattered on my face that I notice on second glance and might scare someone. If they see me.

Deciding to risk it, I get out of the car and glance toward the front office. I spot Kyler through the window. He's smiling at whoever is behind the counter and handing over a credit card. His guard is down, and I can't stop myself from noticing that he is rather handsome, in a rugged sort of way.

I thought he was dark and broody when he first showed up, but the longer he sticks around, annoying me, the more I'm starting to see that's just his work mode. Not surprising, considering he's a protector, but there's still something about him that tells me he's not all sunshine and roses.

As if he has a dark shadow within him that he keeps tightly reined in. I'm tempted to keep poking at it just to see him completely unhinged.

So he can be crazy like you? my wolf asks drolly.

Maybe. That *might actually be fun.*

She sighs heavily. *Our versions of fun have somehow become widely different over the years.*

My wolf isn't wrong, but I depend on her to be different from me. We might be opposites in many ways, and I might bitch about her, but I know her value. I know that I wouldn't have survived murdering Thane and running away without her strength and constant reminders that we'd done the right thing.

I've killed when I've had to a dozen or so times since then and wear the chip on my shoulder proudly, but that doesn't mean I'm without remorse.

Cold and heartless, I am not.

Will I defend myself without hesitation? Absolutely. Will I also lose sleep later overanalyzing every detail of how I might have been able to do things differently? Undoubtedly.

That's another thing that annoys me about Kyler. While he hasn't made all the best decisions, he doesn't just react. He considers options. Even at the worst of times.

I might have given him grief over that earlier and not agree with letting wolves who were trying to kill us go free, but at least he's not an emotionless murderer.

Neither are you, my wolf reminds me as we approach the motel.

The building is rundown with faded, grey paint on the stucco exterior and steel doors that sport rust stains. I just hope the rooms are kept up more than the outside is.

There's a little hallway with an ice machine that isn't running and a vending machine that's barely lit up. Just as I'm about to put some money in to test it, Kyler practically growls from behind me.

"You didn't wait in the car."

I don't bother to turn around. Mostly because that growl is fucking hot, and he doesn't need to see my cheeks flushed. "You took too long."

Where is the smirking man when I need him? That one, I can ignore. I'm pretty sure. But I can't lie. I'm a sucker for gruff and tough.

You realize it's not normal for someone to prefer being choked over coddled, right? my wolf asks, making me snort as I browse my pathetic and possibly stale food options.

You know that I don't care, right? I counter. *At least I'm not sex-obsessed.*

Before she can respond, Kyler reaches his hand around, his forearm brushing over my shoulder and absolutely not making my skin tingle from the contact. "There was only one room left. Here's your key."

I turn sharply to face him, not realizing just how close he is until it's too late to back down without showing how he also *isn't* affecting me. "Then we're going somewhere else."

"No, we're not," he says, looking down at me. His impressive height is a whole head taller than me, and his eyes stare as if they can see more than they should, making my stomach churn. When his challenging smile returns and he's still this close, I realize I might be totally fucked as he adds, "Are you afraid of being alone with me?"

Why is this shifter affecting me like this? *Why? Why? Why?*

My head is shaking, but not for the reason he might think.

I need to get my shit together right the hell now.

I sense the smugness coming from my wolf in waves, and I decide right then to blame my erratic feelings on her.

"I'm not afraid of anything," I finally say, answering his previous question. "You repulse me. Simple as that. I wouldn't want to accidentally rip out your heart and disappoint Dawsyn since she sent you."

I throw that last jab in there since he's already seen I'm perfectly capable of doing so. Except when his smile grows wider and he leans in closer, causing me to press my back against the vending machine, I have a feeling that he's not buying what I'm selling.

"I see you, Sophie." The words leave his mouth and pierce right through my chest, causing the air to *whoosh* right out of my lungs.

He turns and starts walking away. It takes me a solid thirty seconds to recover. Nobody has ever spoken to me like that and made me...speechless.

Who the fuck does this guy think he is?

Now I'm angry, and he's going to see that.

I stomp toward him, eating up the distance he's created with my lengthened strides. When he's within touching range, I fist the back of his shirt, force him to face me again, then slam him against the side of the motel. "Let's get one thing straight. You don't *see* shit. You don't know me and you're not *going* to know me. More importantly, I don't need you. You might have known it was better to get out of that house earlier, but everything after that has been a mess, thanks to you. In the morning, I'm going my own way and you're not going to do anything to stop me. Whatever Dawsyn thought she was doing by sending you to me, it ends now."

As I rip into him, my chest heaves and I find it harder and harder to breathe—especially staring into his grey eyes that aren't nearly as smug as they seemed two seconds ago. When I'm done, there's a weight off my shoulders that I didn't even know I was carrying. Except when he grabs my finger that I also didn't realize I was poking against his chest and that stupid fucking tingle returns, the weight comes right back, twice as heavy as before.

"You're hangry," he states calmly. "I took so long in the motel because I asked the reception to order you a pizza. Now, you're going to go into the room, take a shower, eat the fucking pizza, and sleep. Tomorrow, we can sort out what we are and aren't doing. Not a second sooner."

He's trying to take charge of me, and I...I fucking... lov—hate it.

I throw my hands in the air, because in no way am I going to let him know he's doing anything other than pissing me the hell off. "Whatever."

I take the key that he offered before, this time being the first to walk away. Checking the nearest room number and the one in my hand attached to the key, I continue around the back side of the motel.

There aren't any lights on this side, and the half-full parking lot leads out to a wooded area. I'm tempted to shift and run just to burn off whatever this tension is inside me but decide better of it. Pizza actually sounds damn delicious right now, and my scalp is starting to itch from the shit in my hair.

Finding our unfortunately shared room, I stick the key into the lock and turn the handle. The door sticks, the frame likely warped thanks to weather and time, but a solid shove has it opening.

I glance behind me before stepping inside. Kyler isn't too far behind me, but I don't wait for him. Like a petulant child, I kick the door closed and head straight for the bathroom, not taking even a second to check out the room.

Once I'm locked within the tiled space and have the lights on, I let out a groan of epic frustration. The place is surprisingly clean, but it's Pepto pink. Everywhere.

The old porcelain, jetted tub. The walls. The counter. All of it, varying shades of pink. Well, except for the toilet that has graciously been upgraded over the decades since this place was built, likely in the 1960s.

I turn the showerhead on and get undressed before searching for towels that I find folded in the shape of hearts.

Something tells me this is their version of a suite, and I'm not pleased. Mostly because of the person I'm sharing it with.

You're having quite the conundrum over your feelings, my wolf points out. *Going from one extreme to the other. Maybe you should just settle on one and quit giving yourself whiplash.*

A sneer forms on my face as I step into the shower. *How about you just mind your own business?*

We might be two souls, but we're trapped in the same body, she says matter-of-factly. *Your business is very much my own, fuck you very much.*

My chest rumbles as I let the water run over my hair,

sending red-tinged rivulets running down my body. I've already made my decision. Tomorrow, we're going our own way. I'm going to sneak back onto pack lands, figure out what the hell is going on and why my family seems to be involved, then find the closure I originally went looking for. Alone.

I told Kyler I was done with him, and I meant it. Mostly. Because my wolf is right. One moment, I can't stand him. The next, he's making my skin ripple with feelings I haven't felt in...maybe ever.

That alone makes this complicated, and that's something I don't do. He's not my fated mate. I killed mine. More importantly, I'm not his. With the way my body and wolf have reacted to this man, I'm not willing to gamble with attachments when he could one day leave us without hesitation for the one made just for him. Hell, he might already have her. I could be overthinking this whole situation for no reason. Either way, I'm done.

This is my past that I need to deal with on my own. I need to know that I've moved on from my teenage trauma, and it needs to be done alone.

Why? My wolf asks, her voice—almost shockingly—filled with the utmost respect. *We've been on our own for years and I've understood why, but if you're truly ready to move forward with your life, putting the past behind you, then isn't it time we start doing things differently?*

She makes another good point, but not with Kyler. He's still problematic, and I'm not going to waver from that decision. On top of that, I don't trust him. I feel more than certain he's hiding something from me. I don't like that.

You don't trust anyone, my wolf reminds me. *But that isn't what I'm arguing here. Dawsyn sent Kyler to help us. She said as much in her text. She's your alpha. Or she will be soon. You should trust her.*

I hear you, but—

She cuts me off. *No buts. You're still part of the East Texas pack. If things go well here, that could change, but until then, trust your alpha. She warned you to stay away, knew you wouldn't, and sent reinforcements for a reason. One that has already been validated when men were waiting for you to show up, ready to kill you.*

Why can't she just continue to be the horny, little wolf in my head instead of making so much fucking sense?

I'm tired and hungry and I don't want to think about this any longer, is all I have left to say.

Thankfully, she accepts that and I finish showering without any other verbal slaps to the face. I dry off and wrap the towel around me, wishing I'd grabbed my bag out of the trunk before getting out of the car.

That is until I smell sausage and pepperoni filtering through the air. I have the bathroom door open a half second later, but I only take one step before I'm stopped in my tracks.

Kyler is standing there with his back to me, dressed only in a pair of black boxer briefs. My eyes dance over his wide shoulders, down his back that's covered in more black and grey tattoos, over his sculpted ass, then across his muscled thighs that I immediately imagine straining as he holds me against the wall, pounding into me.

He turns around, showing off his broad chest and muscled stomach and... Nope. I refuse to look any lower when he can see what my eyes are doing.

"Pizza is here," he says, as if I can't manage to figure that out myself, but it's the challenge in his eyes that gets to me the most. He's nearly naked on purpose, and I refuse to let him win. Not even when he openly stares at my towel-clad body, raising one brow that can only be described as appreciation for what he's seeing.

Fuck me. I'm in deep shit if I don't get the hell out of here first thing tomorrow.

Chapter Nine

Kyler

I shouldn't be pleased with how easily I piss off Sophie, but I am. That proves she feels something for me, which is better than her being indifferent. Plus, she makes it almost too easy to push her buttons with how tightly wound she is. My wolf still doesn't agree with my choice to do so—at least I assume so by his continued silence—but that's a problem to be worked out later.

Right now, I need Maciah to call me back, and I need Sophie to eat before she actually bites my head off.

Having been a protector for over ten years, I consider myself more than capable in most situations, but this she-wolf has shown me that I can still be taken by surprise, and I don't intend to underestimate her again.

Not that I'll tell her this, but I regret not listening to her about the cabin. The magic should have been enough and it wasn't. Sophie's gut had known that, even if she hadn't pushed me hard to get me to change my mind.

I hadn't even considered the possibility of being found, but I should have.

My wolf makes an odd noise, but he still doesn't say anything.

Before I step back into the room with our newly delivered pizzas, I peek at the half moon in the sky and inhale deeply.

I miss you, Cara, but I can't help from thinking that you're the one who pushed me here. To this job and to this woman. Is it her? Is Sophie the one who will make sure I don't spend the rest of my life wishing for death so that I can find you again?

Even as a wolf shifter, I've never believed in ghosts, but since losing Cara, I've felt and seen too many things to not believe that her soul is somewhere out there, watching over me.

It could just be the heat from the pizza in my hands, but once again, there's a warmth in my chest, pressing in, comforting me.

With a contented sigh, I go back into the room, feeling lighter than I have in quite some time. I set the food down and strip off my damp pants and shirt. I'd gotten enough blood off me that I only looked dirty as opposed to a murderer, but I still need to change. Or more accurately, get dry.

I'd stashed all my shit in the cabin and only had time to grab Sophie's clothes when we fled. So, by the time I remember I have nothing else here, I'm standing near the door in nothing other than my boxers. Instead of putting my stained shirt and pants back on, I stretch and take my time, even when I hear the shower shut off and the bathroom door open.

Slowly, I turn around and find Sophie openly staring at me. I can't stop myself from smirking as I say, "Pizza is here."

Her eyes narrow, as if I've insulted her. "No shit."

She's only wearing a towel, and I watch as she struts forward, gripping the cotton of her towel with one hand and snagging a box of pizza with her other.

"I'm eating in the bathroom," she announces, turning on her heel.

I should let her, but I don't. Sophie can't keep trying to run from me. Not when I'm certain she's not actually running from *me*.

My fingers wrap around her bicep to stop her forward momentum, but all I manage to do is jerk her arm back, and the hand that was holding her towel to her body comes with it.

In a matter of seconds, she's once again naked. Since we're not in any danger, I don't stop my eyes from roaming over her firm backside. There isn't a dimple in her perfect, creamy skin, and her muscles flex as she spins around, hiding herself.

Sophie holds the pizza box above her tits, blocking my view of anything lower unless I choose to step back, which I don't intend on doing. Giving her space feels like the wrong move.

Her eyes snap up toward mine, flickering with rage. "What the fuck is your problem?"

I ignore the venom in her words, because something

tells me that it only disguises the same attraction that I'm feeling.

My body moves forward, the edges of the hot pizza box now pressing against both of our chests, the scent of food wafting between us. "I'm not the one with a problem, princess."

Her eyes widen. "*Princess*? You're even more stupid than I already thought if you want to keep calling me that."

I can understand why she doesn't believe the nickname to be fitting, but that's exactly why I've used it twice now.

My lips curve upward as I reach for the box between us. When she notices my movements, she backs up. "Don't you touch my food, asshole. I *will* hurt you."

"Will you?" I taunt, closing the distance she's trying to create between us while she wields the pizza like a shield. "Because I know you can, but I don't believe you will."

Her mouth opens slightly, but no words come out. She's trapped against the wall next to the bathroom door. One step to the left and she could escape behind that door, but she's staying put, glaring up at me with all the indignation I expect.

Between the hard lines of fury that frame her oval face, I watch for the more subtle signs that tell me I'm not wrong in my thoughts.

The mere fact that she's yet to punch me in the face or throw another verbal dig at me tells me I'm not. On top of that, I notice the hitch in her breathing as her shoulders move ever so slightly, the way her cheeks are painted in maroon, and how her teeth tug at her lower lip without ever actually peeking out.

I shouldn't do what I'm about to, but I need to know. I need to know if I'm reading her correctly and even myself. Or if I've completely fucked up by taking this job.

With the pizza still between us, I push it down toward her stomach, wrap a hand around her neck, not missing the zap of energy from the contact as I wait one full second for her to knee me in the balls. When she doesn't, my mouth crashes down on her lips and I kiss her.

My tongue pushes forward, and she doesn't shove me away, but she does bite me. Though, I'm not sure if it's her way of defending herself or trying to mark me. The latter surprisingly has a primal need rising within me that even my wolf can't deny.

Soon, she's pushing up onto her toes, moving closer to me, and I don't worry about the possibility of her not wanting this as much as I do any longer.

I tangle my fingers with her wet strands, tasting every corner of her mouth as I inch nearer. With my free hand, I start to pull the food from between us, and her grip on the cardboard loosens, but only long enough for her left nipple to brush against my chest, sending a rush of lust coursing through me.

"No," she growls, but she still doesn't back away.

I take this to mean she still wants me to kiss her, but also requires her shield to stay in place.

Her nails dig into my forearm above the pizza, and there's a rumble in her chest that has my wolf finally awakening.

His piqued curiosity isn't something that he can deny any longer, causing a growl to escape from me as well, but the moment is cut much shorter than I hoped it would be.

Sophie rips her mouth away from mine and finally shoves me away. "What the fuck was that?"

"If you don't know what that was, then—"

She cuts me off, throwing one hand in the air. "Gods, you're the most infuriating man I've ever met."

Her comment has me smirking, but she doesn't see the action as she turns for the bathroom and slams the door behind her, still holding her now-possibly-ruined dinner.

Maybe I shouldn't have done that, given our current states of dress—or lack thereof—but I needed to know and now I do.

Sophie feels the same attraction that I do, and mine wasn't just fabricated by a shitty, emotional day. It had been something I was willing to consider, given where my thoughts had been when I was at the gravesite earlier and the brief conversations between me and my wolf.

I've never heard of second chance mates, and maybe this isn't that, but my pull toward this woman is more than surface level. I confirmed that when the first zap of energy sparked between us and the several others that came after.

Now, I just need to figure out if I'm going to be patient enough for her to get over herself and see what happens. Or if this is still the bad idea I was willing to consider it might be before I kissed that untrusting, stubborn woman.

Chapter Ten

Sophie

The tips of my fingers press over my swollen lips, and for the first time that I can remember in my life, I've completely forgotten about food.

Kyler kissed me. Like, *really* fucking kissed me. Marked and owned my mouth like it'd been made for him, and I didn't stop him. Even when I had multiple opportunities to do so.

I told you that you wanted him, my wolf says, and I picture her smug, wolfy eyes staring at me.

This is too complicated, I say, feeling defeated but having no clue over what, exactly. *I came here to find closure. Not...whatever he is.*

That's life. There will always be obstacles and you have to decide which ones are worth tackling, she replies sincerely before ruining the moment by adding, *And* tackling *that man might be the best thing we ever do.*

With a groan, I let my head drop back against the wall as I slide to the floor, dropping my food as I do. Son of a bitch. And I'm naked. Not only was I letting Kyler ravage me, I had been two seconds away from *accidentally* tripping and landing on his dick.

Okay, maybe things didn't come that close, but he isn't really dressed—or at least he wasn't—and if I hadn't found my strength...

I cannot think about that. The images those thoughts provoke aren't good for my mental state.

Instead, I reach for the pizza box just a couple of feet from me and open the lid. My lower lip turns down when I see the greasy pie has been mangled. Still, that doesn't stop me from taking two pieces, turning them into a meat pizza sandwich, and refocusing my thoughts.

Well, food first. I need to get my priorities straight.

The now-lukewarm slices don't taste nearly as good as I wish, but I chew slowly, savoring them as if they're that burger I had at the diner just the other day.

Though there's a decent chance that if I hadn't been in such a food-bliss that day, I wouldn't have decided to chase my past and I wouldn't be in this situation, so maybe I don't love that burger like I thought.

You're certifiable, my wolf drones, but I ignore her, eating my pizza sandwich, sitting naked on pink tile, and having no clue what I'm going to do next.

I haven't felt this way since I was a teenager, hiding out in Central Park—lost, alone, unsure if the choices I've made are right or wrong.

When I expect my wolf to either say something profound or snarky, she remains quiet, forcing me to truly be alone with my thoughts.

Not what I was hoping for, but I know I need to break things down before I can get my head right, so that's what I do.

I went back to East Texas because my gut was telling me that I needed to find closure. Not with that pack, but with the one I was born into.

Doing so sounded like the best idea ever, even more so when Dawsyn told me that I shouldn't go back to my old pack because they were having issues. But thinking back on it, she never did tell me anything other than the alpha was gone, the beta was dead, and someone else was running the show with Astor Crowe mixed into the shitstorm.

That only intrigued me more, but I didn't stop to question anything. Not like I should have. I'd just made the decision to get back to South Carolina as soon as possible, and that's what I did.

Not even when Kyler showed up, trying to stop me, did I question things. I still charged forward, intent on doing what I wanted. While I don't think that was necessarily wrong, I'm starting to realize that I'm missing information.

Where was my family? Why were people waiting for me—or at least someone—to show up at the house?

And why the hell is Kyler here in the first place? If Dawsyn had wanted to stop me, she could have done so at the pack. She might not officially be alpha, but she still holds power and could have commanded others to restrain me. Yet, she didn't, which makes me feel like I'm still making the right choice by being here.

So many fucking questions, but I'm not finding a single answer here, naked on the bathroom floor.

As I push myself up and walk toward the bathroom mirror, I take in my flushed complexion, red lips, and tangled hair, sighing once again.

I might be ready to find answers before I decide to act again, but I have another problem that I don't want to act on or figure out.

Kyler is...something. I won't lie anymore. He's sexy beyond reason with his light-grey eyes, dark hair, strong jawline, and... *Nope*. I'm done focusing on his other... attributes.

Before I can even consider what I may or may not allow to happen again, I need to know what he knows. He doesn't seem like the type to blindly follow orders, so he must know what's going on and what this has to do with me.

I dress in my clothes from earlier, make a mental note to go get my bag from the car after I'm done interrogating Kyler, and then brush my hair with my fingers. There are still knots, but it's better than two minutes ago.

Grabbing the pizza box, I exit the bathroom and scan the room. There's one bed, but there's also a couch, which Kyler is sitting on, eating his own food, still not dressed.

Asshole probably thinks he can taunt me with his nakedness, but that's not going to happen. Not a second time.

There's a television hanging from the wall and a

dresser beneath that. Normally, I'd poke through the drawers to see if there's anything interesting to find, but I have business to sort out first.

I sit on the bed, crossing my legs, placing the pizza in front of me, and facing Kyler. I make myself another sandwich with two slices and devour a couple of bites before addressing him.

"Why are you here?" I ask without preamble, keeping my back ramrod straight.

"We're not going to dis—"

I point a finger at him and stiffly shake my head. "Whatever *that* was, it isn't to be discussed anytime soon. Answer my question."

His lips twitch at the corners. "Got it. I'm here because my boss sent me to stop you from getting yourself killed."

"Why would he think I was going to die?" I press. "How would he have known there was any danger waiting for me when I showed up at my family home?"

He shrugs, chewing another bite of food before answering. "I don't know. I didn't ask. I just knew you needed my help, so I showed up."

My chest rumbles, the sound echoing around us. "Bullshit. You're telling me you didn't ask any questions about this job before taking it?"

There's a twitch above his right eye before he nods. "It's not my job to ask questions. I get an assignment, I complete it, I move on to the next one."

No fucking way am I buying that. He may have screwed up with the cabin, but I saw something in him.

Something that told me he's a lot smarter than I wanted to believe, even if he'd made a mistake.

He's hiding details from me. I guess that shouldn't surprise me since a part of me didn't trust him to begin with. Fine. He can have his little secret. I'll just have to ask my questions a little differently.

"What are you supposed to do with me now that you have me?" Fuck me. That came out way more sexual than I intended and the bastard knows it, judging by the way his brows raise.

"We didn't have *that* particular conversation—"

I cut him off again. "You know what I mean." I take an angry bite of food to prevent myself from overreacting, a sure sign that he's getting to me in all the wrong ways.

He finally sobers, setting his pizza box to the side, and it takes every ounce of strength that I hold within my body to not allow my eyes to avert any farther south of his face.

"Listen, Sophie," he starts, thankfully not seeming to notice the battle I'm fighting. "All I know is that you're in danger and I'm here to keep you alive. I heard that the pack is a mess, but I don't know why yet."

That twitch reappears above his eye. His tell.

Why doesn't he or his boss want me to know what's going on with my old pack?

My wolf finally chimes back in. *It has something to do with us.*

Well, no shit, I say. *But what?*

Maybe it's Astor, she replies. *He could be trying to lure you in.*

I mean, I did kill his only son, but it's not as if I've been hiding all these years. The man has had every opportunity to get to me if he wanted retribution.

Ask Kyler what he knows about him, she suggests.

"What do you know about Astor Crowe?" My eyes watch his face, expecting the twitch to return, but instead, he tilts his head in confusion.

"I don't know who he is." There's a slight hesitation in his words, but nothing else.

Could be nothing, but that doesn't mean we're done here.

"What about the pack alpha?" I ask. "Do you know he's missing and why that might be?"

His lips flatten. "I know what you're doing, and you're only wasting time."

"Why would you—" I'm cut off when the sound of a phone ringing fills the room.

Kyler gets up, and I'm tempted to punch myself in the face when I finally break and allow myself another look at his tantalizing body.

Every dip from his array of muscles, the bulge beneath his black boxer briefs, even the scars on his skin... He's hot as sin. and I desperately wish I wouldn't notice.

"Hello?" Kyler answers his phone while I listen in.

"Are you with Sophie?" a man I assume is his boss asks.

"I am," Kyler replies. "We're in a motel over two hours from the pack."

"Go outside."

With those two words, I'm on my feet. "I don't fucking think so."

Kyler groans and turns toward me, holding up a finger for me to be quiet, but that's not happening. I reach out and twist his hand to the point that if he fights back, a bone is going to break. "You're not talking about me or that pack without *me* being present. Do I make myself clear?"

"Put her on the phone," the man says, then I grin and release Kyler before holding out my hand.

"I wouldn't get so excited," Kyler mutters before placing the device on my palm.

Ignoring his pissy attitude, I say, "This is Sophie."

"You know you've been a pain in my ass every time that I've had to send someone after you," he says gruffly, giving me pause until I remember this is Kyler's boss. Not some random person who sounds like he knows more about me than he should.

It's more likely he's been around since the beginning of the protectors, especially if he's bringing up when I ran away. Though, that thought has me flicking my gaze toward Kyler.

Does he already know I killed my own mate? While I don't regret what I did, I don't flaunt that knowledge around, either.

"I'd say I'm sorry, but I don't like to lie," I finally say. "In my defense, I didn't ask for help. You're welcome to call your dog home."

That has Kyler growling from across the room where he's finally getting dressed again.

I realize I'm also a wolf shifter just like him, but I've never been one to follow orders, making me the furthest thing from a human pet.

"Kyler isn't leaving his post anytime soon," the man on the phone says. "Do you know who I am?"

"No, but I have a feeling you're going to tell me." I'm not trying to be rude, but I can't help being annoyed when I'm certain that they're trying to keep secrets from me.

"My name is Maciah," he says sternly. "Your alpha is my niece and specifically asked me to make sure that nothing bad happens to you."

I knew Dawsyn was responsible for Kyler showing up, but I hadn't realized it was because she's related to his damn boss. That's something I feel like I should have learned over the years, but I guess that's what I get for keeping my distance.

"I need to speak with Kyler privately about the situation unfolding at the pack, and it has nothing to do with you," he continues. "Are you going to force him to restrain you so he can exit the room, or are you going to allow him to do his job?"

My wolf is already conjuring images of us being tied to the bed, but we're not left alone and we're not at all mad about it.

I hate you, I snarl at her before going back to the phone conversation.

"Where is my family?" I ask before answering. "I

went to their house and people were there waiting for someone to kill."

I realize now that they might not have been there for me. They could have been anticipating my parents or sister. And if even one of them is out there, alone and being hunted, I'm going to find them.

Maciah is quiet, and I have a feeling he's going to try to keep the truth from me.

"If you lie to me and I find out," I warn, "I don't care who you are. Dawsyn's uncle, Kyler's boss, the biggest, baddest wolf out there. If you don't tell me what I need to know and something happens to them, I will hold you personally responsible."

"Excuse me," he nearly yells. "I am *not* a wolf."

Out of all that, that's what he's most upset about? This makes me grin. "Then, how the hell are you the uncle to my soon-to-be alpha?"

"Because I am," he practically growls.

"Clearly, I've offended you," I say. "That was not my intention. I realize I threatened you, but that's different."

Considering his profession, he should understand this. Once he calms down, anyway.

"For future reference, I'm a vampire and one you don't want to piss off," Maciah replies with less bite. "And your family hasn't been seen yet by any of my people. That is the truth. Now, can I speak privately with Kyler without you making any further threats?"

I chew on the inside of my cheek before I finally reply. "Sure. Have your boy talk. I'll be right here with my pizza."

I throw the phone back to Kyler. He catches it easily as I say, "Don't come back for at least ten minutes. I need a break from your ugly face. And if you want any more of your pizza, I'd take it with you. I make no promises it will be here when you return."

He raises a brow at me. "But will you be?"

I reach for my food, only briefly glancing back at him. "I guess you'll just have to wait and find out."

Chapter Eleven

Kyler

I can't be sure if this whole situation is in a perpetual downward spiral or if there's still a chance of recovering. Between Sophie not being happy with my presence, the things I'm not supposed to share with her, nearly being caught, and last but certainly not least, our mutual attraction, this could go either way.

Considering the intensity in her eyes as she stared at my body that I purposefully left on display for as long as possible, I know even if she denies she felt anything with that kiss, she'll be full of shit.

But that's a problem to deal with later.

Maciah calling instead of texting me first tells me that something else has happened.

Once I make my way outside, I double-check that Sophie hasn't followed me. I wouldn't be surprised if she did or cracks the door open in an attempt to use her wolf hearing to listen in on our conversation. That alone has me watching the motel room from where I stand. Once I'm as certain as I can be that Sophie isn't eavesdropping, I give Maciah the all-clear to speak freely.

"We have a problem," he says first.

"I assumed as much," I reply. "What happened?"

"Sophie showing up complicated matters, just as I thought it would," Maciah explains. "The trap was for someone else, but as soon as Astor figured out it was her in that house, he changed his plans and is intent on having her now."

"What does that mean?" I ask, keeping my voice low just in case.

"It means that they have history, as I told you before, and while he hasn't bothered with her before, thanks to us threatening him with the full force of East Texas all those years ago, it seems her return has made him forget our arrangement," he tells me, but he pauses before dropping a bomb I don't expect. "Sophie killed his son."

It would be great if I could ask if he's sure, but after what I've seen, I have no doubt it's true.

"What did the guy do?" This woman might be a killer, but something tells me she doesn't murder because she gets some sort of thrill out of the action.

Maciah is silent, then I hear tapping as if he's typing something on the phone. "They were mates."

I nearly choke before I'm able to reply. "As in fated mates?"

"That's my understanding," he says. "Sophie was only sixteen when she met Astor's son—Thane. He was in his twenties. Considered himself a prince and his father a king, and thought that his mate was his property."

Regardless of the seriousness of this story, I laugh, because I can't imagine someone treating this particular she-wolf as property, much less getting away with it. How someone who should have been close to her thought he could is beyond me.

"It's worse," Maciah explains. "From what River told me, Thane tried to force her to officially mate with him, knowing she was a teenager."

Any enjoyment I might have gotten from this story is stripped away within an instant. My chest burns with rage, and even more, my wolf snarls from deep within. "*Tried to*? As in, he didn't succeed?"

Men who force themselves on anyone deserve to be killed, but to do so to your fated mate? The one you're supposed to protect until your dying breath and cherish more than your own life? I can't even fathom the thought.

If Thane wasn't already dead, I'd be hunting him down tonight regardless of Maciah's answer.

"No, Sophie killed him when he continued to push things and threaten her," he says. "She ran away for the second time after that. We didn't realize just how bad things were the first time we brought her back to the pack for her parents. Two of our men found her, and once they learned why she ran away again, we agreed it was best to place the girl within the protection of the East Texas pack."

Understanding Sophie and her...*overzealous* ways is

getting easier by the second. She still isn't over what she felt forced to do when she was basically a child.

"And Astor suddenly wants his retribution, even though it's been over ten years and regardless of the risk that a pack twice the size of his would decimate him," I state, making sure I'm reading the situation clearly.

"From the sounds of it, yes," Maciah answers. "I'm going to be sending River in tomorrow. He's familiar with this pack. His dad was the previous beta, but it's been years since River lived there. He'll be pretending that he left because he didn't agree with ideologies there and wanted out, but under new leadership, he thought maybe he could come home. If Astor and York—the current acting alpha—buy his story, River is going to have to do things he wouldn't normally. I need you to still trust him."

I've worked with River several times over the years. He's a solid protector and has never given me any reason to doubt where his loyalties lie, but it's not me I'm worried about.

"I'll make sure Sophie knows to—"

Maciah stops me. "No, Kyler. She can't know any of this."

A deep crease forms between my brows as I continue to watch the motel room. "Why?"

"She's been away from her pack for too long, and she's too emotionally involved," he says sternly. "That girl has been running for most of her life. I don't know what made her want to come back to South Carolina now, when everything is going to shit, but something is off. I'm not saying it's with Sophie, but we don't know her, either. She will still get our protection, but I'm not willing to risk the lives of good people because she demands to know more than she needs to. This is bigger than her and more than I can share in detail, even with you right now."

I can't disagree with him. Not just because he's my boss, but because I also understand. None of this feels like a coincidence. Not Sophie showing up, not me being the one sent to protect her, not the secrets I have a feeling are only just starting to be uncovered.

"I'm going to need to give her something," I say, knowing there's no way I can go back into that room and not tell her anything without her threatening me.

Maciah sighs. "After that brief conversation, I expected that. Tell her that our guy on the inside—Cane —is searching for her family, and as soon as we know there aren't innocents in the way, we will be attacking."

"Cane Bridges?" I ask. "He's who's been there, feeding you information?"

"He is. I didn't know you knew him."

I don't personally, but I've heard stories. He doesn't always play by the rules, so I'm surprised Maciah trusted him to infiltrate the pack, but I don't say that. Not when I don't have any proof of the things I've heard and he's already there. It's not as if anything can be done.

"Just heard of him," I say. "I'll look him up on the directory, so we have a fresh image of what he looks like and don't accidentally kill him."

Maciah laughs. "That would be preferred. I'll be in

touch. Keep Sophie in check as best you can, stay under the radar, and Kyler?"

"Yeah?"

"Don't let her get away."

He ends the call as I mutter, "Easier said than done."

As I make my way back to the room, Sophie's shadow moves past the curtains. At least she didn't sneak out the bathroom window while I was busy.

Walking into the room, I find her sitting on the bed near two empty pizza boxes. She grins at me and rubs her belly. "That was so much better than the chips and candy I had in the car."

"Your *relationship* with food isn't normal," I say, walking past her to use the bathroom.

She gets up and heads toward the door. "I'm going to go get another change of clothes."

"No, you're not," I say, a little taken aback, considering she didn't immediately want to know what Maciah wanted to talk privately about.

Add that to the fact that she's trying to leave the room, and something isn't right. Again.

By the time her hand touches the handle on the door, I'm right behind her and spinning her back around. It wasn't my intention to pin her against the wall, but that's where she ends up as I look down at her and say, "We only leave this room together."

She stares back up at me with defiance. "Are you going to try to force me to stay by your side, Kyler?"

The challenge in her tone isn't missed. Not by a long shot. "Are you going to continue to be a child about this entire situation instead of accepting that I'm here to help?"

The dig has the desired effect. Her jaw tightens, and there's a slight rumble in her chest. "I'm not a child."

She's right about that. In fact, she's more woman than I should probably attempt to handle, but I'm not going anywhere, and neither is she. At least, not without me.

"Then show me that by waiting for me," I say, purposefully challenging her wolf by staring into her eyes, unblinking. Though I do make sure not to touch her. At least not now. This moment isn't about our shared attraction. It's about reminding Sophie that she isn't the only powerful wolf in the room.

There's a flicker of something with her light-green gaze that I can't quite translate, but whatever was there disappears quickly. "Fine. I'll wait."

This she-wolf... I don't know what I'm going to do with her.

Protect her, my wolf mutters unpleasantly.

I rein in my shock at his acceptance to our situation and tread carefully as I give Sophie one last hard look before leaving her against the door as I head toward the bathroom again.

We'll do our job, I reply to my wolf, voice filled with confidence. *Sophie won't be hurt. Not again.*

Thinking about her fated mate and what she went through makes my blood boil all over again. Thankfully, my wolf's emotions seem to match mine for the first time in much too long.

At least he understands that she deserves our help, even if he's not willing to admit that she's a good match for us.

Selfishly, I also can't ignore the fact that both of us no longer have our fated mates. Not in this lifetime. I know Cara wouldn't want me to live out my life alone. She'd said as much in the end and I'd already decided that earlier, but to have found someone so soon that I feel a connection to and who I don't have to fear being ripped away from me... That gives me even more reason to believe none of this is coincidental. At least, not my being here.

I finish in the bathroom and when I step back into the room, I'm shocked to see Sophie standing there. I half-expected her to have walked out the door as soon as I no longer had eyes on her.

Before I can say anything about appreciating her waiting, she nods toward the outside. "Let's go."

As much as I hope she will start to trust me, I have a feeling that things are going to get much worse before they can even attempt to be civil. Regardless, I have no intention of backing down.

Not from this wolf or even her unwillingness to admit her feelings with words. I'll break her down eventually, and something tells me that she'll secretly enjoy every torturous second of fighting me, which makes whatever shit we're undoubtedly about to get mixed up in worth dealing with.

Chapter Twelve

Sophie

Getting my clothes doesn't quite go as I think it will. One minute, I feel like I can take control of this situation and get my shit together, and the next...Kyler is buying me cake.

And not just any cake. A heavenly, *death by chocolate* kind of delicacy. Three layers of the moistest cake that melt in my mouth, separated by a chocolate mousse, and covered in ganache frosting, then topped with sprinkles.

Honestly, I can't care about anything else at the moment. And between Kyler ordering me pizza and now surprising me with cake, I can't deny I want to get naked all over again.

Instead, I'm sitting in the passenger's seat of my car, eating my treat with a plastic fork and waiting for Kyler to come back from the store, where he's getting some "much needed supplies," according to him.

He might have even said what those are, but I

stopped hearing him the moment he pulled into the bakery and said he'd be back with something for me.

Should I give a shit that he's manipulating me with this dessert after I teasingly told him I was basically dating food? Probably, but I don't. Not even in the slightest.

By the time I get to the last quarter of the cake, I pause and think maybe I should save Kyler a slice, but that thought doesn't linger long. If he wanted some, he should have gotten his own.

As I dig into the final piece, he returns with an overflowing cart of stuff. When he opens the back door of the car and starts tossing bags in, I just shake my head. I don't even want to know.

Well, unless there's more cake, but I actually think I've hit my limit for the night. Maybe.

Kyler peeks over my shoulder. "How nice of you to save me a crumb."

"You can even lick the plate," I reply wittily, making him laugh.

The sound makes my chest tighten. No. I'm supposed to be in a committed relationship with food. Not this man.

Who said anything about committing? my wolf says accusingly. *It could just be sex.*

Except I see the way Kyler looks at me. He might have owned my mouth like a savage, but I have a feeling this man isn't just looking to get laid. If he were, why in the world would he pick a murdering, stubborn wolf shifter who's also supposed to be the woman he's protecting?

He wouldn't.

Under any other circumstances, I'd be running for the hills, but this isn't just about whatever is going on with Kyler and me. It's about my family.

I can't run now. Even if they weren't there for me when I needed them most, I won't abandon them now. Not when I have a feeling they're possibly in trouble because of me.

Nightmares used to plague me that Astor would hunt me down and take my life just as I'd taken his son's. Yet as the years passed, I'd never even felt an attempt was taken at my life outside of the stupid situations I put myself into. I thought maybe I was in the clear.

That might have been my biggest mistake. I knew Thane's family was twisted.

You couldn't have known he'd be playing the long game, my wolf says, *and you still don't. This might not have anything to do with you.*

But what if it does? I counter. *What if my choosing to come back has put them all in danger?*

You can't control the actions of others. I'm not saying we need to leave, but you need to stop making this about yourself.

Her words almost feel like a slap to the face. That hasn't been... I mean maybe a little, but not without just cause. Right?

They were waiting at my parents' house. The first shifter tried to kill me, and the others gave chase, but still, as I recount their actions, it's what any guard would have done if assigned to watch over a house.

I'm not part of their pack. I don't share a connection with them. I'm nobody. An intruder to be dealt with.

Fuck. Have I been making a bigger deal out of this than I should have been the whole time?

No, my wolf says. *We came here for closure and your family isn't around, preventing that. I just need you to realize this might have nothing to do with you.*

Kyler slides into the driver's seat, and I take a few subtle, deep breaths. Once again, my wolf proves just how wise she is and how much I need her. I allow myself a moment of silence to accept what she's said and realize I may have overreacted a bit. Still, I don't regret coming here, and I'm not leaving until I know what the hell is happening.

It doesn't matter that nothing has gone as planned or that I might feel even more lost than I did before showing up in South Carolina. I'm going to finish what I started and get the closure I feel rather certain that I need to move on with my life once and for all.

Now you just need to listen to me about Kyler, and everything can be perfect in our life, she muses with a slight laugh.

Now you're pushing it, Wolf.

Her chuckle grows louder, but I'm relieved of having to continue that conversation when Kyler finally speaks.

"I got you some clothes," he says. "I wasn't sure how much you had with you."

My head turns swiftly toward him. "Why?"

"Why would I do something nice for you?" he asks, a layer of confusion in his voice. "Has nobody done anything in your life just because they could?"

The fact that I have to truly think about and can still only come up with Roman and Cait taking me in and allowing me to process things in the ways I needed... Yeah, I might have more issues in my life than just needing closure from my family.

Instead of delving into my fucked-up head any more, I merely shrug. "A time or two."

He doesn't say anything else, and his hands tighten around the steering wheel.

"Did something happen in the store?" I ask since this is the first time he's been so tense since finding me. I should be pleased. It makes it easier to stay away from him, but I also want to make sure there isn't anything further to worry about.

"No." His reply is clipped, and I don't believe him, but also, I'm realizing that I never got around to interrogating him about his call with Maciah.

"What did Maciah want to talk privately about with you?" I turn a little in my seat to watch his face as I ask the question.

Though I don't get the response I expect.

His lips lightly turn upward. "Me telling you would no longer make it a private conversation."

I roll my eyes. "Did you really think I wasn't going to demand to know what the hell is going on?"

"A man can hope," he jokes, his body relaxing again. "He wanted to inform me that another protector named

Cane is inside the pack and relaying information as he can. He hasn't seen your family and it's not his primary job to find them, but if they're seen, the information will be passed along."

That doesn't seem like something that would need to be discussed *privately*.

"What else?" I press, still watching him.

Kyler's brow raises as he glances briefly at me. "You really want to know?"

"I wouldn't have asked if I didn't."

"He wanted to make sure I hadn't crossed any lines with you." Kyler says the words so casually, but they immediately make me regret asking.

I want to ask what he said, but I also don't want to have this conversation. Not when I still feel so conflicted about anything that has to do with this man.

"Not that you asked," he adds cockily as I stare out the window, "but I told him we were maintaining a professional relationship. Hope you don't mind me lying."

The smugness in his tone has me wanting to backhand him, but I refrain from resorting to violence. Picturing my hands around his neck only leads me to conjure up other images that I'd rather not.

"He also asked me to find out if you remember anything about your pack that could be helpful in this situation," Kyler says and this time, I have no problem giving him attention.

"Like what?" I ask.

"Places to enter that might be less guarded, hiding

areas, where they might be holding the alpha if he's not actually missing. Anything like that."

My first thought is to refuse telling him anything of the sort. Pack loyalty runs deep through shifters. When I really consider my life, though, I have no pack. South Carolina isn't my home, and whatever fleeting thought I had about coming back here, it isn't going to be to stay.

East Texas is technically my home, but I've denied them in more ways than I can count. They should have ousted me the day I became an adult. The fact that they haven't and even still had the forethought to send help my way... I know I've made a mistake.

Well, maybe not a mistake, but I have ignored the good things in my life for far too long and I'm done doing so.

I'll find my family. Make sure they're okay—again, that wolf shifter loyalty making things harder—then I'll say my goodbyes. I need to sever ties once and for all so that I can return to Texas, watch Dawsyn become Alpha, and settle my ass down. I'm done running.

Even thinking those thoughts has my shoulders relaxing and my wolf humming in approval.

Contentment fills my body, making me feel lighter than I have since I was a young girl. I'm allowing myself this moment to accept what I've decided is foreign, but I know this is the right path for me.

Soul deep, there is a sense of peace that I've avoided for far too long. No more guilt. No more searching for distraction. No more pretending the past doesn't exist or that it has to define who I am.

Just no more.

Before I know it, we're back at the motel, but when Kyler stops the car, he doesn't get out. Instead, he stares at me with concern filling his light-grey eyes. "I didn't mean to pry about your old pack. If you don't want to share what you know, you don't have to. Not that you don't already know that, just know I won't bother you about it if—"

I cut him off with a wave of my hand. I let my thoughts go rampant for a moment and completely forgot he'd even asked me about the pack weaknesses.

"No," I say. "I'll tell you what I remember. I just... I'm in a food coma. Too much chocolate."

The lie falls easily from my lips, because there is no way in hell that I'm telling him about the revelations I've had tonight.

"Well, let's get the car unloaded and to bed, then," he says, opening his door and getting out.

I let out a sigh of relief that he doesn't press me for more.

Getting out, I help grab bags, surprised to find bottles of water, med kits, snacks, clothes, and what appears to be useful hunting items like knives, dark clothes, and scent removal spray. Not that the latter would entirely work, but it might confuse a younger wolf for a hot second.

We get everything inside, and Kyler tosses me one of the bags he grabbed. "This has clothes for you."

I don't know how he knew my size and don't ask. I don't want to be rude when he's actually been pretty fantastic this entire time, if I'm being honest. Well, aside from thinking that cabin was safe and throwing me out a window and...

Maybe I shouldn't think too hard and just be grateful.

"Thanks," I finally say before heading to the bathroom to change. I've been naked in front of him more than once, but the less I dislike him, the more I realize I should keep myself covered.

Why? my wolf asks. *You're having all these revelations. What about Kyler? Doesn't he deserve one?*

He might deserve it, but he's not getting one, I say as I use the bathroom. *I've made my choice. I want to go back to East Texas when this is all done. I want to find a home and the peace that comes with that. Kyler is a protector. He isn't settled anywhere.*

Maybe he wants the same things you do, she says. I briefly let myself wonder if that could be true, but I stop before I can get too far into that fantasy. He has a fated mate out there somewhere. I won't risk having my heart broken for a second time.

Not even for someone who seems to understand my crass ways and doesn't appear to be judging me for my actions.

I wash my hands and face, then get dressed. She says nothing else on the matter, because I'm right. Kyler isn't just a hookup. He could be something more—I'm not too stubborn to deny that—and the risk is too great that he'll stumble on his fated mate one day and forget all about us.

There is a large men's shirt and loose sleep shorts, both black, in the bag that I assume are supposed to be pajamas. At least he didn't get me something with flowers or hearts on them.

Lace would have been better, my wolf says, making me laugh as I change clothes.

Only in your dreams, Wolfy.

Shoving my dirty and ruined clothes into the garbage, I search the new bag for a toothbrush. Gods, he really is too good. Tucking the rest of the items into the corner of the bathroom to go through better tomorrow, I at least brush my teeth before heading to bed. It's getting late, and it's been a long fucking day. I'm ready for sleep, especially after all the sugar I've eaten.

Once finished at the sink, I open the door and step forward without really watching where I'm going, running right into Kyler. He's standing there with his fist raised as if he were just about to knock on the door.

Our chests are pressed together, and I have to tilt my head back to see his face. "I was just going to make sure you knew there was a toothbrush and toothpaste in the bag as well since I heard you cleaning up."

I can now see his own in his other hand, but my eyes go right back to his face—more specifically, his mouth.

Damn him. Why does being this close to him make my skin tingle and heat? Why are my hands itching to claw at his chest before grabbing his cheeks to bring him closer?

I shouldn't do any of those things, but the longer I

allow the thoughts to swirl within my mind, the darker his gaze grows, as if he knows just what I'm thinking.

"Sophie," he says, almost as a warning, but I don't know if that's for me or him.

"Oh, fuck it," I mutter.

I'll deal with the consequences of this choice later.

I jump up, wrap my arms and legs around him, and kiss him without allowing myself to overthink the action.

He drops the items he was holding and has his hands on me just as quickly, one holding my ass and squeezing while the other gets entwined in my hair. He's kissing me back with matched enthusiasm, our tongues tangling as if neither has tasted anything so delectable in decades.

A moan leaves me and is swallowed by Kyler as he adjusts his stance to pin me against the wall. The moment he has more leverage, his hips move forward, and I almost cry out in pleasure.

His hard cock grinds against me and gives just as good as he does while I'm still kissing the hell out of him. My nails dig into his shoulders as the sounds leaving me get louder.

What the hell is happening to me? Am I about to have an orgasm just from a bit of dry humping and a make-out session?

I've hardly gotten off during sex in the past, so this is...new territory.

My skin feels as if it's going to melt off, and there's a tightening at my core that is painful to the point of being euphoric.

Kyler growls and practically slams us both into the

wall as we claw at each other, amping up the shared friction between us.

I can barely breathe and have to break the kiss, dropping my head back. He takes that opportunity to force my head to the side and expose my neck.

His tongue traces over the sensitive skin and teeth lightly scrape across my tendons, while at the same time, his thighs are still grinding against me.

Fuck, this is too much. I can't... I'm going to...

"Kyler," I cry out his name, the sound full of breath yet winded all at the same time as everything in me shatters from the inside out. Any control I thought I had was just wrecked beyond repair.

He holds me tighter against him, his movements slowing, and reality comes crashing down all at once.

What have I just done?

Chapter Thirteen

Kyler

All I'd been trying to do was make sure she had a toothbrush. I had no intention of pushing for more, even if my wolf had shocked the hell out of me earlier by giving me his permission to do so.

Do what you want.

Those four words had tumbled randomly into my thoughts as I was done loading all the items that I'd bought into the car. I tried to get him to talk to me, but he wouldn't add anything.

The more I considered what to do next, the more withdrawn I'd become, and I was ready to fall asleep, hoping for clarity to come with the sunrise. But with the way Sophie looked up at me, I couldn't help myself.

And it seemed neither could she, given she was the one to launch herself at me.

There wasn't a single part of me that had wanted to stop, but I knew the moment she came apart in my arms that I'd lost her.

The fear filling her eyes wasn't hard to miss. Maybe it was wrong, but I let her escape back to the bathroom as she mumbled something about needing to take a piss.

She slammed the door and has been hidden behind it for at least five minutes. I decide to brush my teeth in the room, using a plastic cup from next to the coffee maker and a bottle of water. By the time I'm done and have changed into a pair of grey sweatpants, she still isn't out.

I'm tempted to knock on the door and check on her, but something tells me that it's better for her to work this out on her own.

I grab an extra blanket from one of the drawers in the dresser and head to the couch. I turn the main light out and leave a lamp on next to the bed. As soon as I lay my head down, I finally hear the bathroom door creak.

My eyes watch the dark corner of the room, and the silhouette of Sophie slowly comes closer to the light.

"I just..." she says, but the words trail off.

"It's okay, Sophie," I promise. "I'm not going to rush you into something you're not ready for."

Even if my cock is aching and there's nothing that I can do about it with her right here. At least nothing I'm *willing* to do, knowing it would likely make her feel guilty.

She doesn't say anything as she crawls into the bed. I watch her face as she reaches to turn out the light. The deep crease between her eyes worries me, but the fact that she didn't stubbornly choose to sleep in the bathroom tells me that she's not completely ashamed of me making her come.

"Sleep well," I add when I can hear her rustling under the blankets.

She's quiet for a beat before responding, "You, too."

Yeah, that's not going to happen. Not when I know she's within touching distance. Between her reservations and my wolf's oddly given approval, though, I also know that I shouldn't and can't reach for her.

JUST AS I ASSUMED IT WOULD, SLEEP ELUDES ME. I listen to Sophie toss and turn for most of the night. It isn't until after three that her breathing begins to settle into an even rhythm. So, when I see the sun peeking through the curtain just before six in the morning, I keep quiet.

I head to the shower, taking new clothes with me, and get ready for the day. When I'm done, she's still out, so I make my way outside, ignoring the desire to watch her sleep or brush her hair out of her face or press my lips against her creamy skin.

The morning air is chilled, but it doesn't bother me. Not when everything inside me feels so charged.

I head to the main office to grab coffee. Every step away from the room feels wrong. There's something pulling me back. Not the tether of a mate bond that I would recognize, having experienced it before, but there's some sort of connection to Sophie.

She has to feel it as well. After last night, there's no denying that. Still, I meant what I said before. I'm not going to rush her into anything. Though, I also have no intention of stopping her from throwing herself at me when the need strikes.

There's nobody behind the desk when I slip into the office area. I quickly grab my coffee and just as I make an escape, I hear someone humming and getting closer.

Not that I'm trying to hide. I just don't feel like making small talk with a human.

Okay, and maybe because I can't stand the thought of staying away from the room any longer than this. My stride lengthens, and I'm back at the door to the room in under a minute.

There's a tightness in my chest, and I have to close my eyes, resting my forehead against the door as I level out my breathing.

What the hell is wrong with me?

I haven't felt this out of control since...

Cara.

But that can't be right. This isn't a fated mate bond. Sure, there are feelings—desire and the need to protect Sophie—but that's a far cry from when I met Cara. She had literally brought me to my knees.

It's our second chance, my wolf says, this time without the hostility I've grown used to sensing from him over the last couple of days.

What do you mean? I ask, because I've heard of fated and chosen mates, but nothing about second chances. The way he said those two words makes me believe they mean something more than a surface-level second chance at happiness.

I was visited by our creator, The Moon Goddess, he replies reverently. *She told me to stop fighting you and to remember that everything happens for a reason. That if I embraced the draw to Sophie, I would understand.*

Understand what? I feel confident I know what he's saying, but I need to hear the words from my wolf. I need to know that the discontentment between us won't continue.

Sophie is our second-chance fated mate, he confirms, just as I hope. *I'm sorry I was so angry before. I just didn't want to...*

He doesn't need to finish, and I don't make him. *I know, and we're not going to forget Cara. I believe she led us here.*

She and the great Luna both, he says, this time with a layer of confidence that lightens the tension in my chest that's been there since the moment he became upset at Cara's gravesite.

Thank you, I reply with a smile growing on my face. I reach for the handle to go back into the motel room, but Sophie is already opening the door.

"What are you doing out here?" she demands, then she spots the coffee in my hand that I haven't even taken a sip of. "Oh. Perfect. I need this."

She steals the cup from me and turns back toward the room. "Why are you up at this ungodly hour?" she asks after taking a drink.

"I'm a morning person," I reply simply. Telling her I couldn't sleep with her so close yet so far away might be a bit too much this early in the day.

Sophie groans and shakes her head. "Of course you are."

I start to make coffee, this time in the room since I don't have to worry about waking her up, and I swear I can feel her eyes on me. The need to turn around is strong, but I'm not stupid. If I push her, regardless of what my wolf just told me, she will run.

"What do you want to do today?" I ask without looking back at her.

I hear movement on the bed, the sheets shifting beneath her. "Do you have any more of those cloaking spells?"

My single serving of coffee finishes, and I grab the cup to add sugar before answering her. "Not likely. Everything I brought with me was in that cabin. The wolves likely already searched and took what was there."

"How do you get them?" she asks, and I finally turn to face her.

Her cheeks have a red tinge to them, her chestnut hair is mussed—likely from all the tossing and turning last night—and her green eyes seem a bit red, but damn if I don't still find her beautiful.

"Kyler?" she says, and it takes me a second to remember that she asked me a question before I got distracted with her presence.

"From the main protector headquarters or one of the safehouses, but the nearest one is about four hours from here, taking us even farther from the pack," I answer, then I take a drink, hoping that some caffeine will keep me focused.

Sophie's mouth flattens. "That won't work. There's a supernatural bar two towns over. We can go there for anything we might need."

"Isn't that a risk?" I ask, worried that wolves from her old pack might frequent there since she knows about it and she could be spotted.

"Don't you worry about me." She smirks. "Now, I'm going to finish my coffee and if you want me to spill all my old pack's secrets, then you better have breakfast ready for me when I get out of the shower."

She takes several gulps from her cup, then stands from the bed and saunters into the bathroom, seemingly without a care in the world. I watch her ass as she goes, unable to hold back my grin.

Breaking past her defenses just might be one of the greatest challenges of my life. Even if all I have to do is continue to supply her with food.

Chapter Fourteen

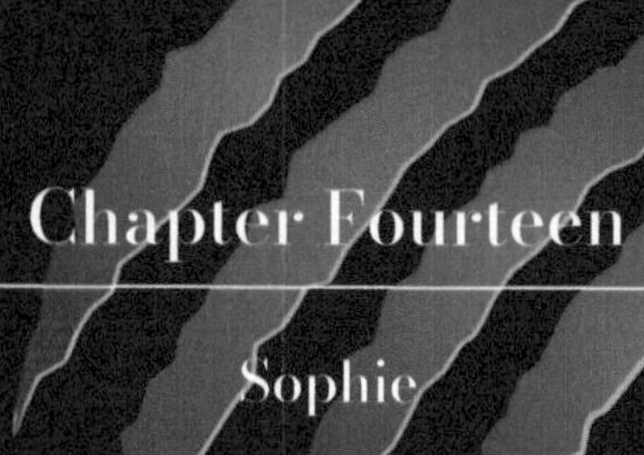

Sophie

Kyler didn't disappoint when I got out of the shower. He had an array of items for me to choose from, including Pop-Tarts, donut holes, granola bars, and even a few selections of fruit.

When I grab a banana to go with my donut holes, he laughs. "Oh, good. You don't survive only on sugar and carbs."

"Nope." I smack my lips together. "But I could."

I wouldn't allow it, my wolf says. *Meat is needed unless you want me to start biting random people.*

Well, that could be fun.

Don't even consider it, she growls, making me laugh.

I don't think I could, even if I wanted to drive her mad. I love a juicy burger and steak just as much as she does.

"Are you ready to go?" he asks as I finish the donuts.

I start shoving the things I didn't eat into a bag. "Just

as soon as I grab enough snacks to replenish my emergency food stash."

He grins and raises a brow. "Is that what you call your glove box?"

"Honestly, that's one of the more stupid names for random objects that humans have come up with," I say with slight annoyance. "Who has ever used that compartment to store *gloves* in? Not me. Not anyone I know."

Ever since I realized how idiotic the name was, I've called it either my mini-cabinet or emergency food stash. Things that actually make sense. Because you know, I'm not the crazy one.

"Right," he muses. "Well, let's get going. If we get to the bar early, there should be less people there that we need to worry about."

"You'd think," I mutter, slinging the filled grocery bag over my shoulder. I grab my keys off the dresser. "I'm driving."

I've let this man drive me around too much. It's time I took charge.

Because you've been doing that so well, my wolf snickers. *Last night especially.*

Shut your dirty mouth, I growl. *I was... Whatever. Just because I lost it once doesn't mean I can't keep my shit together today.*

And you're still lying to yourself. Her mocking laugh echoes through my mind like church bells.

Maybe she's right. Okay, most likely. Especially

because the moment I exit the motel room, my body wants to stop and wait for Kyler to catch up.

That desire makes absolutely zero sense. He isn't ours. He belongs to someone else. This is only supposed to be a fleeting attraction. Except, the longer I'm around him, the more I slip up and allow myself to touch him, the more drawn to this man I feel.

I couldn't sleep for shit last night. So many times, I opened my mouth to demand he get into the bed with me, but I knew where that would lead...

To multiple glorious orgasms, my wolf finishes for me.

This time, I don't bother arguing with her. If that man can make me fall apart just by dry humping me, then I can't even imagine what he can do when we're both naked. The thought is almost too much to even consider.

I walk faster toward my car, throw the bag of snacks in the passenger's seat, and get behind the wheel. Yeah, the distraction of driving is just what I need.

No, you need that man's dick inside you before we combust, my wolf titters.

A rumble releases from my chest. "Stop."

Kyler is just opening his door, of course, and peeks his head into the car. "Did you forget something?"

I hate you, I say to my wolf before shaking my head at Kyler. "Just get in."

All the while, she laughs at me and I have to bite my cheek, using the pain to get my shit together.

Drive the car to the bar, get a cloaking spell so we can sneak back onto the pack lands, and find my family.

Nothing else matters right now, because more than anything, I just want to get the hell away from this place now that I'm here.

How I could have considered coming back to South Carolina and staying is beyond me. All this area brings are bad memories that I need to put behind me.

I pull out of the parking lot and head for the highway that will take us toward the bar. It used to be open twenty-four hours a day and hopefully still is or we'll be driving thirty minutes in the wrong direction only to sit there for who knows how long until they open.

"Once we have the cloaking spells, I know where we need to go to sneak back into the pack," I say, switching lanes and keeping my gaze fixed on the road instead of the man next to me.

"Why do you want to go back there?" he asks with possibly a little suspicion in his voice.

"I told you I'm not stopping until I know my family is safe," I reply sharply. "And I want to see that with my own eyes. Someone from your work saying they're fine isn't enough."

That doesn't give me the closure I want, either.

"You were going to tell me about the weak points in the pack?" he mentions, not-so-subtly changing the subject.

I consider calling him out on it but don't bother. I'm driving, and there's nothing he can do to prevent me from going where I want.

"Just remember all this information is more than ten

years old," I say first. "Before yesterday, I hadn't been back there since I...relocated to East Texas."

I expect him to ask why, but he doesn't. Maybe he already knows, but I would think he'd mention being aware that I killed my own mate. So I continue. "The pack house has a basement and there's a window that I've snuck through before. It's on the south side of the building, and that part of the house was never used for anything, but I wouldn't bet on that being the case now. The farther west into the pack lands you go, the closer you get to government land that doesn't see a lot of traffic, thanks to the terrain. This would be the best place to sneak in."

"Why didn't you go that way before, then?" Kyler asks, his voice curious instead of accusing.

"Because I'm not here for the pack," I reply honestly. "I'm here to see my parents and sister. Nothing more, nothing less."

Again, I expect him to question why after all this time, but he merely nods at me to continue.

I hesitate, once more feeling as if I can't trust him. An undeniable attraction is one thing. Telling him more than he needs to know is something else entirely.

You're not telling him anything that can hurt people, my wolf reminds me. *They already have a man on the inside. This is just showing him that he can trust you.*

But do we trust him? I ask, waiting for her reply before continuing to speak to Kyler.

She mulls over her answer, and the words that come next are full of confidence. *I think you both have secrets and your own reasons for keeping them. Trust isn't necessarily what you need to focus on. Do you believe that he's here with good intentions? Because I do. And for now, that's enough.*

It's easy to agree with her. Though, I'm not sure if that's because she's right or because for the first time in over a decade, I want to have met someone worth believing in.

"Guards rotate the grounds in pairs," I finally continue, having made my decision, even if I'm not sure why. "There are schedules they stick to. Once you figure those out, you'll find the other temporary blind spots. That is, if they haven't upgraded to things like video surveillance or motion detectors."

Kyler's hand lifts, but he settles it back onto his thigh. "Thank you for sharing that with me."

I only nod and turn up the radio. I'm no longer in the mood to chat, not even when it's my turn to ask the questions.

Five and a half songs and another twenty minutes later, we arrive at Bee's Bar. Interestingly enough, nobody has ever met "Bee." At least that was the case last time I was in this area. I assume it's because Bee doesn't exist, and someone just wanted a name that would make people talk. Job well done, Stranger.

This time, Kyler doesn't hesitate to reach out and grab my wrist as I turn off the car. "Wait."

My eyes move from his hand that's currently branding my skin to his face. "I'd let go if I were you."

The threat is real. I don't want to hurt him, but this

isn't the motel room. We're here to get a spell that will help me find my family without getting caught. I won't tolerate him distracting me.

One by one, his fingers lift, and he pulls his arm back. I expect there to be a mark where he was touching, but my skin is completely normal.

"I was just going to suggest that we need to stick together," he says. "We didn't discuss a plan and I don't want—"

"You don't want me to run away?" I cut in, finishing what I assume he's thinking but might not actually say.

"That's not where I was going with that." He sneers, his eyes darkening just a few shades. "Unless you haven't told me about a friend you might have inside here, we shouldn't trust anyone else. Sticking together will keep us from being put in a situation we don't have time for if you want to get back to the pack today."

I unbuckle, glancing over at him with a smirk embedded on my face. Getting into a *situation* just might be the highlight of my day. "I guess we will just see how things go."

Without waiting for his response, I get out of the car and head toward the bar's entrance. The place is rundown on the outside. Water and rust stains trickle down the grey-but-probably-should-be-white siding. The windows are covered in a dark film that's cracked, but you still can't see through it. Weeds are growing out of every crack in the asphalt while spiders and other bugs have made homes beneath the overhang.

Every reason for someone to want to avoid this place. Unless you're supernatural.

As soon as my hand touches the handle on the warped door, a soothing energy sweeps through my body, warming me from the inside out.

Without any issue, I pull the door open and step inside. A human would have been filled with dread and unease, encouraging them to turn around and leave.

When the outside world disappears, the true image of Bee's Bar comes into view. Black marble floors and high ceilings with small lights dangling down, creating an ambient glow. The high-top tables have wooden surfaces and shiny, metal stools around them that match the sleek bar top.

Behind the counter is just one worker with four other patrons sitting on the barstools. Kyler enters behind me, a quiet rumble in his chest that I ignore as I finish my perusal of the place.

The barkeep is a wolf shifter, but not one I recognize. His auburn hair and dark eyes land on me. "Welcome. Sit wherever you'd like."

As he acknowledges us, the others sitting at the counter turn to see the new arrivals. The closest to us is a vampire with reddish-brown eyes. A good one from what I've heard about that particular color. The darker eyes typically mean they don't live feed but use blood bags.

Next to him is a warlock, which would be helpful if his eyes didn't turn nearly black when he sees Kyler behind me. I glance back. "A friend of yours?"

He shakes his head. "Just someone I've had a run-in with on a previous job."

"Right." This is starting out swimmingly.

There's a pair of wolf shifters who aren't paying attention to us any longer and have already gone back to their day drinking.

"We can sit at one of the tables," I say. "It's early. Another magic user will come along eventually."

Kyler stays right on my heels as I walk across the bar. I stop at the back corner, where we can see both the main door we just came through and the hallway that leads to the bathroom—and still keep an eye on the bar.

However long it takes, I'm not leaving this place until we have cloaking spells. Even if the man next to me seems like he'd rather be anywhere else in the world right now.

Chapter Fifteen

Kyler

My job isn't always easy. Especially when I have to take away someone's father for doing shit he shouldn't be, like selling dark objects to good people without telling them of the consequences.

Evander's father was one of them. I haven't seen him since the day I hauled his dad off, but there he is at the bar, giving me his back and probably cursing me.

I possibly should have considered letting Sophie come here on her own. Not that I'm afraid of the warlock. My presence just doesn't seem to be helping at this point.

Though luck seems to be on our side. Evander leaves within the hour, we order lunch and drinks, and we only have to wait two more hours for a group of witches to arrive.

There are three of them, each with different-colored hair, but they all share the same deep-blue eyes with a lighter ring around them. They could be sisters, or they could just share magic a little too much with each other. Either way, I don't care as long as they help us.

The longer we're here, the more comfortable Sophie grows, and something tells me this is the last place we should let our guards down, even if the bar is supposed to be a neutral zone for all supernaturals.

"Which one?" she asks, her gaze pointed toward the trio of witches.

"Why do we have to pick one?" I counter. "Can't we just approach them?"

She rears back, and her eyes widen in disbelief. "And you're a protector? Honestly, I'm a little surprised you've lasted this long."

I really shouldn't ask, but I can't help myself. "Why?"

"That's a longer answer than we have time for," she quips. "But as far as the witches are concerned, you should never approach them together. You need to watch them, figure out which one is the weakest link, then wait until she's vulnerable. Compliment her, tell her she's the only one who can help you, then get what you want."

As much as I wish it didn't, her plan actually has logic. Well, almost. "When you say 'you,' are you referring to yourself or me?"

The smirk on her face doesn't bode well for me. "Depends on which team she's playing for."

Putting Sophie's plan into action, we watch the three witches. There's a redhead, a blonde, and one with purple hair. The latter is loud and does the most talking, which quickly removes her from the equation.

My first thought is that it's going to be the blonde that we approach, but a few minutes later, Sophie gets up to head to the bar without saying a damn word to me and goes ahead with her own plan.

I'm tempted to follow, but I stay put as she stops, only a few seats away from the trio.

The blonde has eyes on her, and before Sophie can even order a drink, the witch is on the prowl. Using my wolf hearing, I listen in on the conversation, immediately glad I didn't join her.

The blonde nods my way. "Your man not capable of buying you a drink himself?"

Sophie's laugh carries across the bar. "Oh, he's not mine. Just a friend."

"A male friend who looks like *that* and you're not hooking up?" the blonde muses, a smirk rising on her ruby-red lips. "I was right about you."

"Under certain circumstances, you just might have been," Sophie says saucily, "but not today. I'm just here for a drink and good food."

The blonde gives Sophie another onceover. "Pity. Let me know if you change your mind."

She winks in return, takes her drink, then heads back toward our table while I openly gape at her, wondering under which *circumstances* the blonde would have had a chance and trying not to picture more than I should.

"Oh, put your tongue back in your mouth, dog," she teases, keeping her voice low. "She never had a chance with me. I just needed to see if my senses were still spot on." Sophie sits a little taller in her seat. "Clearly, they are, which means you're going after the redhead. She's going to be the easiest to get the cloaking spells from."

"Right," I say slowly, then I quiet my voice. "And you're sure the redhead wouldn't prefer you over me?"

"Positive. While you were watching me, she was watching you."

My eyes flick toward the bar and as soon as they do, I find the redhead looking at me. She quickly averts her gaze, takes a long pull of her fruity cocktail, then excuses herself to use the bathroom.

"Go shoot your shot, lover boy," Sophie teases. "And don't miss. I'm ready to get the hell out of here."

"Are you implying—"

"That you should do whatever you have to in order to get the cloaking spells?" she finishes for me and not for the first time. "Abso-fucking-lutely."

When I stand, I know I'm about to regret ever taking this job, but there's nothing I can do now. Sophie is mine. She's...

Holy shit. I nearly stumble as I make my way across the bar, and it takes every bit of strength within me to remain standing. I've just called this woman mine.

I knew this morning that I'm drawn to her, and because of my wolf that she's our second chance mate, but to call another *mine*? I expect the thought to, I don't know, hurt, feel wrong, seem like a betrayal... Yet, the more I consider the truth in the words, the more right everything within my world becomes.

Sophie might not be mine for all eternity, but she can be for this lifetime. And I can be hers.

Continuing with the mission, I follow the redhead down the hallway that Sophie earlier said leads to the restrooms. The second I turn the corner, out of sight from any of the other patrons, I'm pushed against a wall and there are nails lightly scraping over my cheeks, then down my neck.

"I knew you'd follow me," the redhead's sultry voice whispers. "I've seen you staring all night."

So much for this one being docile and easy to manipulate.

Her body presses against mine, and my wolf growls so loudly that the sounds escape from between my lips, but the witch only takes that as encouragement.

"That's right, Wolfy," she purrs. "I can take care of you like no one ever has."

Her hands start moving down my chest, but I grab her wrists, halting any touching she intends on doing. Sophie was clear that I needed to seduce this witch into giving us the cloaking spells, but the thought of this redhead touching me is not worth getting what we want. We'll find another way.

Except before I can put an end to things on my own, Sophie appears behind the woman with a knife in her hand, pressing the blade to the witch's throat.

"Touch him again and I'll cut your vocal cords out," Sophie hisses menacingly, and I can't stop the grin from appearing on my face.

Especially when I see the slits in her eyes, telling me that it's not just Sophie's jealousy showing, it's also her wolf's.

The redhead's hand lifts from my chest. "I thought you said he was just your friend."

"I lied," Sophie growls. "Now, give us two cloaking spells for the inconvenience of your presence and I just might let you live."

"My sisters would hunt you down if you harmed me," the witch threatens, but while she's bold enough to put hands on me, she's not frightening either of us with her words.

"And they would meet the same fate as you if they did," Sophie says without missing a beat. "Now, the cloaking spells."

The witch reaches inside her jacket, and I tense, expecting her to fight back, but instead, she retrieves two small vials filled with clear liquid. "I'll need to conjure it. I don't just keep this shit on me."

The disdain in her voice isn't missed, but still, Sophie doesn't remove the knife from the witch's neck.

"Do it quickly," I advise. "You won't see us again."

She chuckles darkly. "That's what you hope."

Sophie uses her other hand with claws already extended and positions them over the redhead's chest. "Say something stupid again and see what happens. I ripped a wolf shifter's heart out yesterday. A witch's today will be no hardship. I can find a cloaking spell anywhere. You can't live without your heart."

Jealous Sophie is really something else. Not that I want to piss her off all the time, but I have to admit, I'm slightly entertained.

The witch presses her palms together and starts to

mutter a spell, which thankfully sounds vaguely familiar. Perks of having a few witches as protectors to provide these things before we go out on missions.

When she's done and opens her hand, the vials are no longer clear, but the light-purple color they should be for the spell.

I pluck them from her palm and tuck both into my front pocket. "Nice doing business with you," I say as I gladly step away from her.

When Sophie doesn't follow, I turn around and see her whispering something in the witch's ear that has the latter's eyes going wide and face paling.

Sophie then pats her on the shoulder and moves toward me.

I raise a brow at her, wanting an explanation, but all she does is shrug. "Girl stuff. You wouldn't understand."

I might not, but that doesn't mean I'm not more than curious about what the hell just happened and if Sophie's willing to admit she's just staked a claim on me.

We leave the bar without any issues and Sophie throws me her keys. "Your turn to drive."

"Your car, but sure, I'll continue to drive you around," I muse, but she doesn't even crack a smile.

When we're both in the car, I quickly start it and pull out of the parking lot, heading back south toward the pack. It doesn't matter that Sophie might have put the fear of the gods in that witch—I'm not sticking around to see what, if anything, she tells her sisters.

Once we're a mile down the road and I don't sense

anyone following us, I glance over at Sophie. "What did you tell the redhead?"

"I told you, girl stuff."

There's no stopping the smile that appears on my face. "Like how I'm yours and she better not even think of me in her dreams again or you'll kill her?"

The way she stiffens tells me that I'm at least close, which is good enough for me.

"No, that couldn't be it," I amend, keeping my voice light. "I'm sure it was something about asking about which shampoo she uses."

Sophie doesn't respond, but I'm not done with her yet. Not by a long shot. "We have a couple of hours until we're near the pack again. Why don't we trade questions?"

This finally has her turning to face me. "Trade questions? What do you mean?"

"You ask me something about myself, and I'll ask something about you in return," I explain, not surprised she's never done this with anyone else.

She's quiet for a minute but then sighs. "Fine. I'll go first. Why did you become a protector?"

I doubt she has any idea how serious this conversation is about to get, but I'm not going to lie to her.

"My fated mate died in a freak car accident," I say solemnly. "When I didn't think I had anything else left to live for, I decided to help give others the chance at the life I had lost."

I steal a glance at her, but she's turned toward the

window and I can't see her face. The disappointment that floods through me only increases when she doesn't say anything else.

Maybe she intended for whatever pull she's having toward me to be temporary and casual. Maybe her wolf has no clue what we are like mine figured out. Her knowing my fated mate is gone would prove there are no obstacles for us to be together. Does that freak her out? If so, should I consider that a good thing? Or a bad one?

No answers come to me, and as the seconds tick by, I know I should ask a question of my own, but I can't form the words. Not when I don't know if what I've just said has ruined any chance I thought I had with this labyrinth of a woman.

Chapter Sixteen

Sophie

I should say something. I should tell him that I understand in some small way. But I can't. As if locked away, the words won't leave my mouth, staying there as thoughts to torture me with.

But he'd understand, my wolf says softly. *He hasn't judged you yet, and I doubt he's going to start now.*

He did still kiss me after I ripped out another wolf shifter's heart, but that's different. Killing my fated mate was personal.

And it saved your life in more ways than one, my wolf reminds me.

That it had. I would have been treated as a possession, forced to do things I wouldn't want to, be someone I wasn't. All that and probably more if I hadn't defended myself against Thane.

As I keep my gaze averted out the window, my fingers lightly rub over my ribs where the most prominent scar on my body remains. I try to stop the onslaught of memories, but with my emotions all twisted, there's no avoiding the nightmare.

I'm sitting by the river, alone as usual, thanks to my friends not standing up for me against the shit Thane's been saying. Running away didn't work the first time, but as the days continue to pass and that creep of a mate stares at me with his dark, menacing eyes, I know I won't last here.

Even my wolf is anxious to run. We're not safe in our pack any longer.

Worse, I'll be packless at only sixteen.

I throw a stone across the water, watching as it skips along the surface before disappearing into the current.

My stomach grumbles. I should have brought snacks, but I wasn't thinking about food when I escaped out my bedroom window. No, all my mind could focus on were my mother's words.

"Just be a good mate and everything will be fine, Sophie. I promise, it's easier this way."

She wants me to bend to Thane's will. At sixteen. Sure, most of my friends have already had sex, but I've gotten off more from having a slice of cake than eyeballing the "men" around here.

The thought of letting my fated mate force me to do something I don't feel ready for makes me want to vomit. Even more so because my mother believes obeying the fucker is the right choice.

The sun has already set, and it's getting darker by the

minute. Between that and my aching belly, I decide it's time to go, but the moment I start to stand, the hair on the back of my neck begins to rise.

He's here.

Run, *my wolf says, but it's too late.*

Thane's wolf is breathing hard from behind me, and I wouldn't be fast enough. I force a smile to my face and turn around. Dark, narrowed eyes glare at me, and I try not to panic so he can't sense my fear.

"Hi, Thane," I say, strengthening my smile.

I expect him to shift back to his human form, but he doesn't. Instead, his voice echoes inside my head thanks to our pack bond.

It's time, Sophie, *he says gruffly.*

"Time for what?" I ask out loud. *The thought of even being inside his head repulses me, something that isn't normal between fated mates. Then again, most shifters don't feel like pieces of meat for their mates to devour.*

I'm going to mark you and you're going to be mine as of today, *he announces, making my chest tighten with the terror I can no longer hold back.* No more running, Mate. You are mine, and you will obey me.

My head starts to shake on instinct and the action has his wolf growling deeply. I take a step back, but the intensity in his stare only becomes more intrigued.

He wants to hunt me. He wants to destroy me in every way possible.

Even though I know I shouldn't, I turn and run. If I can get to the water, maybe I can swim faster than his wolf.

Except before my feet can reach the shore, his wolf's teeth latch on to my boot, halting my movements and forcing me to fall to the ground.

I try to scramble up, a scream ready to rip from my lungs, and then he pounces on top of me. The front paws of his wolf press down onto my shoulders, and saliva drips from his snarling jowls. You will do as I command, Sophie. The sooner you understand that, the easier this can be for everyone. Don't you realize the discontent you're causing within the pack by refusing me?

I blink, trying to tell myself that I'm not the problem here, but his words still penetrate right to my heart, causing me to believe otherwise.

We need to shift, *my wolf says.* You'll never beat him like this.

There is no beating him, *I reply, already feeling defeated.* The only way out of this is death.

Exactly. *His* death.

Her words make my stomach churn violently. The thought of killing my fated mate makes me want to vomit, but...I also know she's right. Thane has left us no choice. Still, accepting my limited options and taking a life are two different things.

Tears leak down the sides of my face as I consider the best path, but Thane doesn't give me even the blessing of time to think.

Show me your neck, *he demands loudly, making me yelp. His paw smacks across my face.* Don't be so pathetic.

You have to let me end him, *my wolf says, her words*

causing me to shake my head, and I realize too late what a mistake that is.

No? *he roars.* You dare to deny me what is mine?

Before I can protect myself, his claws extend and rip down my side, deep enough that blood starts to seep into the earth beneath me.

Now, Sophie! *my wolf yells, pushing her presence forward until I can no longer refuse her need for control. I know it's the right decision, but he's still my fated mate...*

Our shift takes Thane by surprise, and he's no longer on top of us once we're standing on four feet.

Stand down, Wolf, *he warns, but my girl isn't doing anything of the sort.*

She leaps for him, teeth bared and claws searching for owed blood.

I want to close my eyes and pretend this isn't happening. That what was supposed to be the best thing in my life isn't my worst nightmare. That Thane could maybe one day look at me with any amount of admiration.

But that's not my reality. I've known it since ten seconds after meeting him. I'd only been able to dream of a happier future for mere seconds before he ripped it all away from me.

My wolf's sharp canines puncture into skin for the first time. Fur and blood fill our mouth, making me want to vomit, but I'm not in control. Not now.

Yet as Thane begins to fight back, his own claws going for my spine, I know I need to do this. My wolf isn't alone with this desire to be free of this man.

You little bitch, *he screams in our mind.* I will claim you as is my right, then lock you away until you learn some fucking manners.

No, Thane, *I say with a strength I don't know I have until that moment.* You will never touch me again. I am not *yours.*

Combining my will and energy with my wolf's, we act as one and finish what he started. Our bite increases until bones begin to crack under our unrelenting force. Thane needs to die. He's going to die. Right now.

He continues to fight back, but our surprise attack gave us the upper hand and no amount of clawing at our fur is going to save him. There is no pain to feel right now for us. It's only pure determination to survive.

Finally, his movements slow. Still, my wolf doesn't ease up. She shakes our head several times, and only when we no longer hear his heartbeat does she unclench her jaw.

We need to run, *she says, a sadness I more than understand lacing her words.*

I know. We can't ever come back.

Not when my own mother encouraged me to bend to Thane's will.

A soft touch has me jumping in my seat, and reality comes crashing in. My lungs burn, and there are fresh tears in my eyes from the memories I'd much rather have scrubbed from my mind, never to be thought of again.

"Are you okay, Sophie?" Kyler's kind voice breaks through my rush of emotions.

Still, I can't answer him yet. I can't even turn my head toward him until I know I have my shit together.

It's several minutes later before I turn to him, a grin on my face. "Got a little carsick. Feel free to make fun of me for it."

I expect him to crack a smile in return, but the pinched expression on his face shows that he is anything but convinced of my words.

"You don't have to—"

I cut him off, because I really don't want to lie to him anymore than I already have. "Did you ask your question yet? This was your idea. You can't make me play and then not do the same."

He continues to stare at me when his gaze should be on the road. Still, I know I'm completely safe with him.

Fuck. Where did that come from?

I hardly know this man. I shouldn't... Hell, I can't even argue with myself. I might not entirely trust he's been honest with me, but I can't deny that his motives are true as my wolf previously reminded me. Kyler is here for my benefit and nobody else's.

It takes another few moments, but he finally breaks. "What's your favorite food?"

I gasp, not bothering to hide my outrage. "Excuse me? You want me to pick *one* favorite? That's, like, sacrilegious."

My very real outburst has us both laughing and the tension in my chest loosening ever so slightly.

"Okay. Top three, then," he amends.

"Still not nice, but let's see." I hold my hand up and lift a finger with each item I list. "Cake, obviously. Beef—

and no, I won't choose a particular cut of meat. Hmm, how about chocolate?"

He shakes his head, a grin firmly in place now. "Chocolate doesn't work. Give me something more specific. I've already bent the rule with the question. Give me this."

He's right. Considering how easily he let me have my moment and move on from it, I give him what he asks for. "Brownies, especially when served with ice cream, but also, M&M's. Love those little bits as a good filler snack."

"Good to know," he muses, both hands on the steering wheel and his eyes back on the road. "Your turn again."

Well, let's see if I've learned my lesson about asking questions that can possibly turn much too serious for my liking.

I tap my pointer finger over my chin, using the dramatics to hide the unease I'm still trying to shake. "Where is your favorite place that you've been to for work?"

If this isn't safe, I quit at this game.

"Easy," he says with confidence. "East Texas."

Yep. I give up. I expected his answer to be somewhere tropical or even in the middle of nowhere, but of course, it happens to be the one place I intend on settling down once this shitshow is over.

I told you that he might want the same things as you, my wolf says. *And now you know about his mate.*

Her words are spoken with the utmost respect. Not only for my fragile heart, but toward Kyler's as well.

I want to tell her what he said changes nothing, but I'm not ready for that conversation. Not right now when I've just finished reliving the worst and best moment of my life.

"Why Texas?" I ask, since most people can't stand the heat there unless they grew up in it.

He shakes a finger at me. "That's two questions, but I'll let it slide. Just remember that later. But to answer you, it's the people. When I was there a couple of years ago, they were welcoming, and it had been a long time since I felt like I could have been right at home if I'd stayed."

I want to ask why he didn't, but I know that's too much for me.

"Your turn," is all I say instead.

The smirk on his face deepens, and I have to hold back my groan. What the hell is he thinking about now? Never mind. I don't want to know.

"Have you ever"—*Oh, this should be good*, I think before he finishes—"skinny-dipped with other people?"

My shoulders droop with open disappointment. "Seriously? That's the best you have? I'm a wolf shifter. Nudity isn't really an issue. At least, for most." I raise a brow with that last comment.

He taps on the brakes. "I'll get naked right now. Don't tempt me."

I cover my eyes with my hands and laugh loudly. "Please don't."

And just like that, the trauma of my past has gone back to its locked box, and I find myself enjoying Kyler's company more than I could have ever imagined, considering I held a knife to his throat as our first introduction.

Chapter Seventeen

Kyler

We continue to volley questions back and forth, my lesson learned regarding getting close to anything serious. Seeing her completely shut down and practically frozen in the seat next to me when she'd zoned out terrified me more than I could have imagined. The fact that she wouldn't tell me what was wrong was all the answer I needed.

Me mentioning the death of my fated mate made her remember hers.

I can't think of anything else it could have been, but worse, I had the opportunity to tell her that I already knew about that and didn't take it.

Sophie seems to constantly have one foot out the door with anything that she does. Not that I want to keep secrets from her, but I also don't want her to run before she sees that while we might not be the typical fated mates, we are something that we can't deny. Well, *shouldn't* in my opinion, at least.

The way she started to glow with joy when we were talking about the most random things made me realize I'd done the right thing by not telling her what I know. But that light is quickly diminished when we get closer to the pack lands.

Sophie's guard is back up, and her eyes never stop moving as she directs me to where she believes will be another good place to enter the pack lands.

"Turn left here, then slow down until you see a turnout on the right," she says, voice tight with tension. "We'll be parked on the side of the road this time."

Her hands are clenched into fists, and her jaw is locked as she continues to watch around us.

"We don't have to come back here, Sophie," I say as I turn down the next road. "We have someone on the inside. He'll tell us when he finds your parents."

Her head is shaking before I even finish. "This is my responsibility. I'm not leaving it to a stranger."

I park, and she's out of the car before I can say anything else. Damn stubborn woman.

Turning off the engine, I slide out of the driver's seat and tuck the keys into my pocket. At least this time, she can't threaten to leave me behind.

I reach down and grab the cloaking spells from the pocket in the door before shutting it. Once I have the vials in hand and the car is locked up, I walk toward Sophie, who has made her way to the edge of the trees.

She points a little to the right when I'm standing next to her. "About ten miles east is the pack lands. This right here is all government owned for humans to do... recreational shit in."

"Will we need to worry about staying hidden?" I ask, scanning the trees but not sensing anyone else nearby.

Her head shakes. "Not if we're smart." Then she holds her hand out. "Spell?"

I almost don't give her the vial. I don't think she's emotionally ready for this, but I also know what happens when I try to stop her. I'd rather not be stabbed or have my heart ripped out.

Once she has the spell in hand, I open my vial as well and we drink them at the same time. The liquid goes down smoothly and without me even tasting it. My skin immediately begins to tingle, and a light glow temporarily forms over my body.

As soon as it's gone, I know the spell is in effect and should last about three hours, so we need to be quick.

"We'll need to shift, or we won't make the trek in enough time that we can poke around the pack for long," I tell her. Though she doesn't seem too thrilled about shifting.

"I can run fast on two legs," she says. "It will be fine."

"Don't be a princess," I joke. "If your wolf eats a few rabbits on the way, I won't judge."

The glare she sends me at the use of "princess" again makes my comment worth every death threat she might give me throughout the rest of the day.

"I'm not shifting," she says stubbornly.

"Why?" I saw her wolf in action before. She's badass

and beautiful. Sophie doesn't have any reason to stay in her human form.

Her wolf likes you, my own says, taking me by surprise.

So what?

If Sophie is fighting the attraction, and her wolf isn't, what do you think will happen when she shifts?

Of course it's the animal who points out the sexual tension.

"What if I give you a head start?" I suggest to Sophie. "You can run ahead with your wolf, and I'll follow behind? We'll still be faster that way than running on two legs."

She chews on her lower lip, likely knowing she doesn't have a solid reason to tell me *no*. Even my compromise is ridiculous, but I'm willing to do so to make her more comfortable.

I don't need her shutting down like she did briefly in the car.

You know nothing about women, my wolf says dryly.

Excuse me?

She shut down, because if she tells you about her mate, she's also telling you that she failed.

What the fuck are you talking about? I snap. *You heard what Maciah said about that piece of shit. Sophie wasn't at fault for a single thing.*

And how do you think she felt not having his respect? At not being good enough to wait for? he points out. *Her hand was forced, and while I'm sure she doesn't regret what she did, I'm more than positive it still affects her.*

Could she possibly blame herself for what happened? Looking over at the strong woman I've been getting to know, I want to say that's not possible, but there's a fragileness about her that contradicts that answer.

She's not weak by any means—not in my eyes—but I can see why she might not understand her true value. I fully intend to make sure that no matter what does or doesn't happen between us, she knows how incredible she is moving forward.

After pacing for several more moments, Sophie finally gives in. "Fine. I'll shift. But don't pout when you can't keep up."

She speaks with an edge to her voice that has me wondering if she's trying to cover up more than her attraction.

I back up and start to shift, but before I can fully call my wolf forward, Sophie is already completing the transformation and holds me captive.

Her skin glows for a brief second, then her body begins to contort. The movements happen so quickly and fluidly that if I'd blinked, I might have missed the whole thing.

Her wolf appears, fur golden like a well-aged honey and eyes bright green. When her stare lands on me, I swear she winks, and I have to hand it to my own wolf. He's rather insightful for being so quiet all the damn time.

The she-wolf yips at me, and I understand with ease. I need to shift.

Calling my animal forward, I sense a bit of

excitement within him that I can tell he's trying to hide from me, but that's not necessary. Just because he didn't want this attraction to Sophie—vehemently went against it, even—I'd never rub his change of heart in his face. Not when he had every reason to have reservations.

When we're standing on all fours, Sophie's wolf starts to come closer, then she darts to the left and begins to run.

She wants to be chased, my wolf says, a bit of pride in his tone.

Then I guess we better give chase.

And chase he does, because Sophie's wolf isn't keen on being caught.

We run and run for miles, zigzagging through the trees and never once getting close to her. But the view from behind isn't anything to complain about, either.

They move with not only swift speed but agility that has them leaping off trees and larger rocks, gaining a lead ahead of us. I'm almost too intrigued with them to notice we've begun to circle back and are heading west.

Almost.

That devil of a woman.

She's running toward her family home. She lied to me.

Or she just changed her mind, my wolf says.

Now you're defending her? I'm not sure how I feel about that.

That's not true. I'd rather he takes her side than wish we would stay away from her.

I encourage my wolf to run harder in an attempt to

catch up with them, but that damn she-wolf is quick. It isn't until she begins to slow down that we finally close the growing gap between us.

She stops, staying within the thick foliage, and is shifting back to human form when I finally get close enough.

I follow suit and point a finger at her, then at the vague bit of the house I can see beyond the branches. "This was not part of the plan today."

"I know, but I had to see for myself if the house was still empty," she says. "Just a quick sniff to see if they've been back and then we're done. I won't even go inside."

"Why?" I don't mean to ask the question. It's none of my damn business, but I don't understand why she cares so much about making sure they're okay when it seems rather obvious to me that they were never there for her when she needed them the most. Otherwise, she wouldn't have ended up in East Texas, basically on her own at sixteen.

Her eyes narrow and upper lip lifts into a snarl. "They're my family. It doesn't matter if I haven't seen them in years. I won't abandon them like they—"

She cuts herself off and turns away from me.

Right then, I know without a single doubt my wolf was right. It made sense when he said it, but I assume the rest of her sentence was going to be "did to me" and that is all the confirmation I need.

Thane wasn't the only person in her life who made her feel unworthy.

I reach for her and squeeze her shoulder without

trying to make her look at me. "It's okay, Sophie. We'll check the house, and if they haven't been home, we'll still sneak into the pack."

I want to tell her that they're probably fine even if they haven't been home, but giving false hope isn't part of my job.

She jerks out of my hold and stomps forward. "I'll be back."

Like hell am I going to let her do this by herself this time. If she thinks she can push me away right now, she's about to be really fucking disappointed.

Chapter Eighteen

Making a deal with my wolf is like making one with the devil. She knew I wanted to stop by my family home again and could only make the time to do so if we were in wolf form. She then swore to behave herself with Kyler's wolf, only to alter that promise once she was in control.

I'm not saying I'm going to attack his wolf, but I'm also not saying I won't swish my tail and let him sniff my ass, she muses and as much as I want to be annoyed...I still laugh.

Some days, I don't know what to do with you and others, I don't know what I'd do without you, I reply, specifically not telling her which type today is.

You would die without me every day, so there's that, she says smugly.

No, I'd just be a human, which might be worse than death. Knowing the magic of the world, the freedom to run through the trees, to feel the vibrations of the earth... I wouldn't trade that for anything.

But that's not what I need to be focused on right now. Kyler and the way he looks at me as if he knows all my secrets are making me crankier than my wolf.

He makes me want to tell him everything. The good, the bad, and the ugly—things I've never admitted out loud. And I don't like it.

It's okay to be vulnerable, my wolf says. *Not everyone is an asshole like Thane.*

I hear her words. I know they're true, but that doesn't mean I'm ready to believe them, which is why I'm stomping away from Kyler. Treating him like shit is easier than allowing him to heal the aches I live with every day.

Worse, I know he would and could. I've only known this man for two days, and I may not fully trust him, but I feel confident that his intentions are true.

I don't know why. There's just something in my gut that tells me so. A nudging that I very rarely ignore. Though, I have no problem avoiding thinking about it for a while longer.

Especially as I sneak closer to my family home to scent if they've been back since I was here.

My sister's window is still open from us escaping hastily, and I growl, remembering how Kyler threw me out the small opening.

"I'm not trying to stop you," he says from behind me. "I'm just here as backup."

Now I know my thoughts are *really* fucked. I hadn't

even realized he was following me, and he must have thought my growl was for him. I mean, it was, just not in the way he must think.

I call my wolf forward enough to utilize her advanced senses as I scan the outside of the home. I'm not smelling any fresh scents, and one glance in the window shows the comforter on the bed ruffled, likely from the commotion yesterday. If it had been slept in, I'd expect it to have been made perfectly again.

"They haven't come home," I say despondently.

"That doesn't mean they're in trouble," Kyler tries to assure me, but his words fall on deaf ears.

I know I shouldn't care about the fate of these people when they didn't seem to care about mine, but they're my parents and my baby sister, who isn't a baby any longer. Hell, Jules is... Shit. Seventeen. A year older than I was when I left.

Gods, I hope they haven't forced her to mate with someone. I would decimate this whole pack.

Maybe it's not that I care about my family still. My sister, yes, but my parents... The longer I'm here, the more I'm realizing that I just want the closure from them I should have had years ago. I need confirmation that it wasn't me who was the problem.

I don't know that I'll find what I'm looking for, but I'm sure not going to stop now when I'm so close.

Kyler grabs my arm, his chest rumbling. "We need to go."

His words are a mere whisper, and I turn away from

the window to find his eyes staring above my head, toward the side of the house.

I listen and search for whatever he's sensed, and that's when I catch the scent of four wolves. They're still here, watching the house.

"We can run back to the forest," Kyler says. "With the cloaking spell, they won't know it's you unless they see your face."

"Fuck that," I snarl. "I'm not running from anyone. Not anymore."

Kyler says something else, but I don't hear him. I charge forward, eager to release some of my pent-up emotions.

Ready? I ask my wolf.

Her energy is already pushing forward. *Always.*

"I'm telling you, I saw two people head toward the house," a man's voice says as I shift.

"And I'm telling you I can't sense anyone here," another replies. "You heard Astor. We're only to reveal ourselves if the murdering little bitch shows her face again."

"Come on, Chris," the first one says. "Do you really think Sophie could have done what they're saying? And why would they wait all this time to go after her?"

While it seems as if the cloaking spell is doing its job, I don't get too excited about it. I'm concerned with making sure these guys don't get their hands on me, thinking they can deliver me to that piece-of-shit Astor.

My wolf agrees, pressing forward to gain the upper hand by attacking first. I don't know who these shifters are, even though at least one of them seems to know me. I've purposefully forgotten nearly everyone in this pack and I'm not looking for a friendly reunion.

We come around the corner before they can, my wolf ready for blood. With teeth bared and our speed increasing with every step, we take them by surprise.

There are four, just as I sensed before, but one quickly runs away, which is fine, assuming he's the one who didn't seem to blindly believe everything he's been told.

My teeth latch on to someone's thigh without looking at their face, but my hold only lasts for a brief second before they're shifting and my left eye nearly gets taken out by their claws.

I notice Kyler's umber wolf move past me. He's snapping his jaws like a madman. How sweet of him to come and try to defend my honor, but I've got this.

The pack is my mess, and I'm going to clean it up.

I need Astor to know that he has no power over me. He can have all the fighters in the pack lined up and waiting for me, but I won't back down. I will find my family. I will protect them if need be, and then I can finally be done with this place. Once and for all.

Wolves battle against wolves. We're slashing claws and snapping teeth, spilling blood as we move with practiced efficiency. Though, none of the opposing shifters have fallen yet.

A hit to my back flank sends a sharp pain up my spine, but my wolf doesn't miss a beat as she leaps over another to land on a chocolate-colored wolf. He rolls as we hit him, and we get tangled with his legs.

We scramble to get out of the mess, but before we can back up, his teeth grab our front paw, cutting deeply and locking on tightly.

Knowing an injury like that could shift the odds of this fight quickly, we don't attempt to get free. Instead, using our other paw, my wolf glides her claws across our attacker's chest.

He snarls just enough to loosen his hold, and we get free, but we only make it two steps before there's a sharp pain in our right shoulder.

Fuck! A knife, I practically scream to my wolf.

She doesn't even yelp but can only make it another step before she's falling over, thanks to our left paw already being injured.

This isn't good, she replies.

An older man I feel like I should know stands over me and grabs the hilt of the blade that's still in my shoulder, twisting it deeper. "Be a good little bitch, Sophie, and stay down while I kill your boyfriend."

His voice. I know that deep, gravelly monotone, yet I don't recognize him and not a single guess at his name is coming to me.

It's not Astor, even though he might look a little similar. Twelve years hasn't been long enough to forget that bastard's face. Not when he and his son looked so damned alike.

As much as I wish we didn't have to stay down, the more my wolf tries to move, the more agony we both feel.

We can't let them have us, I tell her, the fear I felt as a teenager coming back fresh, as if it never went away.

They won't touch us, she promises as we watch Kyler's bleeding wolf tear through the remaining wolves. His eyes are glowing, and he's practically foaming at the mouth with rage.

Why the hell is that so hot? I muse to myself.

He cuts through the new arrivals with incredible speed, barely allowing them to touch him before ripping out an eye or tearing through throats.

The man who stabbed me stands idly by, and when there are only two wolves left, he turns back to me. "Looks like I'm going to have to drag you back myself."

When his hazel eyes hit the sun, I'm certain I stop breathing. If I hadn't killed Thane myself, I'd swear this was him. At least the eyes.

But I blink and I realize he's much too old to be my dead fated mate.

Not-Thane grabs my wolf by her neck, then, like a sadistic prick, slams his palm onto the hilt of the knife still protruding from my shoulder. "Just need to be sure you can't get away."

Our eyes search for Kyler as we fight back a whimper. He's still fighting the two other wolves as the man begins to drag us away. We growl, and our back legs that still have no problem working dig into the ground, but there's nowhere for us to find traction.

Not without being able to use our front half.

"I heard you were a fighter," he jeers. "Astor will be

pleased to see that hasn't changed when he has his fun with you."

The fuck he will.

A burst of energy fills my wolf, and we fight back once more, our loud growls hiding the excruciating pain coursing through us as we're forced to put pressure on our front legs.

Though I have a feeling that's nothing compared to the torture Astor will want to put me through, making it slightly easier to ignore.

The man kicks our face with his heavy boot, putting us back in the dirt with what looks like little effort. "Bite me and I'll tell Astor one of the other little shits killed you after I drop your corpse at his feet."

Just as the stranger starts to walk toward the trees again, a shadow moves over us and Kyler's wolf slams into his back.

My wolf is released, and when we try to see what's happening, there's little movement or noise coming from the two of them.

We inch forward, recognizing Kyler's wolf and ignoring the searing agony moving through our body as we do, because not knowing if he's okay isn't an option. And considering how still his wolf is...

It feels as if we've traveled a dozen feet, but it's likely only inches when Kyler's wolf finally lifts his head, snout dripping in crimson.

When our gazes lock, I'm frozen in the moment, and any pain consuming me fades away. All I can see is Kyler within the depths of his nearly silver eyes and the determination he holds to keep me safe.

More than that, there's a draw to him that shouldn't be there. Almost like a... No, that's not possible.

It could be, my wolf says reverently.

A fated mate bond? There's no way. We would have known the moment we saw him, and nobody has ever had two mates.

That we know of, she adds, emotions filling the both of us that we only briefly felt when we met Thane. *Maybe Kyler is the fates' way of giving us a second chance at happiness.*

Second-chance mates? I've never heard of that, but she could be right. As much as I don't want to consider that an option—if I'm wrong, the disappointment just might be my undoing—I do realize that just because we don't know something exists doesn't mean it can't be real.

Kyler is the first to break our connection, shifting back to his human form. The darkness in his eyes isn't something I've seen yet. Is he angry about whatever that just was? Does he not want me?

He's growling and mumbling words I can't comprehend under his breath. There is nothing positive that I can sense coming from him. My heart feels as if it's about to burst.

The fates can't be this cruel. They can't hurt me twice.

Right?

Chapter Nineteen

Sophie

For the first time in as long as I can remember, I'm at a loss as to what I should do. My wolf is severely injured to the point that we can't shift back to human form until we've healed a little more. Kyler is bleeding, but he's also not talking to me. And I'm pretty sure we're...something.

Say the word, Sophie, my wolf taunts. *Mates.*

I don't agree with her. I can't, because the way Kyler is vibrating with fury right now doesn't bode well for my heart if that's true.

Surviving the first asshole mate is one thing, but if Kyler doesn't want a second-chance mate, if I've allowed myself to feel something for him only to be rejected, I don't know what I'll do.

That's not going to happen, she tries to assure me, but as I stare up at him, completely helpless at the moment, and see only rage looking back at me, I'm not so sure.

"I'm going to pick you up," Kyler says before bending down. His words are clipped, and his jaw seems so tight that I wouldn't be surprised if he broke it during the fight. Or maybe that's just because he's so damned furious right now.

He could just be upset because you were almost killed, my wolf says with a layer of hope.

That's a possibility, but my heart is telling me something completely different.

Kyler's shaking hands slide beneath my animal form, seeming mindful of the knife still lodged in my shoulder. "We'll get that out when I don't have to worry about you bleeding out."

Smart choice, but I can't tell him that in my current state.

"I'm going to need to run," he says with a hard edge. "I'm sure more are coming, and we can't be here when they arrive."

His body stiffens with me in his arms, and I want to scream. How could things have changed so quickly? It's not as if I asked for this. He's the one who pursued me before, and now that it could be something real, he's the one who's angry? Not a chance in hell.

My disappointment and self-doubt quickly turn to annoyance that easily forms into my own anger. Kyler doesn't get to kiss me—twice—then make me feel like I tricked him into something I have no control over.

I wiggle in his arms, wanting to get free of his touch, but the movement sends a new shock of pain through my entire body, and I can't hold back the snarl of agony.

"I'm so fucking sorry, Sophie."

Those five words leave me incapable of thought. More accurately, the pain they're laced with. The way his voice grumbles and how his fingers tighten around our fur and the pinched expression on his face that was previously more like a statue...

Is it possible that he's not angry *with* me?

I can't think properly, but my body tingles with something foreign, making me believe that I might have jumped to the wrong conclusions.

You think? my wolf snarks, but I ignore her, badly wishing I could speak to Kyler. Though, maybe it's a good thing I can't talk. My emotions are all over the place and I'm apt to say something stupid.

While Kyler runs, doing his best not to jostle me, I notice a spot of crimson growing bigger beneath his grey shirt.

He's hurt, but the only thing I've sensed from him is his rage. Hell, I was so consumed with my own worries that I didn't even scent the blood on him. The wound on his shoulder isn't the only one he has, either.

Kyler finally stops, his chest heaving as he gently sets me on the ground. "I'm going to pull the knife out now. I don't smell any new blood on you."

My wolf head nods, and he grips the blade at my shoulder but then stops to remove his shirt. "Bite this."

I want to tell him *no* but then realize I'm probably going to soon wish the knife had stayed in place, so I let him shove the cotton material into my mouth.

Once he's done, I get a better look at his chest and

arms. There are several holes in his skin, likely from teeth biting his wolf so deeply that they didn't heal during the shift.

A few of them are still leaking blood, but most of them seem to be healing normally. I want to reach out and…I don't know what, but something. Until he yanks the blade from my shoulder and my entire body clenches with anguish.

Motherfucking hell, that hurts!

Bet you're glad we have the shirt now, my wolf titters, but I pretend she's not there when I hear Kyler mutter, "Shit."

He pulls the shirt from my mouth and presses it over the wound. "You're bleeding more than you should be."

There's a panic in his voice that I don't understand. We have the cloaking spell, which should hide even the scent of our wounds. Unless we hear the wolves coming closer, we're fine. I'll heal soon enough, even if I can't shift back to human form yet.

Kyler presses hard against my fur. "Stop fucking bleeding."

There's a layer of fear to his words that I still can't understand, and I whimper without meaning to. He's scared but shouldn't be, and I don't know how to help him.

"I'm not going to let you die, Sophie." The conviction in his voice is so strong that it sends shivers down my spine.

I know you won't, I think, even though he can't hear me.

He tenses, and his head tilts to the side before he grabs the ruined shirt and bloody knife. "We need to go." His arms scoop me up with ease, even though I know he's hurting, then he begins to run.

Every stride sends a new wave of pain through me that's so strong, I can't focus on our surroundings to know how close someone might be.

Instead, I close my eyes and focus on each breath. One inhale. One exhale. Repeat. A wave of nausea rolls through me, but it ceases the moment Kyler comes to a stop.

When I open my eyes, we're at my car. I don't know how we traveled over ten miles already, but I also wasn't exactly paying attention and might have even passed out for a bit there. He places me in the back and uses the center seatbelt to buckle me in.

"Just in case I have to drive a little crazy," he explains before slamming the door closed and jumping in the driver's seat.

He starts the car and is back on the main road only seconds later.

This isn't good, my wolf groans. *Wolves aren't meant to ride in vehicles.*

Her motion sickness hits me as she speaks. *Do* not *vomit on my seat.*

The responding moans don't bode well for my poor car, but there's nothing I can do. I've never shifted in such a small space before and I'm not about to try for the first time while I'm injured.

It's only another five minutes before Kyler pulls over and opens the back door.

My wolf breaks the seatbelt and nearly knocks Kyler to the ground on her way out of the car. Our breathing is ragged as she tries to get the motion sickness under control.

I think we're good to shift now, I tell her. I can't sense any new blood on us, even though everything still hurts like a bitch.

Then do it, she growls sharply.

With our injuries and her being distracted with trying not to throw up, it's not as easy to draw on our inner transformation magic, but I push through and finally feel the change.

As bones begin to reform, I want to cry. The normally euphoric experience is wrought with agony as my body fights having to recreate itself.

When I'm finally in my human form again, tears stain my cheeks, and I start to drop to my knees. Okay, maybe we weren't ready.

"What the fuck, Sophie?" Kyler practically growls, wrapping his arms around me so that my knees never even touch the ground. "Are you *trying* to die?"

"For your information, no. Not today, anyway." My words are a poor attempt at a joke. He doesn't seem pleased, based on the deepening crease between his brows.

"Let me look at you," he demands, his hands already pulling at my clothes.

"How about you look at yourself?" I suggest. I don't

think he's still bleeding, but his wounds are still very much present.

He grunts, then grabs my shoulders and directs me back to the car. "Sit down."

I open my mouth to disagree with him, but the glare he sends my way has me keeping my snark to myself.

I don't know who has possessed the jovial man from earlier, but I'm just a tiny bit afraid of this one.

Once I'm seated on the edge of the back seat with my feet resting on the ground, Kyler goes around to the trunk and opens it up, digging through shit I didn't even know was back there. He comes back with a med kit in his hand that he places on my lap to open.

I try to watch, but looking over makes my head pound, so I shift my gaze to stare over his shoulder. "I'm going to be fine," I say to him, hoping he doesn't intend to poke at me too much. Otherwise, I'll be repaying the favor.

He doesn't respond, and I'm halfway through asking what he's so furious about so I can stop wondering, but I don't get to finish.

Something cold covers one of my wounds and then burns so badly, I can no longer control my movements. Without consciously doing so, I first punch Kyler in the face then kick him in the balls as I screech, "What the fuck?!"

One of his hands holds his junk, and the other pinches the bridge of his now-bleeding nose. "*What the fuck* is right!"

My hands cover my face as I quickly mutter, "I'm so sorry."

Instead of getting up, he lies back on the ground and just groans.

I think I've officially broken him.

Chapter Twenty

Kyler

I probably should have seen that coming, but my mind is a total fucking mess. Fighting for our lives aside, when my wolf locked gazes with hers, there was something there.

No, not something. A damn bond.

The energy that ignited in our chest and intensity of the pull to go toward her nearly brought me to my knees. If it hadn't been for all the fucking blood and my terror of watching her bleed out just like I'd done with Cara, I would have wept with joy at Sophie's feet.

Thankfully, logical thinking took over. I had to get her out of there and that knife out of her wolf's body. The entire race back to the car, not knowing if more wolves were going to find us, not being sure I had it in me to protect her after the hits I'd taken… It was more than I could handle.

Now, for my trouble, I might have a broken nose and bruised balls.

This day has turned out to be one hell of a roller coaster.

"Seriously, Ky," she pleads, her hands still over her mouth, muffling her words. "I didn't mean to hurt you."

I force myself up from the ground but stay on my knees right in front of her. Gently, I pull her at her wrists until I can see her face. "I'm fine."

"No, you're blee—"

I cut her off, grabbing her cheeks and kissing the hell out of her. I can't wait another moment. My body needs her too damn much.

Her fingers grab on to my shoulders, nails scratching over my skin as she deepens the kiss. Our tongues tangle and this time, there isn't a moment's hesitation from either of us.

Until I realize I need to know something more than I need her touch.

She growls softly when I pull back, making me smile as she pouts. "I wasn't done."

The pad of my thumb brushes over her lips. "Neither was I, but I have a question for you."

That has her tensing and going quiet.

"You felt that back there," I say. "The connection of a bond."

Her eyes go wide, and she shivers beneath my hands before she finally nods.

My excitement increases for only a fraction of a second until she says, "I need to tell you something."

If she's about to tell me that she's been seeing

someone else and doesn't want a second chance at a mate, I'm going to lose my fucking mind.

"I killed my first mate." The words leave her mouth with such shame and terror.

"Sophie." I gather her into my arms, mindful of both our injuries, and hold her gently but close. "You had every right to do what you did. Do not let that piece of shit hurt you any longer."

As soon as she tenses within my hold, I know I've messed up. I shouldn't know about Thane, and she doesn't like that I do, even if she's just told me herself.

She pushes me back, and instead of the rage I expect to see, there's sadness filling her eyes. "I want to leave."

"Sophie, I'm sorry," I start to say, but she holds her hand up, silencing the rest of my apology.

"Not now, Kyler." There's a brief sigh. "Not fucking now."

She stands and goes toward the passenger side of the car, head hanging low in a way I never would have expected from her. That guts me even more.

I pick up the med kit and go back to the trunk. I left extra clothes back here as well, so I slip on a new shirt for myself and grab a sweatshirt for Sophie. She might not want my words or touch right now, but she needs to stay warm to help her healing.

The bag with snacks catches my eye before I close the trunk. A peace offering. Even if she doesn't say a word, if she at least eats the chocolate, I'll know I didn't completely fuck this up.

When I get into the driver's seat, I set two water

bottles down in the cup holder and place the candy bars between them. "Those are for you if you feel like eating."

She stares out the window but doesn't say anything, so I drape the sweatshirt over her legs. "And in case you're cold."

Still, I get the silent treatment, but at least she didn't run away. I'm considering that a sliver of hope that I'm determined not to lose.

I start the car and pull out onto the road. My hands squeeze the steering wheel tightly as I drive. Not only am I worried about Sophie, but even with the cloaking spell still working, we need to make sure we avoid being seen by pack members who might be on the roads.

My wolf healing has already kicked in, but my body is bruised deeply and there are a couple of deeper cuts on my back that I can feel sticking to my shirt. I should have bandaged them, but getting Sophie out of here is more important.

I catch her head turning toward me out of my peripheral vision, but I don't say anything. I said what I said, and I need to wait for her to be ready to speak again.

Seconds turn to minutes, and I can tell she's still looking at something, but without putting my eyes on her, I don't know exactly what. It is slowly driving me mad, a punishment I'm sure she'd no doubt enjoy me going through.

Finally, her hand reaches for me. No, not me. The damned chocolate.

It takes every effort to hide my smile. She may not be

ready to talk, but she took the peace offering. That's something else to hold on to until I can apologize again.

After she eats the candy bar, she chugs the water and then throws the now-empty bottle at my head. Not hard, but with enough force for me to know that the action was intentional.

I use that as an excuse to look at her, hopefully without further pissing her off.

She's lowering the seat back and bunching the sweatshirt up to use as a pillow. Her eyes close and I take in her face. There are no injuries on her cheeks or around her eyes, but I can still see the bruises and wounds on her shoulders and chest. Just the sight of them has my terror rising all over again.

I almost lost her. Before I've even had the chance to really have her.

Fuck. I don't know that I would have survived that.

My wolf finally chimes in. *We wouldn't have.*

She's ours, I tell him in case he has any lingering doubts.

There's a beat of silence before he finally replies, *And we will do whatever it takes to earn her forgiveness.*

It seems like forever since the two of us have been in agreement, but hearing those words from him has me finally smiling. Until Sophie catches me still staring.

Her glare cuts me to the quick, but her sharply spoken words manage to fuel my hope. "Keep your eyes on the damn road."

She doesn't tell me to stop looking at her

permanently, which I take as a win. Even if she rolls over, giving me her back.

Sophie is pissed, and rightly so, but she isn't cutting me out. Not entirely.

I intend to use that to my advantage just as soon as we're both healed, have had some food, and maybe even a little rest.

Tomorrow will be better. It has to be.

Chapter Twenty-One

Sophie

I want to be so fucking furious right now. I want to punch Kyler in his handsome face and kick him in the balls again, twice as hard. I want to have never met him.

Yet at the same time, I don't want to do any of those things.

He knew what I had done—that I had murdered Thane—and he didn't leave. He didn't judge me or make me feel as if I were the monster.

Then the bastard gave me chocolate and a sweatshirt that smells like sandalwood...like *him*.

It's the mate bond, my wolf reminds me. *You can't hate him. We never even hated Thane. We just loved ourselves more.*

Gods, isn't that the truth. I wouldn't have felt so much guilt all this time if I hadn't cared for him as I had.

Now, though? Now, that fucker is becoming more

like a faint memory, and the only things I can see when I close my eyes are Kyler's light-grey eyes, the terror in them when I was bleeding, and the determination on his face to make sure I lived, no matter how much he was hurting at the same time.

I'm not ready to forgive him for not telling me he knew, I say to my wolf, expecting her to argue with me.

You don't have to be, she says, surprising me. *The fact that you didn't beg me to run away from him is enough for now. We've only just found him. There's plenty of time for forgiveness.*

I hope she's right. With the way those wolves were talking, I have a feeling Astor Crowe is hellbent on making sure my time runs out sooner rather than later.

Astor won't touch us. She growls loudly within my mind. *We're not the teenager he remembers, and we have Kyler now. He doesn't need your forgiveness to fight for you.*

No, I don't assume so. He's too damn perfect for that kind of nonsense.

Almost too perfect.

I want to sleep, I tell her. My body aches and my heart would love it if I let out a loud scream, but since that's not possible, rest is the only thing I know will solve one of my problems.

With my back still to Kyler, I nestle into my sweatshirt-pillow and take count of my injuries so that I can figure out how quickly things are healing once I'm awake.

My shoulder is the worst, thanks to being stabbed by the guy I'm beginning to assume is somehow related to Astor and Thane. There are bruises along my arms and I'm near certain on my ribs, but none of those feel broken, thankfully. Both legs are sore, but the few bites I had there are already healed.

With my battle wounds cataloged, I clear my mind and pretend the warmth of the heater blowing over me is coming from Kyler instead of the car.

Maybe one day, I murmur to myself as I drift off to sleep.

MY EYES BURN AS THEY SQUEEZE CLOSED tighter, and my stomach twists painfully, practically shouting at me for food. Yet I'm moving without doing so on my own, making me assume we're still in the car.

Wait. No. I hear the sound of keys and the movement isn't smooth.

I open my eyes to find Kyler's face above mine and my head resting against his chest. He's carrying me inside the motel room, a pinched expression on his face as he does his best to open the door without waking me.

Like I said earlier: Almost too perfect.

"You can put me down," I say, my voice scratchy from sleep.

"I've got you," he replies, finally getting the door to open.

He carries me to the bed, pulls the comforter back, and gently lays me on the mattress before covering me up. "I tried to wake you in the car, but you weren't even flinching, and I didn't want to stay out there when you could be resting in bed."

The sight of blood on my shirt makes me groan. "I need to change. Hell, I need to shower."

I start to move, and Kyler's hands shoot out like he's going to help me sit up, but then he jerks his touch away from me.

Oh, yeah. He thinks I'm still furious with him.

I think I should be, but then, the more I do *think*, I can't find a valid reason to refuse him.

Sure, the mate bond is messing with me, making the pull toward him stronger, but I'm a rational person. I knew before that there was a chance his boss, who had been around when I ran away, had told Kyler what I'd done and maybe even why.

I also can understand that until this connection appeared, he might have been battling some serious feelings between betraying his fated mate, who probably hadn't been a psychopath like mine had been; his obligation to his job; and whatever he was feeling for me.

Maybe it's the exhaustion I feel toward life right now, but there's nothing in me that wants to run or resist any longer. I give in. To my feelings, to the bond I can't exactly feel right at this moment but know is there, and to Kyler. I don't want to fight anymore. I've been fighting for too damn long.

I just want to be done, for someone else to take control.

"Will you help me?" I ask, glancing up at him through my eyelashes.

The way he fights a grin makes me feel even worse for having snapped at him earlier. "Of course. Whatever you need," he says, sliding his hands under my arms and lifting me from the mattress.

Pain shoots through my shoulder, and I pull away from his touch, but only to relieve the pressure there. "Maybe I could work with fresh clothes and a wet washcloth."

There are faint aches of discomfort around my ribs, but nothing that will stop me from moving. My shoulder just needs more time. Muscles typically don't take it well when they've been cut in half, even for a wolf shifter.

Kyler lightly squeezes my knee. "Stay right here."

I watch, expecting him to go to the bathroom for a washcloth, but instead, he goes to the mini-fridge and starts grabbing food. Seriously. How does he know me so well already?

When his back is to me, I notice that bits of his own shirt are stuck to his skin. Either that shirt was sticky when he put it on, or he was hurting much worse than I thought earlier while I'd been focused on myself.

He brings me a premade turkey sandwich, a fresh peach, and a big bag of my favorite potato chips. "Eat this. I'll get you a change of clothes and stuff to clean up in here with."

I barely hear him after "eat this," but I do at least

manage to thank him before I begin stuffing my mouth with sourdough, meat, and cheese.

By the time Kyler returns, I've already demolished the sandwich and taken a bite of the juicy peach. He grins. "Better?"

I nod, realizing that even my shoulder doesn't feel as stiff as I sit up cross-legged on the bed and eat. "Food fixes everything," I say earnestly, taking another nibble out of the sweet fruit.

Kyler takes the spot next to me and looks at me with hopeful eyes. "Everything?"

Like the lady I am, I wipe my mouth with my ruined shirt and set my food down. "Yes, Kyler. I shouldn't have gotten so angry with you earlier. You had no reason to tell me you knew. It's not like it's a huge secret. I'm sure your boss or possibly even someone from East Texas told you. I just...don't like to talk about it."

"I'm still sorry," he replies sweetly. "I should have told you I knew the moment Maciah said something to me. Just so you know, I didn't know until the phone call I took with him outside."

That doesn't really make a difference, but I appreciate him trying to be honest now. I want to say something else, except I'm at a loss for words.

This isn't me. I don't get close to people. I never thought I would have a mate again—not even a chosen one.

Though I don't think that's what Kyler is. This feels different, stronger. Like the universe has been pushing me toward this moment, and I wasn't allowed to have it until I decided to finally find my closure to the past. To begin my second chance.

You weren't ready before, my wolf agrees.

I chuckle. *I don't know that I'm ready now.*

We wouldn't be sitting on this bed if you weren't, and you know it.

Like usual, she's right, but that doesn't mean I'm not terrified.

Still, I meant what I said before. I'm tired of running.

I assume Kyler takes my moment of reflection to mean that I don't accept his previous apology, since he begins to do so again.

"Seriously, Sophie," he pleads. "There's nothing el—"

With my good arm, I reach for the back of his neck, and my chest rumbles. "Shut up, Kyler."

The smirk he gives me before our lips crash together is everything that I need to forget that we were just ambushed and nearly killed. His body continues to move toward mine as I lean back onto the mattress. Our lips never part, even as he settles over me, using one of his arms to lessen the amount of weight he's putting on top of me as his other slowly moves up my side.

I moan from his light touches and the way he devours my mouth. Then, a second later, he stops, turning my sounds of pleasure to ones of annoyance.

He moves away from me and shakes his head. "You were nearly killed. I shouldn't be..."

"You shouldn't stop," I say with a huff. "I'm fine."

"But you almost weren't."

My eyes roll. Hard. "And I almost never came to South Carolina, meaning I almost never met you. Are we going to live life by *almost*?"

Now it's his turn to sigh. "Sophie, we're still bloody. I'm not going to..."

He seems to be having a really hard time finishing sentences, and it's slightly comical.

"What? You're not going to fuck me because of a little blood?" I ask teasingly.

His eyes darken, and in the next second, he's back in my personal space. His face is only an inch from mine as he says, "Oh, I'm going to fuck you, all right, but not the first time. Not until you're...mine."

Oh, hell.

I might have just died and come back to life within the blink of an eye. How is this real right now? How can he be so sweet and then say things that make me feel as if he's about ready to own me, body, mind, and soul?

"First, I'm going to take care of you," he says, only backing up enough to tug at my shirt. "This needs to go."

Before I can even attempt to pull the fabric above my head, he rips through the cotton material, casually tossing it to the side, as if that wasn't completely hot as fuck.

"Are you going to be ripping all my clothes from my body?" I ask, trying to sound as hopeful as I really am.

"Maybe." A sly grin tugs at the corners of his mouth, and I let him do whatever he needs so that we can get to the fun parts of the evening.

The day didn't go at all how I expected. I still have no

idea if my family is safe or already dead, but that's a problem for tomorrow.

Tonight, I'm going to give everything I have over to this man. and I can't wait to see what he does with me. Something tells me there's a beast inside him, one I intend to poke at until he's released.

Chapter Twenty-Two

Kyler

I don't know what time it is, but as I slowly inspect and clean every inch of Sophie's soft skin, I know I won't be rushed. Every curve, scratch, and bruise are to be checked. Only when I have zero doubts about her wellbeing will I give in to my other desires.

My fingers brush lightly over her ribs, and my other hand uses the warm washcloth to press against her shoulder. The stab wound is nearly closed, but that doesn't mean there isn't internal damage still hurting her.

I saw that bastard twist the knife, saw the intent to inflict as much pain as he could upon her. The joy it gave me to rip his throat out was the only reason I hadn't lost my shit before I knew Sophie was going to be okay.

Now, touching her and knowing she isn't angry with me or trying to push me away, nothing else matters. All I can see is her. I feel the heat emanating from her body, hear the rapid beat of her heart. Its tempo increases as I get closer.

"We're mates, Sophie," I tell her, because I need to know that she understands what's about to happen.

She nods, her eyes fluttering closed as her head leans to the side. "Hmm, yes."

I stop touching her. When her eyes shoot open, I know I have her full attention. "Not chosen mates. My wolf says second-chance mates, basically the same as fated ones."

"And if you don't put your hands back on me, we're going to be *nothing* mates," she threatens, but there's a lightness to her tone.

Gently, I cup her face. "Sophie, if I'm right and I keep touching you, then there's no going back. You're mine and I'm yours. Tied together for the rest of this life. I won't let you go, not even if you try to run or tell me that you hate me."

She reaches for my shirt, gripping it tightly with one hand while the other covers her heart then mine. "I know what I'm doing and what will happen when we have sex. The pull between us will become a physical bond, and I have no intention of running from that. I'm giving myself to you, Kyler. Fully and freely."

I've never been an overly emotional person. I can rage with the best of them. But deeper feelings that make my throat ache and eyes burn aren't usually something I experience. Staring into the eyes of this strong, fierce woman who's allowing her walls to come down and not being afraid of jumping right in, though, I know I'll never be the same after this.

There are no words I can form that feel right.

Instead, I pull her closer and kiss the hell out of her, imprinting this moment on my mind to never be forgotten.

My breathing becomes ragged, and I want to pin her to this bed, but I haven't yet finished my inspection.

Or more accurately, she still has too many clothes on, and I want to be the one to undress her.

My lips break away from hers and I trail them down her jaw, then over her neck, nibbling at her skin as I go and enjoying when it pebbles beneath my touch.

Moving down her chest, I place light kisses over the swell of each breast as my hands reach around her back to unclasp her bra.

She tries to help, but I pin her hand down and lightly growl, eliciting a low gasp from her. Each strap falls down her arms, and as I remove the contraption, I give her shoulder one more look. There's a red and jagged scar forming on her shoulder blade. One that I suspect will fade to a light pink by morning.

I press my lips over the wound, then move to face her again, but this time, I get up from the bed and stand next to it, turning her so that she's still facing me.

Her brow raises and a sweet smile plays on her lips. "What do you think you're doing?"

"Getting you naked," I say. Though, that's only partially true. "Do you have a problem with that?"

My fingers reach for the button on her jeans as she says, "Not a single one."

"Good. Now, lie back, be a good girl, and let me do my job."

Just as I suspect, she doesn't take well to the "good girl" comment. Her eyes narrow on me. "I'm not a dog."

But I have no problem pinning her with an intense look of my own. "No, but you are mine."

Her cheeks flush, and she licks her lips while her eyes roam over my body. "Proceed."

The single word has me chuckling under my breath. I unbutton her pants and pull the zipper down, but before I lower the concealing material, I kneel to remove her boots.

She wiggles over the bed. "If you're trying to test my patience, I'm going to fail in about two seconds."

"If you want to know what I'm really capable of, then you'll figure out a way to stay right where you are." My words are rough. She's not the only one being tortured. My hard dick aches from being confined, but I won't be rushed. Not tonight. Not for this first time.

Still, I take her words to heart and yank her shoes off without a second thought. I don't bother to stand back up as I reach for the waistband of her jeans, grabbing those and the underwear beneath them at the same time.

Inch by inch, she's revealed to me. Her body wears the scars of a hard life, but when I look back up at her face, seeing her light-green eyes glowing with trust and yearning, I only see perfection. A woman worthy of love and respect and who should be treasured for all-time.

When I get her jeans to her knees, she kicks them the rest of the way off and shrugs. "Habit."

Right, I think with a grin.

But I don't waste time reprimanding her for losing

patience. Instead, I show her the wait was worth it. My hands grab her thighs and jerk her toward the edge of the bed before I spread her legs open.

Her folds glisten just for me, and I want to take a moment to appreciate how fucking glorious she is, but the desire to taste her is too strong.

My mouth covers her clit and I suck hard before running my tongue over her pussy. Her fingers grip my hair, pressing my face harder between her legs and crying out my name.

"Don't you fucking stop," she demands, but it's not necessary.

I lap at her center, and her entire body shivers beneath me as her thighs press around my ears.

Using my hand, I slowly move my touch over her hips and along her ribs until I find her nipple, pinching hard at the same time as my other hand presses two fingers inside her.

Her back arches, and my upper arm keeps her pinned down as I continue to lick and suck at her center while curling my finger inside her tightening pussy.

She cries out louder, nails digging into my head as her hips surge upward. Her heated skin trembles, and I expect her to come any moment, but she surprises me by sitting up quickly and grabbing my shoulders.

"If I'm going to come right now, it better be around your cock," she says, doing her best to pull me up.

I don't fight her, because I at least got my taste. Rising to my feet, I pull my shirt over my head with one hand, taking note as the fabric gets unstuck from the dried blood on my back. Nothing hurts, so I assume those wounds are healed enough.

Before I can reach for my pants, Sophie already has my zipper undone and is tugging them down. I help her, kicking out of my boots and losing my desire to cherish every moment as her eagerness becomes my own.

She moves back onto the mattress as I rid myself of the constraints. Her legs are still spread for me, and her hair falls in soft waves around her shoulders while she sits up, waiting for me.

I climb onto the bed, my eyes staying trained on hers. "Are you ready?"

Sophie's nod and the accompanying grin on her face makes my heart soar as she says, "More than."

Positioning myself on top of her, I lean forward to kiss her again. Her lips meld to mine, and I sigh with the utmost relief.

I've been lost for so long, and I thought that my life was over. I'll never forget what I had, but I intend to cherish every bit of this second chance.

Reaching between us, I guide my cock to her waiting pussy. As soon as the head brushes against her center, Sophie lifts her hips and closes the distance.

I thrust forward and, in an instant, it's as if I've come home. Her warmth wraps around me while our hips come crashing together, each of us giving as good as the other.

My chest feels as if it's slowly being opened, and tingles rush over my arms before covering the rest of my body.

The bond. It's already forming.

My eyes find Sophie's, and there are tears forming at the corners of hers, but there's a wicked smile on her face that keeps me moving without asking if she's okay.

She grabs my head and kisses me again. Our tongues battle for dominance as I move over her, doing my best to draw out the moment.

Except my new mate has other plans. Her nails dig into my ass cheeks, deepening my thrusts until she's crying out. "Fuck, Kyler."

I ride her harder, giving her what she wants and, if I'm being honest, what I do as well. Our bodies slap together in a tangle of arms and legs as I attempt to touch her everywhere, all at once.

I'm close to coming, and I know she's nearly there by her increased breathing. My speed picks up, and the energy from the bond wraps around me, invisible but heavy. Within seconds, I can no longer tell where Sophie begins and I end.

She is mine. A part of my soul. The woman I would die for.

She's ours, my wolf corrects.

I'm not used to him speaking, but I don't have time to process his true acceptance.

The energy between me and Sophie rocks through my body and I assume hers, because we both cry out and come at the same time.

Fucking hell.

You're telling me.

I hear Sophie's voice in my mind, a confirmation that

the bond has taken root, officially confirming everything my wolf told me before.

That was intense, I say, grinning down at her.

Her nails drag lightly over my back, and she goes back to speaking vocally. "That's one word for it."

"What would be some others?" I tease, peppering kisses around her face.

"Mind-blowing, world-altering, addicting, to name a few." The smile she sends my way as she speaks nearly undoes me.

"*Addicting*, as in you're going to need repeat performances?" I ask while lifting my weight off her, readying to stand so I can clean us both up.

"'Repeat'?" she says with admonishment. "Breakfast, lunch, and dinner. Your cock has just become as necessary as chocolate."

I tilt my head to the side and grin. "Am I seriously being compared to food right now?"

"With as much as you've fed me in the last two days, you should know what a compliment that is," she teases in return, gripping my ass a little tighter.

"I'll try not to be insulted by that." I kiss her once more, then get up.

She grabs my wrist, keeping me close. "Where do you think you're going?"

"To the bathroom to warm the washcloth," I say. "We'll clean up, I'll feed you real food, then you can have your new necessity for dessert. My goal is to trump all food. I'm only supplying it first, so that I can make sure you'll be able to keep up with me."

Her laughter makes my chest expand with so many feelings. "Me? You're the elder here. I can go all night."

I turn back around, take both of her hands, and pin them above her head. "I'm only eight years older, and you'll soon find my stamina will be more than enough."

I nip at her lower lip, then release her, walking away and leaving her speechless. Something I imagine doesn't happen very often for this vivacious shifter.

One who is now all mine.

Chapter Twenty-Three

Sophie

I used to think sex wasn't all people made it out to be. Even my wolf seemed to boast about the act in ways that rarely made sense to me.

Then, I had sex with Kyler Murphy.

Mind fucking blown.

It wasn't me or my lack of understanding. It was all the idiots I chose to settle for.

I think I need to apologize, my wolf adds to my thoughts. *I really thought the problem had been you.*

Geez. Thanks, I think dryly.

On second thought...you did pick all of them. At least initially, she quips. *You just have bad taste. You didn't even want Kyler and look how that turned out.*

Oh, shut your mouth.

I refuse to listen to her on this incredible morning. My body aches in all the best ways. I only slept an hour or two, but I'm more energized and alive than I have been in my entire life.

Kyler is sleeping soundly next to me. My fingers itch to wake him for a proper good morning, but I decide to brush my teeth first.

After getting out of bed slowly, I head to the bathroom. Every step reminds me of the workout I received last night, and the dent in the wall next to the bathroom has an image appearing in my head of when Kyler had my back pressed against the spot, rocking my entire world.

With renewed quickness, I move through the motions of using the bathroom and freshening up. When I open the door back into the room, Kyler is standing next to the bed, grabbing his phone from his previous day's jeans.

"Yeah?" he answers, and I lean my naked body against the dresser, purposely trying to distract him.

But when he looks at me, there's a deep crease forming between his eyes. "What the fuck did you just say to me?" he snaps.

My libido is quickly extinguished as I use my shifter hearing to listen in on his conversation and grab a sheet to cover myself before moving closer to him.

"I said hand her over and you can live," a deep male voice repeats. "She killed my son, then my nephew, and now my brother. I will have her head."

Motherfucking hell.

Astor Crowe.

"Your son was a worthless excuse of a man, and it wasn't Sophie who killed your brother," Kyler snarls in return. "It was me. If you want her head, then you'll want mine, too. I wish you luck in trying to get either."

Kyler moves to hang up, but I shake my head. We need to know if he has leverage. More specifically, my family.

I also want to know how the hell any of this even came about. Where did the previous alpha go? Why is Astor trying to get to me after all this time? Something triggered him, and I want to know what or who, along with what my parents and sister may have to do with any of it, considering they still seem to be...missing.

"Then I'll kill you both," Astor sneers. "I let someone convince me to forego justice once. I won't do it a second time. Not for any reason. Not again. The next time the two of you set foot in my pack lands, you will die."

Fat, fucking chance of that happening, but it's almost endearing that he thinks he has those capabilities.

"Long time, no chat, Astor," I say, deciding to go for a more direct approach. He already wants to kill us. I don't suppose things can get much worse. "How's life?"

"Sophie." The growl that accompanies my name makes me smile. "You have some nerve coming back here."

"Yeah, well, someone once told me that time heals all wounds," I reply casually. "I guess they were wrong."

"I guess so," he says. "Now, how about you save your family from paying for your mistakes and turn yourself over? You do so and I'll consider letting your little boyfriend keep his life."

"Not a chance in hell," Kyler cuts in with a snarl.

"He's feisty," Astor titters. "I didn't expect you to go for another strong alpha male when you so easily disposed of the one the fates gave you."

"Thane wasn't an alpha," I state clearly. "You taught him to be selfish and cruel and to believe that the world owed him for his existence."

"He should have been this pack's next alpha," Astor roars, and a loud thud accompanies his words. "You took that from me, and you will pay."

Interesting. I didn't know Thane had the alpha gene, but then again, I'd never been given the chance to get to know him and had been too terrified to pay close attention to him. He hadn't wanted to form a relationship with me. He wanted to chain me to his side and bend me to his will.

"Well, that sounds fun and all, but I have other plans," I say, purposely sounding bored. "I'll be seeing you, Astor."

"Yes, you will," he replies with a sinister tone as I end the call.

Kyler's creased stare meets mine. "You didn't find out where your parents are."

"He was never going to tell me that, but he did at least confirm he has them," I say, knowing that there had been a chance my family had run. "At least presumably since he mentioned them 'paying the price', but I refused to show him my interest in them. Not when that might make things worse, especially for my little sister. Now, it's time for us to fight."

The disgrace that is the Crowe family is going to end and by my hand. I won't let them harm anyone else or ruin any other lives. Whatever dark hole they crawled out of twelve years ago, Astor is about to wish they'd stayed in it.

I start moving about the room, grabbing clothes to put on, but Kyler grabs my arm, stopping me. "Sophie. Stop."

"No," I retort. "I'm going to kill him."

"We have people on the inside." He starts with that nonsense again.

"And they've told us nothing," I say. "I'm done waiting. I understand if you have to stay back because of your work, but my family won't suffer because of me."

Even if they gave up on me a long time ago. Just because they weren't loyal doesn't mean I have to let that change who I am.

I step away from him, removing his hold from my arm. "I'm getting dressed, and then I'm leaving." My eyes look up at his, pleading with him to understand. "You don't have to come with me. I won't hold that against you, but don't stop me, Kyler. I need you to accept that I can't *not* do this."

"Fuck," he murmurs under his breath, then he closes the distance I've created between us and grabs my face with both of his hands. "I do accept you, but you can't fault me for trying to keep you safe."

"The sooner that son of a bitch is dead, the sooner I'll be safe," I remind him. "I need to get dressed. If you're coming with me, so do you."

I move toward the bathroom and close the door behind me without turning back. Mates or not, I need to finish this. I let Kyler in, and he can stay there, but only if he doesn't hold me back.

You're making the right choice, my wolf finally chimes in, shocking the hell out of me.

Thank you, I tell her as I get dressed. *Hopefully, he'll see it that way as well.*

He will, she says, and I start to brush my hair into a ponytail.

Once I'm as ready as I'm going to get with our limited supplies, I step back into the room. Kyler looks prepared to leave, but then I notice he's holding a crumpled phone within his hand.

"What's wrong?" I ask, my entire body tensing.

"I called my boss, Maciah," Kyler answers gruffly. "I was going to tell him to warn Cane that we were coming, but he hasn't talked to him in nearly twenty-four hours."

"And? Is Cane dead?" I ask, not understanding what has Kyler furious enough to ruin his phone.

He shakes his head. "He's taken Astor's side, and they know where we are. Or they did until I destroyed my phone."

Motherfucking hell.

I grab mine from the dresser, ready to throw it against the wall, but Kyler stops me. "Cane could track me because all protectors can find each other through a beacon on our phones. Yours is fine. I gave Maciah your number. We need it to communicate with him."

My hands form into fists at my side. "So, what? Now we run?"

"Now, we regroup," he corrects. "We will attack Astor, I promise, but we need to get our shit and go. There's another man on the inside named River. He's only just arrived, but I trust him with my life."

"River, as in Dawsyn's best friend River?" I ask, because while I was pretty sure I've never met the man, she's spoken highly of him and I might be willing to beat down my desire for blood if it's him.

"I don't know, but we need to go, Sophie," he pleads with me. "I promise to get you more answers by tonight. Just stay with me."

The damn bond is flaring to life within my chest, encouraging me to fall into Kyler's touch, to trust him to take care of me and let that be that. Yet that's not at all who I am. I don't let other people do things for me. I've mostly had my own back for over a decade now.

I realize that I took this trip to find closure and turn over a new leaf, but that's easier said than done. While I want to tell him *yes* and respect his desire to protect me, I don't think that I can.

Before I'm forced to say something that I might regret, my phone rings. I turn it over and the screen shows an unknown number. I glance at Kyler, not sure I should answer it, but he nods. "It's okay. Maciah is just giving us another update."

Well, that's a hell of a lot faster than I expected, considering we hadn't heard much over the last twenty-four hours. Maybe waiting with Kyler is the best choice.

"Yeah?" I answer curtly.

"Sophie, this is Maciah. May I speak with Kyler?" he asks with a formality I'm not sure I like.

"Sure, you're on speaker. What do you have to say?" The grin on my face can't be hidden. Not when Kyler's shoulders sag and I hear Maciah's sigh through the phone.

"Privately would be preferred," the vampire boss man says.

I chuckle. "And I'd have preferred to be done with this trip already. Sometimes we don't always get what we want."

Kyler shakes his head at me. I'm sure people don't often speak to the leader of the protectors as I have, but my jar of fucks is empty.

"She's my mate, Maciah," Kyler says, taking me by surprise. "You can trust her."

"I have a lot of questions about that, but they'll have to wait," he replies in defeat. "Cane has been dealt with, but your location has been compromised. The two of you need to get the hell out of that motel. Astor's men are closing in on you. They left before he even called you."

"How do you know this?" I ask, because I'm not going to run for no reason. I want to be done with that bullshit.

"Because River got what he needed out of Cane before he killed him," Maciah says sternly, likely not appreciating that not only is one of his men dead, but that he was a traitor as well.

"Though that doesn't mean everything is going as we hope," he adds. "River's story about coming back because he didn't appreciate the leadership before and is hoping he will now isn't easily being believed. Without River getting into Astor's inner circle, I don't know what good he'll be able to do."

Since Kyler couldn't answer my earlier question, I ask Maciah. "Is this River, as in Dawsyn's best friend?"

"Yes. Why do you ask?" he questions immediately.

"Don't worry. I'm not about to drop another bomb on you," I reply. "But you've already had one traitor. I needed to be sure we can trust this guy. Since I trust Dawsyn, then we can do the same for River."

Not that they needed my approval, but my cooperation is probably appreciated and this was the only way they were going to get it.

"I'll give River as much time as I'm able," I add. "If he doesn't have something to tell me about my family soon, then I'm going into that pack with or without the support of either of you."

I swear I can hear the vampire's teeth grinding. "Would you care to add anything helpful or just give us an ultimatum?"

"Tell River to pick a fight with one of Astor's top guards," I say. "He'll need to be prepared to kill him if he wants an in. The best way to get noticed by a psychopath is to be one yourself."

There's a stretch of silence between the three of us. I'm sure they weren't expecting me to suggest murder, but that's the only option we're left with if they have any hope of making this work quickly.

"Thank you, Sophie," Maciah finally says. "I'll be in touch."

"And I'll be on the run. Again," I say with a sigh.

This isn't my first choice, but I can't deny as my eyes meet Kyler's that my heart is more than happy that I won't be alone this time.

Chapter Twenty-Four

Kyler

As soon as we're off the phone, I begin throwing all of our shit into bags and Sophie helps me carry them out to the car. I have no idea where we're going to go, and we don't have any more cloaking spells, so we need to move quickly before someone picks up our scent.

Once everything we need is loaded up, I move toward the driver's seat, but Sophie steals the keys from my hand. "I've got this."

My head tilts to the side. "Not that I don't believe you do, but what's your plan?"

"You'll see." She smirks and slides into the driver's seat, closing the door.

Right. I guess I will.

Moving with urgency, I get to the other side of the car and give the area another cursory glance. I don't sense any supernaturals, and I don't see any eyes peeking through from the trees beyond the motel. Still, I don't like knowing that Astor's men have a head start on us.

Getting in, I slam the door. "Go."

"Already on it." Sophie's foot hits the gas, making the tires squeal, and there's a grin on her face that tells me she's going to enjoy this little race more than I would have thought.

She gets to the main road and heads east. "Where are you going?" I ask since that's the direction back to the pack.

"To our next hideout," she says casually, pressing harder on the accelerator.

"Sophie."

She deepens her voice, mocking me. "Kyler."

"What is your plan?"

She chuckles. "You sure ask a lot of questions when you're nervous. Don't you trust me?"

The car is nearing ninety. It's early enough that the sun hasn't even risen and we're not in a big city, so the roads are mostly clear, but she'll be drawing attention we don't need if we pass the wrong people.

"You know I do," I say, trying to hide my frustration. "But that doesn't mean I don't want to know what we're doing when there are people after us who want us dead."

"We're sitting in a car," she quips, having too much fun with this.

"Don't be difficult, *princess*," I say, hoping to kill her mood enough that she'll finally tell me what the hell she's cooked up.

Except the nickname seems to backfire on me. She

turns her gaze on me briefly and blows me a kiss. "Get used to it."

Son of a bitch.

The car creeps up in speed, and all I can do is hold on and hope nobody stupidly pulls out in front of us and that we don't get pulled over.

Minutes and miles pass before we're nearly back in the pack territory. I've opened my mouth a dozen times to figure out what the hell this crazy mate of mine is thinking but decided better of it each time. Wasting my breath would only encourage her to keep her secrets.

It isn't until we're back at the trailhead from that first night that I finally break. "What the fuck, Sophie? You said you would give River time before we moved in."

She shakes her head at me. "We are. I'm just making sure we're in a position to attack quickly once we have the all-clear."

"By camping out in their back yard?" I say with a growl I can no longer hold back.

While I know Sophie's perfectly capable of taking care of herself, this feels more than risky. Being so close without the proper gear is suicidal.

She shuts the car off and turns to me. "I have a plan."

"One you don't want to share with me."

"Not entirely true." She smirks and reaches for my hand, squeezing it. "I trust you, and I had every intention of sharing said plan with you. I just needed to wait for the right time. You know, in case it didn't work."

Not pleased with her words, my face falls flat. "Are

you saying whatever you set out to do already worked, and now you'll finally tell me what we're doing here?"

"Sorta." She glances out the windshield before looking back at me. "Astor is a cocky bastard. He thinks he has us on the run, which means he expects us to go farther away from the pack. Assuming I was right about that, I figured his wolves would have taken the other highways to try to head us off. I took a direct path *back* to the pack. It was a gamble, but I was right. We didn't pass any other supernaturals, and we've made it here safe and sound."

"But?" I say because this can't be all she's got going through her head.

"But the second part of my plan hangs on the hope that nobody searched that cabin you tried to hide us in the first night," she admits, almost sheepishly. "If they took all your supplies, my plan is fucked and we'll be back on the road in the next ten minutes."

While I don't like that she refused to tell me what she was doing, I can understand why. I wouldn't have taken the same risk. Not because I would have thought she was wrong, but because the mere thought of risking her life isn't something I'm okay with.

But I know while looking at the determination in her eyes, listening to the steady beat of her heart, and from what I've already witnessed, Sophie doesn't hesitate. She takes chances. I'm going to have to get used to that if I don't want to be left behind.

"Then let's go see what's still in that cabin," I say with a smile I hope she takes as confirmation that I trust her and won't tear down her plan. Even if the place was raided and none of my supplies are still there, she had the right idea.

"All right, then." There's a hint of shock on her face, but she moves to get out of the car. At least until she tenses. "Wait."

She reaches back toward me. Well, that's what I think she's doing until I realize she's actually going for the glove box. "I need a snack."

Those four words have me laughing and shaking my head. "Of course you do."

Without a care in the world, she grabs a handful of chocolate and a granola bar. The former is in her mouth before she's even exited the vehicle, and by the time we're both standing at the front of the car, she's inhaled half the bar.

"We'll shift and run for the cabin, find the potions, and conceal the place," I say, checking our surroundings. I can hear wolves in the distance, but I can't scent any of them, which means they're still several miles away and can't smell us, either.

"We'll need to be quiet and quick," I add, mostly as a reminder for her.

She winks at me and starts walking toward the trees. "I've done this a time or two before."

"Snuck onto enemy territory and taken over a human's cabin?" I ask with slight amusement as I catch up to her.

"Something like that," she muses.

This woman has stories, and I can't wait to spend the

rest of our days hearing about them. Today isn't that day, though. With the sun shining above us, there isn't much besides the trees to conceal our movements. That paired with being so close to the pack has me on high alert as we enter the forest before preparing to shift.

My coffee-colored wolf appears just a split second before her honey-colored one. They lock eyes, and just like before, there's a tightening of the connection between. A flare from the bond that draws us together.

I wanted to hate her, my wolf says quietly as he closes the distance between us and them. *Yet her soul is bright and pure, a beacon calling us home.*

For as bloodthirsty as Sophie is, I can understand what my wolf is saying. There is something innocent within her eyes. A younger version of her begging for another chance to live a different life. One I hope to be able to give her.

The two wolves touch heads, eyes closing and just soaking in the moment together. I wish we had more time, but they'll have to get to know each other better another day, in another forest.

We will have all the time in the world, my wolf agrees as he breaks the contact.

Though it's Sophie's wolf who begins sprinting ahead first. We follow after, gladly watching her six and listening for anyone else getting too close.

The sounds of wolves are nearer, but until I can pick up a scent, I don't deter Sophie from her plan. She's been right so far, and I want her to continue to be.

Within five minutes, we're at the back side of the

cabin. The window is closed, and it shouldn't be if nobody else went in there after we fled. My heart sinks, but still, I follow Sophie's lead and shift back to my human form.

She doesn't wait for me as she creeps around the side of the house, inching her way toward the front door. Her eyes are constantly moving, and I watch in awe as she stops, listens, and only proceeds once she considers the potential consequence of each step she takes.

When she turns back to me, I'm right behind her and give her a nod of approval that seems to have the tension in her shoulders loosening slightly.

Sophie gets to the front of the cabin, and neither of us senses anyone close enough to be concerned with. At least not yet, but I have a feeling that will change soon if we don't find the bag of concealment spells that I left behind.

I follow her lead and shift back to our human forms, knowing wolves aren't the best at opening doors. When we get to the entry, I twist the handle, surprised the lock hasn't been busted, but then again, I don't remember locking it once I put up the cloaking spell before.

Before stepping in all the way, I listen and scent out the cabin. With magic no longer present, it's easy to confirm the place is empty. Still, there could be a trap waiting inside. Being aware of that possibility has me moving forward carefully.

I'm not sure what I expect as we get farther into the small space, but finding everything exactly how it had been before isn't it.

Had Astor's wolves not circled back to check the cabin? If we were no longer there, I guess they wouldn't have had a reason, but still, I would have if it had been me.

They lost several wolves that night, mine points out. *Maybe it was an oversight.*

Or maybe it's a trap.

Regardless, if we can find my bag, the trip out here won't be a waste. Thinking back to a few days ago, I recall having first gone to the table to set my stuff down before searching the cabin. When I was done, I grabbed my supplies and headed toward the couch.

As long as nobody has really been here, then this should be easy.

Getting to the couch with Sophie still beside me, I don't see my bag on the cushions. My shoulders drop, and I turn to tell her that we need to go, but she's still moving.

She starts to search around the living room, and I go back to the kitchen in case I'm remembering things wrong thanks to the chaos of the last few days.

Even with my hope lessening, I continue to look around, but two passes through the other side of the house and I come up empty.

I enter back into the living room to tell Sophie we need to go, we've already been here too long, but she's nowhere to be seen.

My heart starts to race, and there's a roaring in my head that I can't seem to get under control.

Outside, my wolf snarls. *Follow the bond.*

In my panic, I forgot that we're connected now. I don't even need to follow the bond. I can just speak with her.

Where the fuck did you go? Apparently, I'm still not calm, even knowing that I can reach her without seeing her.

"Easy, lover boy," she jokes, entering through the front door. "I found the bag and concealed the cabin myself since you were in the bedroom."

I'm rather certain she's trying to kill me by continually putting herself at risk, but I also know there's no changing her. So, instead of bitching about her not at least communicating telepathically with me, I close the distance between us and wrap my arms around her.

My nose goes to her neck, and I take a deep inhale. The desire to mark her surges to the forefront of my thoughts, but I keep my inner beast at bay. This isn't the time.

"You can hold me in bed," she says with a smile on her face as she pulls back. "We got up way too early for the day. I either need a nap or food, and considering we don't know how the rest of the day is going to go, sleep is probably the better choice."

"Fine, but next time, maybe consider telling me what you're doing," I say, following her to the back bedroom. "We have the ability to mind-speak for a reason."

She shrugs. "Never been a fan of it."

My hands wrap around her waist, pulling her tight against my chest as we keep walking. "A little murder doesn't scare you, but having me in your head isn't ideal?"

Even though I keep my tone light, she still stiffens within my grip. "Something like that."

Sophie pulls away, and I know I've said something to upset her, but I have no clue what. It occurs to me that her abandonment issues aren't the only things I'm going to have to contend with.

My mate had a fucked-up adolescence, but I won't stop fighting for her. Not now and not even as the decades pass. I'll be there to remind her how amazing she is every day, for the rest of our lives, even when she doesn't want to hear it.

Chapter Twenty-Five

Sophie

Out of all the shit I've been through in my life, the unknown is probably what scares me the most. I try to shove my worries down into the shadows of my mind, but the more shit that keeps piling up, the harder that becomes.

Kyler is perfect. I've already acknowledged that. He wanted me and didn't stop pursuing me just because I'm a little crazy. Hell, maybe more than a little. He didn't judge me for having killed my fated mate. He hasn't tried to hold me back, even if he doesn't always agree with my choices. More than that, he's fought alongside me when this has nothing to do with him.

The bond I sense pulsing between us is as strong and sure as I'm certain he is. I want to hold tight to the warmth that connection offers me. I want to go all in. I've even said the words, that I give myself to Kyler freely, and meant them.

And yet...I don't understand this bond or how we

can be mates connected like this. I don't understand why he's here with me, and I'm terrified that once he realizes how damaged I really am that he's going to run for the hills.

Even with a fated mate connection, I've seen that pure determination is enough to break through the haze of the warm and fuzzies the fates want us to feel. Kyler could do the same. He could realize that I'm nothing like his first mate, that I can't compare to what an amazing shifter I'm sure she was.

When he does, I know he'll run.

You don't know anything, my wolf says. *Not when it comes to this. Kyler has given us no reason to doubt him. You are fearing things that haven't even happened, and by doing so, you're only harming yourself. Don't ruin this because you're scared.*

But I am scared, I plead with her. *I'm fucking terrified.*

I'm mentally exhausted and want to sleep, but I can't even close my eyes because all I see when I do is Kyler's back and him walking away from me.

I didn't ask for this second chance. I didn't want to have a bond or to feel anchored to someone who could either be my saving grace or destroy me so completely.

I didn't want any of this! I shout in my own head.

My chest pounds, and silent tears fall from my eyes. If I weren't so afraid of waking Kyler, my body would be shaking. Every breath I take burns through my lungs and up my throat.

I can't even stand the thought of mind-speaking with

Kyler because that's just another way I can get attached to him. Another tether tying me to him that I fear he'll one day cut away.

So, instead, you'll push him away and lose him on your own terms? my wolf says sharply. *Sounds like the dumbest bullshit I've ever heard. We are on the cusp of having everything we could need. A pack is waiting with open arms for us back in East Texas. There's a man sleeping beside you who would die to protect you. We're potentially hours from having the closure on our past that we've needed for years. I've stood by and let you choose the wrong path because it's what you needed, but I'm telling you right now that I won't stand by while you push away what I know is going to be the best thing to ever happen to us.*

THE SHITTIEST PART IS THAT I KNOW SHE'S right, but I can't seem to help myself. I don't know what's wrong with me. I want better. I don't want to run any longer. Yet...I don't know how to believe that the rug won't be pulled out from under me.

Nobody can, not entirely. We don't have guarantees in this life, my wolf adds. *Kyler could be taken from us tomorrow. Whether by his choice or someone else's. That doesn't mean we should stop enjoying what we have right now. We've been hurt, abandoned, and betrayed in all the worst ways. I understand why you're scared, but it's time to put on your big girl panties and fucking live, because I'm done running. We take risks with our life all the time. It's time to take one with our heart. For me and for you. We need this.*

She's right. I know it with every fiber of my being. There's just so much fear.

Still, her words and feelings matter. What my wolf wants and says matter. So, I try again. I close my eyes and fight for control of what my mind shows me. I fight to see Kyler smiling at me, to see us in East Texas, to know that there's a pack who would die for us, and we would do the same for them, because pack is home. Pack is family.

Just because my blood turned their backs on me doesn't mean I'm forsaken.

While saying the words eases the agony in my chest, I know believing them will take time. I just needed this moment to allow myself to truly feel the grief I've held on to since I was a teenager.

Maybe now that I've faced it, admitted that it's there, I can finally and truly let go of the weight I've been carrying around.

It's going to take patience and grace, my wolf says. *Two things I have no doubt our new mate has.*

That, I could believe in. That, I would put my faith in and find a way to come out stronger than ever before.

Knowing it's still going to be a process, regardless of what I believe, I decide to take the first step toward allowing myself to truly let Kyler in.

The wall I unconsciously began constructing around my mind and heart the moment I felt the bond snap into place begins to crumble. A brick here, a brick there. Piece by piece, I encourage them to fall. Not completely, because I know that I can't just blink and accept everything will be fine, but I can expose myself enough to let him in a little more every day.

To allow him to feel my true emotions and to let his in.

The moment I unleash my desire for him and fear of the future, Kyler's eyes open and the hand he has draped over my stomach pulls me closer to him.

He sits up and brushes his thumb over my trail of tears. *Sophie.*

His voice sounds in my mind with the utmost care. Gentle and kind.

You're safe with me, he says.

I nod, knowing I need to say something back if I'm going to succeed at this first step. But the words don't want to come. Not in the way they should.

I won't ever leave you, he adds. *There isn't a force powerful enough in this world to rip me from your arms.*

It's a promise I know he can't keep, but the words have me losing my shit all over again. I'm supposed to be this badass wolf shifter who has taken care of herself for years without the help of anyone. Yet in Kyler's arms, with his sweet words, I fall apart. My shield crumbles, and I cry like the child I barely remember being.

My sobs get buried into his chest as he holds me tightly, keeping my body from shattering, as I'm most certain it would without him there.

The tears fall, one after another, for what feels like an eternity. I say nothing and neither does he. But he doesn't have to. Not when I can feel his emotions pulsing through the tether of our bond. His warmth becomes mine. His kindness washes over me. His protectiveness reminds me that I'm not alone. His desire for only me mends the cracks in my heart.

I'm so sorry, I finally tell him when the tears have stopped.

He pulls back just enough that he can see my face. *You have nothing to apologize for.*

I'm not as strong as I pretend to be.

His head shakes, and he smiles softly. *No, you're even stronger, because you have held on to all that pain by yourself and still found a way to live, which is more than most people would be capable of.*

I hold him tighter and try to hide my face again, but he's not having any of that. He grabs my cheeks and forces me to stare into his eyes as he says, *You never have to hide from me, Sophie. I will never shame you for your choices or feelings. You are mine, and that means more to me than just some bond we share.*

Thank you, I say, knowing it's not enough, but that's all I'm able to do. At least with words.

My hands slide over his chest, and I push him back. As he moves, so do I until I'm straddling his waist and he's looking up at me.

Make me forget the pain, Kyler. Make me forget everything but you.

He guides my face toward his and brings our mouths together, kissing me with a ferocity that has my toes curling and my nails scratching at his chest.

Our tongues meet in a battle, but not against each other, *for* one another. He holds me tightly, filling my mind with joy, desire, and need. The last being the most prominent.

This man needs me. My body, my mind, my soul—all of it. He needs me more than his next breath, and the fierceness of that has my heart expanding in my chest, beating in time with his.

I lift my hips and reach under his boxer briefs for his cock, grateful he'd kicked off his jeans before we got in bed earlier. My fingers wrap around the hard and velvety skin, barely able to touch the tips together as I stroke him.

You need to be naked now, Kyler commands roughly, and I have no problem complying.

Between the two of us, we strip away all physical barriers within seconds and I grab hold of him again before positioning him right where I need him.

Still on top, my body slams down, taking the entirety of his hard length in one go. I cry out, my head dropping back. He fills me so completely, and not just physically.

His intensity could consume me, and I've known that since the moment I first kissed him. It's why I've been so afraid, but I don't want to let fear control me. I don't want to ruin the future, like my wolf said. Her words were the reminder I needed. I haven't fought all these years to not enjoy the peace we've finally found.

The stronger those thoughts grow in my mind, the quicker my pace becomes. I don't want to slow or savor this moment. I just want to consume everything this man is offering me.

He seems to understand that, because he pulls me toward him, placing a firm hand at the base of my spine and thrusting his hips up in time with my movements.

Our bodies slap together as our breathing becomes ragged. It's just me and him. There's nothing that I need to fear. I have Kyler, and that's enough. At least it will be.

The roughness of our sex, the pure need being shared between us—it can't be ignored. For full-blooded wolf shifters, we don't have to bite the other to complete the bond. Sex is enough, as we confirmed last night, but I've heard the talk about marking one's mate, to show the world that they're yours... It's supposedly nearly better than bonding.

Feeling the urge to do so and having already admitted that I'm tired of holding back, of keeping my walls in place, I allow my canines to grow. When they're fully extended, I run my tongue over the tips. Kyler's eyes don't miss the action, and I watch as his own elongate.

He's moving up toward me before I can lean forward. Once we're sitting up, his cock still snug within me, I lick the curve of his neck, shivering as the stubble on his face brushes against my cheek.

I can't hold back anymore, and neither can my wolf, who is right there at the surface with me. My bite cuts cleanly through his skin until blood begins to trickle into my mouth. The coppery taste that I've known from fighting doesn't come. Instead, the crimson is sweet and tingles down my throat with that first swallow.

Before I can get greedy, Kyler returns the gesture and his canines puncture my neck. A blast of euphoria explodes within me, starting at my chest, then moving through my veins like a fire that intends to consume me.

I release his neck and ride him harder in our seated position. The need for a release overwhelms me, and if I don't get it, the explosion I just felt might actually become reality.

Kyler holds me, our bodies grinding together, and the tether between us winding tighter. Our stares meet and I only see love within his eyes. Not that I think we've fallen in mere days, but that doesn't mean we can't have love between us.

A care so deep for one another that it can only be such a strong emotion, even if we haven't both completely dove off that cliff.

I have you, Sophie. Now and always.

His words are a whisper in my mind, and a trigger that unleashes my orgasm. My legs wrap firmly around him, keeping the tight pressure between our bodies as I cry out, falling apart in his arms, believing his words as the truth.

This man does have me. In more ways than he's possibly yet to realize.

Chapter Twenty-Six

Kyler

The hurt inside my mate has become my own. Her pains and fears now weigh heavily on my mind, and I have no clue how she's survived all these years on her own, bearing these burdens that never belonged to her in the first place.

I thought she'd let me in before, but I was wrong and stupid to think it could have been so easy. Though, none of that matters now. Sophie is still mine, and even if she shuts me out again, which I'm sure she will, I'm going to be there to fight for the both of us for as long as I need to.

She's sleeping soundly for now and I allow myself to do the same, but it feels as if my eyes are only closed for a minute before the shrill sound of her phone ringing fills the quiet cabin.

Sophie jumps out of bed, eyes wide and arms out, ready to defend herself. It takes another second for her to realize the sound is only her phone that she left on the nightstand.

"This is Sophie." Her voice already sounds wide awake.

I sit up in bed with the sheets around my waist, reaching for her to rejoin me. Surprisingly, she does as River's voice sounds over the speaker.

"I don't have much time, but the plan worked," is the first thing he says. "I *accidentally* spilled a drink on the third man from the top, and he ended up challenging me when I wouldn't apologize."

His voice is gruff, making me think it wasn't an easy fight, but that's the least of my concerns right now and it seems Sophie's as well.

"So, Astor invited you into his inner circle?" she asks. "Did you get into the pack house?"

"I did, and I'm a little confused. I thought your father was a prisoner?" River's words have Sophie tensing next to me.

She closes her eyes and breathes deeply before answering. "I assumed that because they weren't home and Astor said my family would pay for my sins, but there's a possibility he's in on whatever is happening."

"I'm sorry, Sophie, but it's not just a possibility," River says softly, showing compassion for a woman he's never even met. I've seen it from him before, and it's one of the reasons I trust him. "It's reality. Your dad stood right next to Astor. Whatever Astor has been doing, James has been supporting him enough to be part of this inner circle."

Fuck. Had Sophie's own father sent people to kill her when we were alerted by Dawsyn to keep an eye out for

Sophie? I don't know, and part of me hopes we don't find out, but I'll make sure he pays one way or another for even standing beside the man who is threatening his daughter's life.

Sophie's emotions flare between the bond we share. She's hurt, but more than that, she's furious. Though, she seems to be hiding both well.

"You need to keep searching for my mom and sister, River," Sophie says, a low growl echoing within her words. "Especially my sister. Her name is Jules, and no matter what it might look like, she deserves better. If she's not a prisoner, she's been brainwashed. My mother can have that effect."

That last sentence is said with a taste of betrayal so strong that I feel it in my own chest. Sophie's family didn't only let her leave after refusing to join her first fated mate, they were half the reason she did. I'm sure of that by listening to her speak.

"I'll find her, but if you come charging in here, I can't help you," River says. "I have my orders, and while they include finding and extracting your family, if possible, they also include finding out who Astor has sold wolves to. We've been tracking this for months now, and we can't lose this lead."

Sophie's head snaps toward me, and I grimace. I'd forgotten that bit of information.

"What did you just say?" Sophie asks gruffly with her narrowed eyes still on me.

River stays quiet, and I reply since I'm the one she really wants the answer from. "Maciah was already watching Astor from a distance. He found out that Astor is involved in selling wolves to humans. I don't know much more than that, though."

"And you didn't think that was information I should know?" Her clipped words are filled with hurt that weighs down on my shoulders.

"I do," I say earnestly. "But that part of the job wasn't at the forefront of my thoughts for the last few days. You and your family were."

I mean it, Sophie, I say through our bond. *I never would have kept this from you once I knew you were something more if I had thought of it before now.*

Her eyes close, and she rubs the space between her brows before finally replying. "So, let me get this straight. Astor is a true psychopath who has been betraying his own kind. You've had men trying to get close to him, but the only one prior to River who has succeeded ended up switching teams and now he's dead. So, it's up to River and us to not only save my...family, but to take down that motherfucker?"

"Essentially," I reply with a slight smile, hoping she'll find this part of the plan fun and not daunting.

"And why hasn't your boss sent an army to put an end to this?" she asks.

This time, River answers first. "Because the situation is complicated. We have an escaped wolf who gave us the lead, but by the time we knew, the place she'd been was cleared out. We've spent months trying to find more leads, and Astor is the only one. We need people to interrogate to find the others. Leaving them behind isn't possible."

Not only do I see Sophie's face soften, but I can feel her compassion pulsing through our bond. That doesn't seem to change her plans, though.

"But you don't need Astor," she points out. "You just need some of his men."

"Ideally, it would be both," River replies tersely.

Sophie's lips thin. "Well, we don't always get what we want."

As much as I can understand River's position, my mate is at risk every day that Astor lives. I'm not normally a supporter of outright murder, but in this instance, I think I'll make an exception.

"We're not in the business of murdering people, Sophie," River adds. "If we can take Astor alive and punish him under the laws that have been painstakingly put into place, then we will. We need to do this the right way or we're no better than them."

This guy really cares about right and wrong, doesn't he? Sophie asks through our bond.

For as long as I've known him, yes, it's seemed that way, I reply sincerely. *River and I have never been close, but I've always felt I could consider him a friend and trust him when we've worked together.*

And you trust him to find my sister without being swayed by Astor?

Without a moment's hesitation, I reply with, *Absolutely.*

"All right, River," Sophie says. "Considering this new

information, I'll give you one more day. Find my sister, figure out what the hell Astor is up to and where the other captured wolves might be, then find us a way in to end this once and for all. But just one more day. I won't wait longer than that. Not for your laws or for anyone else."

"I can respect that," he replies. "Kyler, do you have enough supplies? Maciah said you had to abandon your post twice."

"We're fine," I reply. "We're actually right outside the pack in the cabin that I originally shielded."

"Excellent plan going back to where they already found you once," he says. "They'd never think to look there again."

The grin on Sophie's face is almost insufferable. "I couldn't agree more."

"I need to take down the shield in my room before they notice, but I'll send word as soon as I'm able. You two stay out of sight until then."

Sophie and I both nod as I reply, "Stay safe, River."

The call ends, and Sophie throws herself back onto the bed. "What a shitshow."

I lean over her and trail my finger over her collarbone. "And we're stuck in this tiny cabin with nothing to do for possibly hours more. Whatever will we do...?"

"Eat," she muses with a saucy grin. "Me."

The blankets get thrown back, and I match her smile. "Wouldn't you know... I'm suddenly famished."

Chapter Twenty-Seven

Kyler's mouth and hands and cock serve as the perfect distraction for the rest of the day. We stay in bed, getting to know each other's bodies and focusing on the good in our lives instead of the shit sandwich River served us earlier.

Hearing my father is working with Astor initially shocked me, but the more time I've had to consider what I remember, I'm not surprised. Yes, it was my mother who wanted me to give in to Thane, but my father also knew. He began having dinners with Astor once he saw how influential the Crowe family seemed to be getting, spouting on about how great our families were going to be and the grand life we were going to live. Even more so once it was realized that Thane was my fated mate.

My dad only seemed to see me as his golden ticket to ranking higher within the pack he'd never quite fit into before Astor's arrival. Now, it seems even without me tying him to Astor, my father has gotten what he wanted.

Still, as I wait on Kyler to bring me food, I stare at the wooden ceiling in the bedroom of this cabin and wonder why my mother isn't at his side. What is she up to? What has Jules been subjected to because of their choices?

Worse, I wonder if my leaving only made life worse for my little sister.

But I don't dwell on that thought, because I can't change the past, but I can fight to protect her now. Something I'm more than eager to do.

With a grimace on his face, Kyler comes back into the bedroom holding a tray with two bowls on it. "I have spaghetti from a can or chicken noodle soup. Neither of them seems appealing, but you've eaten all the good stuff I bought at the store."

"I'll take the spaghetti," I say, knowing it's pretty hard to screw up chicken noodle soup, even in a can. Kyler can have the safer meal. He deserves that and more after the orgasms he's given me.

He hands me the bowl with trepidation. "Are you sure?"

"I've eaten so much random shit in my time on the road," I say with a grin. "This can't be that bad."

To prove my point, I grab the fork and swirl it around until there's a mound of noodles at the end, then shove the utensil in my mouth. "Mmmm, so good."

I practically choke on the words, but still, I try to chew and swallow. I need some sort of food before the fight, or I'll be a cranky bitch. I laugh to myself. Maybe that would be a good thing.

Kyler's hand pats my back as I struggle to swallow. "Seriously, Soph. Spit that out. I'll go kill something."

My lashes flutter up at him. "Sweeter words have never been spoken."

"I'll be right back." He leans to kiss me, lightly touching his lips to mine.

My fingers curl around his shirt, holding him closer and deepening the kiss. "Hurry up," I mutter.

The smile he sends my way nearly takes my breath away as I watch every step he takes until he disappears out the door.

As fucked as life seems right now, I'm also finally feeling incredibly lucky. In fact, I should call Dawsyn and thank her for putting her nose where I previously didn't think it belonged. Hell, I owe her a massive apology as well.

She might not officially be Alpha yet, but I lied to her, and she knew it yet still did what she could to protect me. I've taken advantage of the pack's kindness for far too long.

I get up and throw a shirt on before grabbing my phone. When I pick it up, I see there's a text from an unknown number.

How the hell did I miss this?

Opening the message, there are no words with it, but there is a picture. It's of my mother and sister. I zoom in on their faces. My sister's eyes are closed, and there are dark circles beneath them. Her fair cheeks are hollow, and her dirty-blonde hair is matted as if she hasn't properly bathed in weeks. Her head is down, her chin touching her chest, and her bony legs are pulled up to her ribs.

That motherfucker.

My mother is clean...ish, but still thinner than I ever remember. Her green eyes, much like my own, are trained on my sister and her thin lips are pulled downward. Still, her clothes are free of dirt and there aren't signs of abuse on her like there are on my sister.

How could my mother and father allow this to happen? I knew what they'd been willing to let me go through, but Thane had been my fated mate. A part of me understood their reasoning, even if I didn't agree with it.

Jules, though? She's just a child.

She's a year older than you were when we left, my wolf reminds me.

I know, but she looks so much more innocent than I felt all those years ago.

A message comes through, and I immediately click on it.

Unknown: Who else has to die for your stupidity, Sophie?

Me: You. You will die.

The phone gets slammed on the bed, and I'm up searching for my clothes. I'm done waiting. I won't let Jules get further hurt by the idiocy of our parents.

I find the rest of what I need to dress and head to the bathroom to clean up. In no time at all, I'm covered by a wrinkled, black T-shirt and dark-blue jeans with my socks on, but I still need to find my boots. First, though, I take a peek in the mirror.

My long brunette hair is a tangled mess, but that's easily tamed with my fingers. My normally light-green eyes are closer to emerald thanks to my heightened emotions, darkening from the outside toward the center. I've killed dozens of times before, and today, I will kill for my family, even if that's only my sister now.

Just as I tie my hair back into a ponytail, Kyler walks into the cabin, his proud voice echoing through the small space. "Snagged two rabbits."

"They're going to have to wait," I tell him, stepping out of the bathroom. "We're getting my sister. Now."

He drops the dead animals on the floor and is standing in front of me, hands on my shoulders. "What happened?"

Instead of using my words, I show him the picture, giving him a moment to see what I already have. The rumble that builds in his chest tells me I'm not overreacting.

"Who sent that to you?" he asks, his grip on my shoulders getting tighter as I tuck my phone back into my pocket.

"I assume Astor, but it was an unknown number," I answer, moving past him toward our bags, where I'm pretty sure the hunting items he bought before are stashed.

"We need to call River," he says, not seeming to understand my urgency.

I don't reply, because it doesn't matter what River

says. I'm not waiting.

"Sophie." Kyler's voice is low and much closer than I expect.

When I still don't say anything, he grabs my waist and turns me until I'm looking at him. "You have a picture. Nothing else. We need to know where your sister is before we go in there. We're outnumbered. Don't waste this chance to save her."

I open my mouth to yell at him, but my wolf stops me.

He makes a point, she says. *We will only get one chance, and as much as you may hate the idea, we need help. Help that Kyler's people can provide.*

Motherfucking hell.

"Two hours," I say between gritted teeth, then I shove my phone at him. "Call whoever you need to and tell them, stolen wolves or not, I'm going in there tonight to get my sister and to kill that son of a bitch."

His hand slowly moves up my face, cupping my cheeks. "I promise you won't regret this."

"I better not, or a hell of a lot more people are going to be dead before tomorrow morning."

That's one promise I know I can keep, and from the way Kyler nods at me and his mouth flattens, he knows it too.

———

IT'S BEEN ONE HOUR AND FIFTY-SIX MINUTES. Kyler is pacing in front of the unlit fireplace, and I'm sitting on the couch, my foot tapping on the hardwood floor as I watch the clock on the wall.

"He's going to call back," Kyler tells me, having more faith in River than I do.

Not that I think he's incapable of doing his job, but I don't know that he's had enough time to become close enough to Astor within the window I've given him.

Yes, I'm aware that waiting could yield less casualties, but that's not what my brain is capable of focusing on right now. I need blood. I need retribution. I need to save my sister. That is all that matters to me, so until I have those things, reasonable thoughts are taking a back seat.

Murder is our friend today, my wolf says, a ring of glee in her voice. *Their blood will be spilled, and it will be the second-best thing we've ever done.*

What's the first? I assume it's killing Thane, but I'm curious what she thinks.

Letting our mate fuck us into oblivion.

I nearly choke but cover my surprise with a cough. Kyler's eyes land on me, a brow raising.

"Are you okay?" he asks, his gaze roaming over my body.

"Just fine," I reply. "It's time to leave."

Technically, River has two minutes left, but I can't sit here any longer, having no clue if my sister's life remains intact with every minute we waste.

Just as I stand, the phone rings. The cocky grin on Kyler's face has my eyes rolling as he answers River's call.

"What do you have for us?" Kyler asks as I force myself to sit back down.

River's voice is low and quiet. "Jules is being offered as a prize and kept on the top floor of the pack house somewhere. Whoever brings Sophie to Astor will win the girl as their mate to do with as they please."

"I will castrate any man who thinks he even has a chance of that happening," I say with a loud snarl.

There's some rustling, and then River is whispering again. "Talk softer or this call is over. I've been working my ass off, proving myself over the last twelve hours for you, and I'm not letting the two of you ruin that now."

I want to tell him to fuck off, but the adult in me takes a steady breath, allowing my shoulders to rise and fall with the heavy action. "What else have you learned?" I ask more calmly.

Kyler comes to sit next to me, bringing the phone with him. His hand wraps around mine, offering support that I don't realize I need until it's there.

"Jules is the prize, but she's being kept hidden with your mother, who has more freedom, from the sounds of it. Though, she hasn't left your sister that I've seen. I haven't asked any questions about her, just revealed my interest in claiming...the prize."

I growl, not meaning to. I know—or at least hope I know—that River doesn't mean what he's said, but even just the thought... If anything happens to Jules, I don't know how I'll ever forgive myself for leaving her and staying gone all these years.

River continues. "Considering I left when I was eighteen and haven't been back for anything more than a quick visit, thanks to school and work, Astor has had no problem believing my disdain for the old pack ways. Especially since I've given him details about the alpha that he didn't previously have. Apparently, the alpha Joseph Lane is actually missing. Astor didn't kill him, but he'd very much like to."

"And what if what you've done to prove yourself gets him killed?" Kyler asks, and I selfishly think that it doesn't matter as long as it saves my sister.

Yep. Worst person in the world right here.

"It won't," River says confidently. "I had Maciah send others to the places and people I knew about. They'll beat any of Astor's wolves there, and they'll also make sure a trail of information to Lane's potential whereabouts is left behind, further cementing my position with him."

"You won't need to do that," I say, doing my best to keep my tone even. "We're coming there tonight, River. I won't wait to be attacked or leave my sister to be *won*."

"You're not at risk in the cabin," he promises. "Not one wolf has caught your scent out there."

"But my sister isn't safe there." I growl. "What if Astor changes his mind? What if he kills her? He already sent me a picture of her cowering on the floor. Astor doesn't seem like he's above killing Jules if it means drawing me out."

River pauses, and I know he's not in the best position right now, but I don't feel guilty for pressuring him. I need something good to happen, and it needs to be today.

"I know," he finally says with a sigh. "I can win her,

and I can keep her safe. Will you trust me to do that without putting either of your lives in danger? Another day will give us the time to get protectors in place, ready to attack with you and for me to get eyes on Jules. Otherwise, you not only won't save your sister, but you'll also get yourself and the rest of us killed by being unprepared."

Kyler's grip on my hand tightens. He's been quiet for most of this conversation. Without needing to look at him, I know he agrees with River. I want to do the same, yet verbalizing the words isn't easy.

It's not that I have a death wish or want to be selfish with my choice, risking other lives, but I walked away from Jules once without considering the consequences. Now, I'm paying for that choice.

If I don't go after her sooner rather than later and something happens...

"She's too valuable, Sophie," Kyler says softly. "Yes, I won't lie. I think there's a chance that she could be hurt, but at most, it will be a broken bone that will heal quickly. We've waited this long. Let Astor confirm the information River has given him is accurate, then River can offer more. He can even tell Astor where our car is."

River cuts in. "Actually, that's a great idea and could speed things up considerably. I can go out after we hang up, find the vehicle, and tell Astor I want Jules as my prize now instead of later for my efforts. Between the leads on the alpha and possibly getting him closer to you, he won't be able to deny my value. There's a decent chance I can have your sister at my side within two hours.

After that, Maciah should have everyone else ready. By midnight, we can attack. That's only five more hours."

And yet, that sounds like an eternity.

Kyler's stare is on me, watching my face and pleading with me to understand. It's not that I don't understand, though. I do. And I see the reason. I just don't want to.

I won't make a promise that I can't keep, Kyler says through our bond, *but I do know that we can believe in River and that I will do everything in my power to keep your sister safe, just as I would you. That includes telling you what you don't want to hear. River is right. We need to wait just a little longer.*

My eyes close and I lean forward, settling my face into my hands. I want to ask Kyler to knock me out. I don't know how I'll wait otherwise.

Yet I know I need to find a way.

I've been running all my life, and I said I was done with that. This is my time to prove it. I can't run into this fight on my own. Not only because I could fail in saving Jules, but because I'm not alone anymore.

I haven't been for a long time, and I don't want to continue to pretend otherwise. I said I was done, and now I need to prove I meant what I said.

Lifting my head, I glance at Kyler first, then nod. "We attack at midnight, River. No later. And if you don't have my sister away from that bastard before then, you're going to see firsthand just how bloodthirsty my wolf can be."

Chapter Twenty Eight

Kyler

Keeping Sophie distracted for five more hours while getting calls from Maciah and texts from River that aren't confirming Jules's safety isn't easy. I've gone as far as nailing the windows shut so that I will at least hear her try to bust them open, and I put furniture in front of the two exits.

None of that has stopped her from trying to escape early, but I've at least been able to get to her before she's gone outside the safety of our shield, blowing our cover.

What's worse is that even food hasn't tempted her. I cooked the rabbits I caught, and she refuses to even look at them.

"It's almost midnight, and River hasn't confirmed that he has my sister," she snarls, sitting on the couch that's now positioned in front of the main door of the cabin. Her arms are crossed, and her eyes seem to focus on anything other than me, but I'm not taking offense.

Everything is going to work out better because we waited. I'll take her thanks later.

"He told us only fifteen minutes ago that he was headed to meet with Astor," I remind her. "If River is too eager, he'll blow his cover. Have some—"

Her cold eyes cut to me. "If you say *patience* one more time, I will...hurt you."

Thankfully, our bond has seemed to prevent her from threatening my life. Still, I take her seriously, because the last thing I need is for her to be upset about me placating her.

Her phone pings with a text that I assume is from River, but the deep rumble that comes from her chest tells me otherwise.

"If that's not River in this picture, I'm going to kill him myself and there isn't anything you can say to stop me," she says menacingly. "And if it is River, I'm still going to break something on his body. Maybe two somethings."

She shoves the phone at me, and I look at the photo she's just received. It's of River and her sister. He's holding Jules by the throat, tight enough that I can see the shadow of indents from his fingers on her neck. Her eyes are pinched closed, fresh tears stain her cheeks, and a new black eye appears to be forming on the left side of her face.

River is grinning sadistically, and he's licking her cheek. His other hand has a fist full of her rear end, and the darkness in his eyes is nearly enough to convince me he's no longer on our side. Yet I don't panic.

We already knew he was going to have to do things to prove himself. This is just part of the act. Even if it's hard to see.

Another picture comes through. This one a little blurry, as River is shown dragging Jules by the back of her neck out of the room. She's clearly fighting back; her hands are clawing at his back, and her body is lowered to the ground as if she's trying to use her dead weight to stop him.

Just a little longer, kid, I think. Soon, she'll know she's safe, but until then, Jules believing her life just essentially ended is necessary.

"That's River, right?" Sophie asks, coming back to me.

I nod but don't get to respond as I see a text following the pictures.

Unknown: Your sister is about to experience things she won't soon be able to forget while you hide instead of owning up to your sins. What a terrible sibling you've turned out to be.

Sophie grabs my shirt with both hands and jerks me against her. "We need to go. Now."

"She's safe," I remind her. "River won't actually hurt her."

"I don't fucking care, Kyler!" she roars. "I'm leaving this house, and I won't let you stop me again."

Another text comes through.

River: I can't tell Jules that she's safe, but she is. I'm locking her in a crate in my room on the first floor while I give the all-clear signal to the others

waiting. It's the third bedroom on the left when you go down the second hallway in case you can get to her before I do. Ten minutes and it's go time.

"Ten minutes, Sophie," I plead with her. "River was waiting until he got your sister, and now they're all moving into position. We're going to get her. Just ten more minutes."

Her chest is heaving, and she's refusing to look at me, but I won't let her pull away. Not when I've only just found her, and especially not after the breakdown she had when we were in bed.

I close the distance she's created between us in three long strides. My palms gently cup her face, and I force her eyes to look at me. "I know you're scared, but you have dozens of people here to help you and to save your sister, including me. Even if you can't believe in any of them, believe in me."

Her lower lip quivers, but no tears fill her eyes. "If you're wrong, if something happens to her, it won't just be me that I'll never be able to forgive. I don't want to hate you like I know I'll hate myself. I know you won't deserve it, but I won't be able to stop my emotions."

My arms wrap around her, and I hold her close, kissing the top of her head. "It's not going to come to that. We're going to go in there, stop Astor, and take your sister away from that pack. Anything else is unacceptable."

She's shaking her head against my chest. "No." She pulls away, her eyes darker than I've yet to see them. "We won't *stop* Astor. I will *kill* him. Whatever your boss wants with him, it's not going to happen if it hasn't already. I will end that son of a bitch tonight."

Not that I don't understand why she needs to kill Astor, but I can't help myself from thinking about the stolen wolves. Wondering how many of them are children, how much they might be tortured. Keeping Astor alive just a while longer could be the only way to save those who have been taken. Passing up that opportunity seems wrong.

Though, I'm not telling her that. Not now.

"Let's get our things," I tell her, leaning in to kiss her, but she turns her head, and my lips barely brush against her cheek.

"Yeah, let's do that." Her dry tone makes my stomach sink.

Sophie, I say sharply through our bond.

She pauses but doesn't turn around.

You're my mate, and I will do whatever I can to protect you and make you happy, I tell her, hoping the words will help, but I frown when her shoulders stiffen.

And what if whatever you can *do isn't enough?* she asks indifferently. *The deeper we get into this, the more I see that we're not the same. That's okay, but I won't be someone else now that we've bonded, and I don't expect you to be. You saw what I'm capable of. There will be bloodshed tonight. I'm not a protector, and I don't care about protector laws. My feelings for you don't change what I need.*

This isn't fucking happening. Not right now. Not before we're about to head into a fight that could get us both killed if we're not at our best.

Once again, I move forward and spin her around just as she's about to enter the bedroom. I push her against the wall and pin her there, demanding her full attention.

"Enough," I snap, my face only inches from hers. "I get that you've had shitty things happen to you, but I'm not one of them. I'm your mate, and even if we don't agree, I will always support you. My job is not more important than you, but I also expect you to respect who I am. I consider the wellbeing of others, even at my own expense. And while your needs come above all others, can't Astor being captured be enough until we save the others? Then, end him."

Her face softens, but her eyes harden. "No. I need blood, and I need it tonight. It's who *I* am."

"No—"

"Yes, Kyler," she says pointedly. "I'm not trying to hurt you, but I'm selfish enough not to back down from this. I also won't lie to you. I want to push you away right now because that's easier than disappointing you, but admitting that doesn't change anything. I'm going to kill Astor."

My forehead presses to hers, and my heart aches for the hurt she's been holding on to for far too long. When she doesn't shove me away or storm off, I close my eyes and focus on my thoughts. Though, it isn't words that speak the loudest within my mind, it's my feelings for Sophie.

I'm her mate. First and foremost. Taking a deep breath and calming my emotions, I can admit that my preference to keep Astor alive is more about the protector in me taking root than about who I am. Murder in self-defense isn't something I've shied away from, and defending the life of my mate is the most important thing to me.

Yet, I've basically just said otherwise to her.

The moment I accepted this incredible woman into my life, I made the choice to forsake everything else without realizing it. Her happiness. Her peace. Those are what matter to me. Leaving Astor alive won't give her that. There must be others out there who know where the stolen shifters are.

We will find them. We have to, because not allowing my mate this comfort of knowing Astor can never hurt her or anyone she cares about again is no longer acceptable.

"I'm sorry, Sophie," I tell her solemnly. "You're right. Astor needs to die, and there's nothing wrong with you needing that to happen. I was thinking like a protector, but that's not all I am any longer. I'm yours, and that holds priority over everything else."

Our stares lock and slowly, she releases the wall that I could feel her building back up between us. Neither of us moves for several seconds as we soak in one another's emotions and acknowledge the shared truths along with the hurt, the fear, and the need to protect one another.

We're going into a pack that wants us dead. That's not to be taken lightly, and even though Sophie was ready to run right in, I feel her sense of awareness growing through our bond.

"Thank you," I tell her. Not only for letting me back in, but for allowing me to understand her a little better.

We've known each other for mere days. Just because I would die for her today doesn't mean I truly know her. Spending the rest of my life learning every nuance of hers is an experience I'd regret missing out on.

She pushes up onto her toes and, this time, kisses me first. "Thank you."

I press her harder against the wall, deepening the contact, but only for a few seconds. We have somewhere else to be, and I won't lessen the importance of this task by allowing myself to get distracted with desire.

My mouth moves along her jawline and to her neck, where I breathe her in, needing just a moment longer to soak in my mate and strengthen the connection that hums between us.

The invisible tether that ties us together, one created by a magic I don't understand, pulses in time with our heartbeats. I latch on to that energy and send every hope and want I'm wishing for through it.

Today won't be the day I die, and it won't be the day I lose another mate. We're going to do what needs to be done and not look back.

"Let's do this," I tell her again, this time, meaning it more than before.

She nods and stares at me with a smile that takes my breath away. "Let's."

We go into the bedroom and gather the knives I bought before. Our wolves will likely do most of the action, but it's never a bad thing to be overprepared.

Especially not when the person I know I can't lose is going to be putting her life at the highest risk.

Chapter Twenty-Nine

Sophie

Having a mate after being on my own for so many years isn't easy. I'm so used to doing whatever I want, not caring what anyone else thinks. I know Kyler was coming from a good place about leaving Astor alive and I'm trying to do better, but it's not as easy as just wanting those things.

Coming back to South Carolina has opened old wounds I can't leave exposed. For me, this has to end tonight. I'll help follow leads if needed for the other shifters, whatever the protectors need.

Except letting Astor continue to breathe air longer than necessary.

Kyler seems to have come around to my reasoning. Not that I want him to bend his beliefs for me just to get my way, but this is bigger than I know how to explain. Thankfully, he hasn't asked me to. Mostly because I can't see much beyond wanting Astor's heart ripped from his chest at the moment.

We're as ready as we're going to get. We've used the last two cloaking spells and stepped outside the cabin. Everything is eerily quiet. Not even the animals living in the forest are making noises, as if they know war is coming.

Kyler grabs my hand and looks down at me. I expect him to smile, but he doesn't. Then again, this isn't really a situation for that.

"I'm going to be right at your side," he promises. "You're not alone."

"I know." I squeeze his hand back. "Now, let's remind Astor and everyone else who stands with him what happens when they fuck with the wrong shifter."

We separate, and I begin to call my wolf forward. She's been supportive in a silent way as I've processed a lot of these pent-up emotions, but the time for that isn't now. Now, I need her to be the ferocious beast I know she's capable of.

I am feeling rather ravenous since you were being stubborn about not eating while we waited for news on Jules, she muses.

I'm not opposed to it now, I tell her. *Let's go hunting.*

The transformation sends shivers of warmth from the magic throughout my body, allowing me to revel in the manipulation of my body as I change from human to animal.

When we're on all fours, my wolf's attention goes right to Kyler. I've yet to really give her much time with his wolf and now really isn't the time, but when they head for each other, I have no objections.

His head nestles protectively over hers, and they both make content rumbling noises as they stand next to each other, soaking in the bond that ties all four of us together. A tranquility moves through us, and I smile to myself, remembering that no matter how frightening it might seem to depend on someone, it's these little moments that will make the hard ones all worth it.

These times when the world feels as if it's stopped just for us. When the devotion Kyler and his wolf have for us is stronger than any fear we've ever had. When the loneliness I thought would never leave is nothing more than a distant memory.

In those few moments, I can let everything else go.

Even though we're not technically a pack, River and I will be able to communicate through our wolves as protectors, Kyler tells me as we part and start to run toward the pack. *He says that there are two hunting parties out looking for us, lessening the amount of people at the pack. He told them about your car and is sending people to the cabin now that we've left.*

That works for me, I reply, enjoying the feeling of freedom that's pulsing through my wolf as she runs through the dense forest. The moon is high in the sky, the air is cool, and the sky is dark. A perfect setting for her.

I mean... my wolf starts. I'd rather be letting this sexy wolf beside us chase me through the woods, allowing the anticipation of him catching us to fuel my desire, but sure, it's a pretty night.

She's nearly insufferable, but I wouldn't trade her for the world.

How exactly can you communicate with River? I ask after realizing I've never heard of that being possible outside of pack and fated mates.

When we're inducted as protectors, we meet with a witch, he explains as we run. *She ties us together with magic that's similar to an alpha's without the pack requirements.*

Huh. A loophole of sorts. Weird, but I let it go.

We continue running, our speed increasing and Kyler keeping up with us, staying at our side. We're quiet for the rest of the way, listening for sounds of other wolves. I can scent them out there, but none seem to be coming close to us.

River says we need to enter on the north side, Kyler says. *There are families in those homes, but they shouldn't bother an unknown wolf as long as we don't linger. Most of the pack is just trying to survive in hopes that their alpha returns.*

Does River actually know where Joseph is? I ask since he seemed to know enough to convince Astor he was helpful in the hunt for the alpha.

Not that I'm aware of, because Maciah has also been looking for him, wondering how the hell any of this even happened.

I have a few guesses, but now isn't the time. We're getting closer to the pack, and it's time to act.

We're going to need to split up, I tell Kyler, and the

way his wolf snarls at us makes me laugh. *Do you not trust that I can take care of myself?*

My wolf apologizes for the misstep, he says, but there's another growl from the animal telling me otherwise.

It's okay, I reply with another chuckle. *I can handle overprotectiveness as long as you can handle me kicking your ass.*

Now it's Kyler's turn to laugh. *Another day.*

How about—I don't get to finish speaking. The wind is knocked from our lungs, and my wolf's body is suddenly ten feet from the path we were on.

As we roll over, another wolf is jumping for us, teeth dripping with saliva and claws ready to destroy.

Not today, motherfucker, my wolf sneers as she envisions the blood of this asshole covering the forest floor.

We get out of the way and back on our feet, but there are more coming. So much for the pack having fewer wolves around while we moved in.

Kyler is battling his own group of wolves. There are five total. Once again, I've been underestimated, with only two of them coming for me.

Just means we can play with these two idiots a little, my wolf muses.

No, we need to be ready to help Kyler, and these might not be the only ones around, I tell her as we scan the area. *We need to pretend this fight could be never-ending and be done with each wolf quickly. Jules needs us.*

That final thought sobers my wolf and has her attacking first instead of playing coy.

Our claws extend, digging into the cool earth beneath us, and we push forward, colliding with the two wolves. There's a silver one on the left that gets knocked down from the impact and an ebony one that goes to the ground but is back up quickly.

She licks her sharp teeth and charges for us again. My wolf lowers and we roll to our side, using our claws to gut the attacking shifter.

The black wolf whimpers but doesn't go down, not even with a part of her intestines hanging out of her stomach.

Guess she's a fighter like us, I say, hating that anyone who should have been my packmate had my life been different has to die, but also not feeling bad enough to back down. Anyone who would fight for Astor doesn't deserve to enjoy this life.

The silver wolf is back in the game as well. He nudges the darker one, and she snaps at him, but I'm not one for reunions. Not when lives I care about are on the line.

We attack again, this time going for the ebony wolf's neck. Surviving a broken neck isn't as easy as ignoring your guts hanging out.

She's quick, though, and spins around. Our bite lands on her shoulder just as the other wolf plows into our side for the second time. Does this asshole think he's a bull instead of a wolf?

We're back on our feet and notice Kyler has one wolf down already, but he's bleeding from his right flank.

We need to finish this, I tell my wolf, but it's more of a reminder for me that there's more on the line tonight than Jules and killing Astor. This isn't just about me anymore. I've found a mate and brought him into this nightmare. I need to make sure he survives as well. Anything else isn't an option unless my own death comes with it.

The two wolves attack us at the same time, but the darker one is slowing down. I ignore the silver one in favor of finishing the other. Getting a neck bite in is going to be difficult with both of them this close, so we go for her stomach again.

My wolf's claws snag the bit of intestines that are already showing, and she pulls hard. Not once, but twice. Blood gushes from the other wolf's stomach, and organs begin to drop to the ground. Her eyes widen, and she starts to teeter. The black one behind me howls, a sorrowful sound that makes me hurt for my enemy.

Based on that chilling cry, I assume they were mates, but I can't not defend my own life. This is the price they chose to pay when they decided working for a psychopath was more important than doing what is right.

The male wolf comes for me as the female falls to the ground, the life leaving her eyes.

I'm ready for him, but that doesn't mean he's going to be easy to defeat. We circle each other and my wolf calculates the best plan of action.

He's out of his mind with grief, she says. *We need to put him down quickly. The best way to do that is—*

Her words stop as we watch with mild astonishment as the wolf's left eye suddenly has an arrow sticking through it and going out the back of his head. Another follows quickly after, landing right at the center of his chest.

What the fuck was that? The smell of decaying flesh hits me a second later. *Vampires.*

Yet that's the least of my worries when I hear Kyler's snarls.

We race for our mate but come to a halt as a woman dressed in all black with long, dark hair and wielding a dagger cuts in front of me, beheading two wolves with just as many swings.

She turns around and waves her free hand at me. "You must be Sophie. I'm Amersyn."

The name rings a bell, but I don't recognize her. At least her eyes are a muddy red, telling me that she feeds from a bag and not a corpse.

I shift and by the time I'm on two feet again, so is Kyler. He's at my side in the next second and is looking around. "Where's Maciah?"

"Dealing with the group that was coming in from the south," the vampire says, then she smirks. "He thought he could come out in the field again without bringing me. I laughed in his face. At least now I can prove I was right."

"We had them handled," I tell her, not meaning to be defensive, but I don't need a vampire taking credit for a fight that we were nearly done with.

She smiles, and the action is friendly instead of condescending like I expect. "Yes, you did, but do you know how long it's been since I've gotten in on the fun?"

She slides her dagger in the sheath on her hip and rolls her neck, revealing the bow on her back. "Too long."

Howls sound from closer to the pack, and another figure comes speeding through the shadows, stopping at Amersyn's side. He looks her over, seeming to check every inch of her body before he turns to nod at Kyler. "Everyone's in place. River is fighting for Astor still until we all arrive and then he'll break cover. We need to hurry."

Finally, someone else who's ready to charge in. It only took two damn days.

The male vampire nods at me. "Sophie. I'm Maciah."

Another howl sounds through the night. "Yeah, I think proper introductions need to wait." My eyes meet Kyler's, and he nods, stepping away from me.

I'll be right by your side, he promises as we both start to shift. By the time we're on four feet again, the vampires are gone and we take off at top speeds toward the pack.

It's time to end this nightmare, I tell my wolf, whose chest rumbles in agreement as she moves with little effort between the trees, taking a path that used to be familiar to us.

We start to pass by the homes of the other shifters. The lights are off, but the reflection of eyes through the windows isn't hard to see. At least the entire pack hasn't been infected with Astor's bullshit. Just those like my father.

Continuing on, we arrive at the pack house. There are wolves and vampires battling Astor's chosen warriors.

The fight seems to lean heavily toward our side, assuming the wolves protecting the vampires are with Maciah.

A looming and rather significantly large shadow flies over our heads, and I'm forced to do a double take to understand what I'm seeing. I'd heard of the dragons that had begun appearing around some of the packs and communities, but hearing about them and seeing them are two totally different things.

With dark-red scales and a wingspan possibly wider than the pack house, the enormous beast soars over the crowd, then releases a stream of fire from his mouth that splits the crowd and catches several people on fire before he lands.

I lose sight of him as he flies around the back side of the house. Right then, I know I have to admit that everyone else was smart to stop me. There would have been no chance of saving Jules if I'd shown up with just Kyler yesterday, as I wanted. We would have died, and it would have been for nothing.

That serves to motivate me more than anything, though. I have the help I need—possibly more than necessary—and I'm going to take advantage of that before anything has a chance to go to shit.

My wolf brushes her head against the side of Kyler's who seems to have stopped as well to take in the already bloody battle. As we touch, a charge of energy moves between us.

We're ready, she says to me, and without a flicker of hesitation, we race into the battle with our mate at our side, just as he promised.

Chapter Thirty

Sophie

As we move into the thick of the fight, Maciah runs past us, touching the back of our neck before doing the same to Kyler. When I see my mate, there's a glowing smudge on his fur, like bright, shimmering silver paint.

The vampire marked us, so his people know we're not the enemy, my wolf says as I come to the same conclusion.

That's preferrable. With a quick look around, I see other marks, most of them placed on the backs of heads, likely done before they arrived. I don't have time to count how many are on our side.

A sharp howl sounds, and I feel others begin to move in on me. *We need to get inside the pack house,* I tell Kyler. *And we're going to have to fight our way there.*

Not a problem. He leaps in front of me, teeth snapping together and a sexy rumble echoing from his chest. Two wolves try to come for me, but he somehow manages to kick one of them to the side while ripping out the throat of the other.

His snout is covered in blood when he turns back to me, eyes bright with adrenaline. I expect him to say something, but instead, he jumps over me and is on top of another wolf in the next breath.

By the time I turn around, the other attacking shifter has a broken neck and Kyler is sauntering toward me like the beast he is. A sexy fucking beast.

That was hot, I tell him before heading toward the house.

And it felt good.

Of course it did. He's a man at heart, and he was protecting his mate. Testosterone is a powerful thing in a fight with the right motivation.

This time, though, it's my turn to remind Kyler who I am. As he takes the lead to enter the pack house, another wolf begins to stalk him, staying low to the ground and toward the shadows but not hidden enough to remain unseen. At least by me.

I slow down, making myself less noticeable, going as far as turning my body away from my mate. *You have a wolf on your right,* I tell Kyler. *Don't look. I've got him.*

Here I am trying to be nice by warning him about what I'm going to do, and he does exactly what I tell him not to, ruining my fun.

As soon as the two wolves make eye contact, the stalker leaps forward, teeth bared and claws out. Kyler doesn't back down, and I wouldn't expect him to, but that doesn't mean I'm not annoyed enough to charge in between them.

My wolf agrees. *We already had one kill taken from us tonight. Mate or not, he doesn't get to take the second.*

She pushes forward, this time running into Kyler enough to throw him off-balance before using our back end to push him away from the attacking wolf. With quick movements, we swipe out once, twice, and then a third time. The first hit took an eye out, the second cut through his throat, and the third hit his head hard enough that the wolf fell to the ground.

He isn't dead, and we're leaning in to finish the job when a young woman's voice rips through the air. "Help! Please, help!"

Jules.

Our kill is quickly forgotten as we race for the pack house entrance. The door is already open, and Kyler is right on our heels.

Is that your sister? he asks, and I wish I could say *yes* with certainty, but I can only assume since I haven't heard her voice in over a decade.

I catch the sight of someone going up the stairs and dark blonde hair hanging upside-down over his back. *There,* I tell Kyler as I start to shift.

As much as I love my wolf and appreciate her skills in a fight, it's my turn.

Kyler follows my movements and is at my back by the time I reach the stairs. I can't see anyone any longer, and I have no idea who had the female I assume is my sister, but I'm going to find them.

My foot lands on the first step of the stairs, and I have to take a steady breath. The last time I was here... I shake my head. No. This isn't a time for nightmare lane. I save my sister. I kill Astor. I leave. Nothing more, nothing less. My parents are on their own. I've had brief musings of whether they should die as well, considering they allowed this to happen to Jules and put me in a position to have to kill, forever changing my life.

If they'd never supported the Crowes...

Nope. Not going there, either.

Another scream echoes through the house and has my steps increasing in length, taking the stairs three at a time.

Are you sure you want to do this? Kyler asks through our bond.

I don't miss his choice of words. "Want to" instead of "can." He knows I can, and I do, too. But just because I'm capable of something doesn't mean there isn't a risk. I'm not cocky enough to believe I'm invincible.

There are a million scenarios I can fabricate proving it would be a bad idea for me to continue, but all I can picture is my sister's hollowed face in that picture. I allow myself to imagine what she had to go through to look that way. That's enough to know that I not only *want* to do this, but that I need to.

I've got this, I finally reply as we reach the landing on the second floor, but that's not where I stop. The alpha's room is on the third floor, and I have no doubt in my mind, even without the alpha gene in his pathetic body,

Astor has taken it upon himself to move in as if he were one.

We hurry forward, but when we get to the last set of stairs, there's a familiar face there bringing me to a halt.

"Mom?"

She nods, tears shining in her green eyes. "Hi, baby girl."

My heart hammers in my chest. The picture didn't show her age, but I can't miss the changes now. Her hair is greyer than the light brown I remember, and wrinkles line her eyes and mouth. She's lost even more weight than I thought and seems like a shell of the woman I used to know.

I brush away the softer parts of me that want to hug my mother for the first time in too many years and step forward to move past her.

She holds her hand out. "You need to stop, Sophie."

I shake my head. "There is nothing you can do to stop me from doing what you couldn't. Jules deserves better."

The last sentence is spoken with a disgust I have no desire to hide, which makes my mother flinch. "He won't hurt her."

I laugh, and I'm tempted to punch her in the face, because Astor has clearly already done more than hurt Jules, based on the picture I saw. He's traumatized her.

"Have you gone blind?" My voice raises, but Kyler presses his palm over my spine, reminding me to keep calm. This is a fight that's more than personal for me, but

I need to stay levelheaded, or I might as well walk away now.

"Astor already hurt her," I say with an even tone. "I saw the picture. You were with her. How can you not see what I do?"

She's shaking her head, and her hands are flailing. "It's not him. It's never been him. It was always..."

"What, Mom?" I snap, losing patience and unable to hide my disappointment in the woman she's become. "You always have an excuse. I used to hate you for that, but now, I just pity you."

I shove past her, feeling the heat of Kyler right behind me. Though, when I turn around, he's stopped to help my mother sit on the steps. He whispers something in her ear, and she sobs loudly, the sound like a knife to my chest.

"Run, Sophie!" the voice that must be my sister yells before she starts to cry. "You never should have come back."

Her weeping breaks my heart. "I never should have left" is what I want to tell her, but I won't show weakness in front of the enemy. I won't show him how much I care. Astor only needs to see how much I hate him and intend to murder him.

I step forward and pause at the door, double-checking that the knives I stashed in my boots and the one clipped to the back of my pants are still in place. Okay, and maybe to get my nerves in check.

You're not alone, Sophie, Kyler reminds me, and I turn to face him.

His jaw is tight, and his shoulders shake with built-up tension. I know he wishes I weren't here, that this wasn't my fight, but the fact that he's not stopping me now is all I need to know that he's my person. No matter what happens next, I'm thankful it was him sent to stop me, even if he didn't succeed.

I squeeze his hand and offer him a small smile. *I know.*

Together, we enter the room where Jules's voice came from. My eyes scan the area quickly, and I count seven shifters hiding in the shadows, two next to Astor, one of who is holding on to my sister, and then my father on his left.

He hasn't aged as much as my mother. He still has the same brunet hair and dark-blue eyes, though his nose is a little more crooked than I remember.

"Sophie," he says to me, voice indifferent. "Welcome home."

I huff with a smirk. "Quite the welcome party you threw."

My stare moves to Astor next, and bile churns in my stomach. He still looks so much like Thane did, and memories try to force their way forward, but my bond with Kyler is stronger than my past. All I have to do is think about the mate I should have had first and any thoughts of the one I killed slowly disappear.

Astor sneers. "I've waited too long for this moment." His dark eyes leer at me, and I do the same back to him. He's dressed in charcoal slacks with a matching suitcoat and white dress shirt beneath, presumably trying to exude the power he doesn't actually hold. His hands are shoved in his pockets, and he rocks back and forth on his black loafers as if he doesn't have a care in the world, but I see past all that. I see the fury in his stare.

He can't hide what I've lived with myself since the day I killed his son. A rage that is blamed on the world for the choices we've had to make.

I want to look away, to check on my sister as I hear her whimper, but I won't back down from this man. He needs to know that I'm not the little girl he last saw. That I'm not afraid of him.

The room is quiet until my father starts to speak. "She's here. Now, it's time for you—"

Astor doesn't let him finish, and I'm left wondering what the hell just happened as a knife that seems to come out of nowhere is drug across my father's throat. Astor's chest rumbles as he grimaces. "You've served your purpose, and I'm done listening to your petulant voice, James."

I watch, doing nothing as the man whose DNA runs through me drops to his knees, holding his throat. Our eyes meet, and he blinks rapidly, but I can't feel anything for him. Not sadness, not the drive to want to help him, not even relief. There's just nothing.

He did nothing for me before, and I'm doing the same for him.

Why is your sister smiling? Kyler asks me and I finally move my stare.

She's being held by a man I don't pay attention to. Her shoulders are sagging in what I can only assume is relief, and she seems to watch our father die with pure glee.

"I can see you're confused," Astor says with a little too much enjoyment. "Let me catch you up. He is your father." He points the knife toward my father's unmoving body, then at Jules. "But he isn't hers. Though, by your lack of reaction to his death, maybe he's nothing to both of you. Pity."

The only *pity* is that Astor kept my father alive as long as he had.

As much as I want to maintain control of my actions, when my gaze snaps back toward my sister and she refuses to look at me, I can't stop the words from leaving my mouth. "What the fuck are you talking about?"

The laugh that pours out of Astor grates on my nerves, because I've just given him exactly what he wanted: my emotions.

He grabs Jules by the back of the head, jerking her out of the other shifter's arms. "She's mine."

The way he says those two words has my head pounding and my vision blurring with ire. At first, I think he's trying to tell me that he's already claimed Jules as his mate, but then my mother's previous words start to come back to me.

It wasn't him.

She said Astor hadn't been the one to physically hurt Jules. Astor just said James wasn't her father, then answered with her being his.

As in his daughter.

Never before have I hated my parents more than I do now. How could my mother have... I don't know, and honestly, I don't want to.

My hardened gaze moves toward the man I wish I wasn't related to. The one who inflicted pain on my baby sister. He's still unmoving, but I listen for a heartbeat anyway because if he's not already dead, I intend to take his life myself. Unfortunately, I hear nothing until Astor starts to laugh again.

"I see from the disgust on your face, you're starting to piece things together," he says, shoving my sister out of his grasp. She yelps, and I know that even if Astor never raised a fist to her, he's still responsible for a lot of her hurt.

His wolves begin to come closer, and I start to pay them more attention. There are a few that I remember from my childhood. Ones I might have even called friends long ago. Yet, each of them is ready to destroy me for a man who couldn't care less about them.

I glance back at my sister, wondering what chance she might have of escaping on her own, and when I pay more attention to the man behind her, I have to take a second look. Dark-hazel eyes, auburn hair, full lips.

Is that River? I ask Kyler quickly, regretting not having taken the opportunity to look closer at the picture that was texted to me of him and Jules earlier.

Yes, your sister might not know it, but she's safe.

Holy shit. How did I not remember his name when his face was so clearly embedded in my memory as one of the protectors who found me in New York and took me to East Texas?

I don't know, but I recognize him now and feel even better about him being in charge of my sister. Especially when I see her rest her head against his chest.

With that knowledge, I know it's time to act. Astor needs to die, and the people fighting for him will follow suit or stand down. The choice will be up to them as soon as I know Jules is out of the crossfire.

"What do you think you're going to do, Sophie?" Astor taunts, gesturing to the men around him. "You've come here with help, and I'll give you credit for that because I didn't expect anyone to give a shit about you. But you're here in this room, facing me, with only one other. You have no chance of survival." His lip curls into a snarl. "You were a pathetic excuse for a wolf shifter when my son found you, and it seems nothing has changed. He knew it and I know it still. Hell, even your parents did. Why do you think they were so eager to let you go with him? Nobody wanted you, but my son was willing to teach you and you killed him for it. Now, I finally get to right that wrong."

Nobody wanted you.

He's right. I was nothing when I killed his son. I was a lowly wolf shifter in a massive pack. I might have never become anything, and just a week ago, Astor's words might have had the power to weaken me, but not today. Not any longer.

I'm not pathetic.

I used to hate the fates for pairing me with such a

horrible mate, while deep down wondering if it was what I deserved, but now, I can see the truth.

The fates didn't send me a shitty mate because I'm unwanted or unworthy. They sent Thane to me because I'm strong enough to end their fucked-up family, and I'm going to. Right the hell now.

Chapter Thirty-One

Sophie

I don't have to tell Kyler that we're ready to attack. He's moving before I am, shifting into his wolf right in the middle of the room. I'm tempted to do the same, but I watch Astor. When he stays in his human form, I have no problem doing the same.

Out of the corner of my eye, I catch River carrying Jules out of the room, and I'm grateful that he's keeping her safe but also disappointed that he's not going to be able to help right away in the fight. We're severely outnumbered, but there's no backing down at this point.

Before anyone else can shift, Kyler's wolf has already shredded the stomachs and throats of two others. Maybe we won't be outnumbered for long.

Astor reaches for where Jules was just seconds ago, but he's missed his chance at using my sister as his shield.

I reach for the knife behind my back, grip it tightly between my fingers, then punch the asshole in the face, the hilt of the blade acting like a fist pack and deepening the impact of my hit.

Astor seems to be prepared for that, because he grabs my wrist and forces my hand to turn back toward me. "You should have stabbed me while you had the chance."

Instead of allowing the knife to puncture my chest, I release the blade, letting it fall to the ground. But it's not the only one in play. Astor already slit my father's throat, and I see him reaching toward his suitcoat, likely wanting to kill me the same way.

Moving for the other knives I have on me, I realize I'm not going to be quick enough and instead start to do a partial shift. My claws are better than a blade any day.

Except before I can swipe out, I'm shoved out of the way, landing on my hip with a hard thud. When I look up, I expect to be glaring at Kyler, but it's not him.

It's my mother.

She's standing there, her body tangled with Astor's as they fall to the floor. I expect her to push away from him once they land, but instead, she leans into him like he's the love of her life, nuzzling the side of her face against his chest.

Yet she and my father were fated mates. How could she care for this monster of a man? How could she have let him touch her, see what he's done, and still seem to be affectionate with him?

Disdain for the woman who gave me life rises up until I can no longer contain my emotions. With a roar that rumbles through the room, I get to my feet and charge forward, but as I'm about to attack them both, everything changes.

Astor shoves my mother off of him, and she's rolled over. The knife that had been intended for me is protruding from her chest.

Our gazes lock for the briefest of seconds as she whispers, "I'm sorry, baby girl."

I'm paralyzed. I can't move. Had that been affection I saw on her face? Was it the peace that her fight was over? I don't think I'll ever know, but I can see now that she sacrificed herself to save me. After all this time, she finally chose me.

And now she's dying.

What have I done?

No, not me. Astor. This isn't my fault. It's his. For being a Class A prick, for raising his son to be just like him, and for not walking away while he had the chance.

There's no saving my mother, but I offer her a solace, even if she may not deserve it.

I kneel at her side and hold her hand for the brief second that I have. "It's okay, Mom. I forgive you, and I'll take care of Jules."

Her eyes flutter closed as she attempts to nod. Her lips part, but no more words leave her mouth. Just like that, both of my parents are dead.

Now, it's time to make sure this son of a bitch can never hurt another person.

Except I've allowed myself to be distracted for too long.

Astor is already back on his feet, and his fingers grip the hair at the base of my neck, jerking me back up.

I push up, relieving the pressure on my skull and this time when I face him, my claws are out and ready for blood. A partial shift takes strict concentration, and while there is still plenty of fighting happening around us, all I see is Astor.

"Don't worry. You'll see your parents again real soon," he taunts, no longer armed and not seeming prepared for a bloody fight.

Instead of engaging in a pointless conversation, I lean into his grasp, ready to finish this nightmare, but before I can rip his heart from his chest, a gunshot goes off, the boom loud and painful on my sensitive ears. There's a reason that wolves prefer blades over guns, and this is one of them.

My head is stunned, and it takes another moment that I don't have to keep moving. While Astor no longer has a hold on my hair, there's now a searing pain in my chest.

One glance down and I see there's blood pooling through my shirt. No. Not me. Not now. Not when I'm so close to...

Astor leans in, smirking, then grabs my throat, keeping me upright when my body would prefer to fall to the ground. "I told you I would have my revenge. I stupidly allowed your mother to convince me to let you go all those years ago so that I wouldn't draw the attention of the protectors, allowing them to ruin the bigger picture. I did, however, promise her that if you ever showed your face here that I would kill you."

His chuckle casts hot breath across my face, and I'm close to vomiting on his shiny, black shoes.

"And you couldn't have returned at a better time," he continues. "With your death, I'll have everything I've always wanted."

"You'll still be nothing," I spit. "Even more, you'll have nothing. Even if the protectors don't stop you and by some crazy chance the pack doesn't revolt against you, they won't respect you. They'll only fear you. And if you think that's something to be proud of, you're even more of an idiot than I thought."

His hold around my neck gets tighter, and the pain in my chest expands, moving to my stomach and down my arms. If Astor weren't holding me, I'd be in a heap on the ground.

The bullet went all the way through, my wolf says. *As long as we don't bleed out, we can survive this.*

Or as long as we aren't choked to death, I reply, not really seeing a way out.

That's right when Kyler's wolf finally sees me. The growl that thunders through the room rivals any other, but he won't make it to me in time.

Spots start to dance in my vision as he yells for me in my mind. I hate to do it, but I shut him out of my mind even further than I already had.

I close down the mate bond, not wanting him to carry my pain or fear with him when he's still under attack. I won't be the reason both of us die today. Plus, my wolf is much too excited, and concentrating on anything other than surviving isn't possible right now. Not even for our mate.

"You're going to die, Sophie," Astor whispers into my ear. "Just give in and allow the world to move on, like you should have done."

What is your plan? I ask her, ignoring his delight at the possibility of my death.

Give up, she says, taking me by surprise and filling me with disappointment. She scoffs. *Seriously? You think I'm ready to die when we've only just begun to live? Give up and let me take charge, you idiot.*

That, I can do. Though I don't know why I didn't think of it before.

Because I'm the brains of this operation, she jokes. *You're just the body.*

Not bothering to argue with her, considering the fire that's beginning to burn through my body, shutting my organs down, I close my eyes and let my muscles relax.

The energy of the shift begins to shimmer around my skin, but it's weak thanks to my injuries and lack of oxygen. Possibly too weak.

Don't be so quick to believe we're hopeless, my wolf says, her presence stirring stronger within my mind. *I've got this.*

Astor's nails start to cut through my skin. "That's it. Just fucking die."

The venom in his voice, the desire to get what he wants... It's enough to send a surge of adrenaline through me. That boost intensifies my shifter magic, and the change finally takes root.

It's slow and Astor catches on too quickly, but he can't stop me. Not now.

"Shoot her again," he roars, but no other gunshots go off and he adds, "Put that down, child. You don't know what you're doing."

"Yes, I do," Jules's voice sounds from behind me. "I'm doing what I should have done long ago."

By the time I'm on all fours and can see my little sister, there are tears in her eyes and her hands are shaking as they hold the pistol between them.

No, I won't let her be like me. She won't be a murderer at seventeen.

My wolf moves into action. Every step she takes sends a wave of new agony through our body, but there's no stopping us now. At least not until Astor's blood coats our mouth.

My wolf pounces on him while he's still looking at Jules, and we knock him to the ground, not at all gracefully. Astor nearly gets back up, but we claw into his thigh, halting his movements enough to pin him to the floor.

"You're inferior in every way," he says with a desperation I don't miss. "You can't kill me."

Watch me, I say, even though he can't hear me.

"Enough!" a deep, booming voice yells through the room, one filled with alpha power that has my wolf nearly yelping from the intensity of the command. "Everyone, yield."

"You better kill me now," Astor whispers. "You won't get another chance."

He wants to die, my wolf says. *He's lost. Whoever that is, he can't beat him.*

As much as I hate to give this man what he wants...

He needs to die.

With the alpha command to yield still pulsing through the room, it isn't easy to move forward, but my wolf isn't weak. Not like we've been told. Not like I might have almost just believed. She's powerful and wise and a fucking badass.

She fights through the energy around us and opens her mouth. Astor grins, his eyes on us the entire time. Sadistic and crazy. Two things that don't mix well.

"I said, *yield*," the voice says, much closer than before, but it's too late.

We've won.

Our claw rips into Astor's chest, quickly followed by our teeth that sink into his heart, tearing into the organ. Our head jerks back and forth as blood fills our mouth then drips onto the ground beneath us. Even when there's nothing left to recognize in his chest, my wolf claws at that bastard for good measure. It almost feels wrong when he's not fighting back, but ridding the world of this man is something I won't ever regret.

I was meant to end this family.

Yes, Thane was my fated mate and one day I'll meet him again, but I have to believe that we'll both be different...better in our next lifetime.

When his body goes limp under us, my wolf falls to

the side and relinquishes control. *It's done. You need to shift back and let Kyler back in before he murders the alpha and gets himself killed.*

Gods, I really am the worst mate ever.

Before I shift, I catch sight of an older man with a fresh scar on his left cheek, and by the glower on his face, I assume he's not too pleased that I overpowered his command, but that's a problem to deal with later.

I draw on my shifter magic, pull the energy from my core, and at the same time, I open the bond back up with Kyler.

His rage instantly fills me, but so does his love and fear. I grasp on to the intensity of his emotions, taking strength from him and using it to allow me to shift back to my human form.

The process, while still painful thanks to my gunshot wound, is quicker than I expect. I can't stand up when I change, and I expect to be yelled at by not only the alpha, but by my mate. Yet there's nothing but silence when I look around.

"Let him through," the alpha above me finally says and Kyler is holding me in the next second, cradling my body to his chest.

He looks up at the alpha. "She was only defending herself."

I can hear the plea in Kyler's voice, but I can speak for myself. I don't get the chance, though.

The newcomer bends down and meets my stare. "Sophie Thomson, you defied a direct order." His eyes darken, but there's a flicker of something else in them as he continues, "but I'm not your alpha. Roman will deal with you when you go home."

Yeah, he'll pat me on the back and tell me how proud he is of me, but something tells me this man knows that.

"I'm going to take my sister with me," I say, not asking, because it's not up for debate.

He nods and looks around, likely taking in all the bloodshed. "That's probably for the best."

Maciah and Amersyn blur into the room, coming to a halt near us.

"Joseph," Maciah says, and the alpha stands.

I glance up at them from Kyler's shaking arms. Amersyn winks at me, then gives me a thumbs-up before she moves farther away with Maciah and the alpha.

Finally, I give my mate the attention he more than deserves. I expect him to reprimand me—in fact, I'm almost hoping for it—but instead, he leans closer and presses his lips to my forehead. "You are everything I didn't know I needed."

He squeezes me tighter, and I finally wince. "I was shot."

His head shakes, a dark laugh escaping him. "Yeah, I saw that," he says dryly, pushing his palm firmly over my chest. "You're healing already or I would be a lot more pissed off right now."

"So, you're not going to yell at me?" I ask him with a grin that I should probably keep to myself.

He chuckles again, and the sound is still more wicked than soothing. "Oh, you closed down our bond link. There will be plenty of yelling to be had, but first, I'm going to get you and your sister the hell away from this place."

Seriously, how many times is he going to prove just how damned perfect he is?

I might be covered in blood and surrounded by dead bodies, including those of my parents, but for the first time in my life, I'm free.

Free from the demons of my past. And I'm not alone. More importantly, I never will be again.

Chapter Thirty Two

Kyler

I'm holding Sophie, but I still can't breathe. My muscles won't unclench, my heart won't stop hammering in my chest, and the need to kill every person who even looks at my mate pulses loudly within my mind.

She almost died. She was shot. She risked herself to end that bastard.

And I didn't do a fucking thing to help her.

Yes, you did, my wolf says. *You kept the others from getting to her. You made it so that she had a chance to do what she needed to do on her own.*

He's already told me this more than a few times in the last several minutes, but I can't accept what he's saying. I can't relinquish the pain and guilt that I wasn't enough.

You defeated six other fully-trained-for-battle wolf shifters without help, my wolf adds. *I'd say that's more than enough.*

I'm not used to him giving me pep talks, which makes it easier to ignore him. But I hear the words and maybe I'll believe them in time. When Sophie's life no longer feels as if it's on the line.

Taking another deep inhale, I remain calm on the outside for my mate, but now it's my turn to block her out. She doesn't need my guilt right now. Not when this mess isn't actually over. Not until we've officially left this place behind. Even then, who the hell knows.

"Where's Jules?" Sophie asks, and I realize I also haven't seen River. He should have been helping me. If he had been, I'd have gotten to my mate and maybe she wouldn't have been shot.

I look around as Sophie does, but we don't see her sister.

Joseph nods toward the hallway. "She's out there with River." The grimace on his face doesn't bode well for my friend or possibly for my mate. "He's not doing well."

Seems it would be my friend, then.

Sophie struggles to get out of my arms, but I'm not ready to let her go yet. Even with the injuries I sustained in the fight, I manage to stand up with her still cradled against me. I carry her toward the hallway and find Maciah standing with another man I don't recognize as Amersyn tries to remove Jules from the situation, but the young wolf refuses to move.

"I won't leave him," she cries. "He saved me, and I told him I hated him, even though he's my-my-my…

mine." Her sobs grow louder as she cries over River's body.

"Holy shit," Sophie whispers. "You have to let me down."

"Why?" I don't understand what has her sounding as if she's in a bit of shock.

"River is her fated mate."

Well, that would do it.

I don't know how Sophie knows, but I know her sister needs her right now. Considering my mate missed out on being there for Jules for too many years already, I force myself to let her go.

Sophie gets to her feet, a little unsteady, but she doesn't have to walk far to get to her sister. She bends down and holds the young girl, talking softly into her ear.

"Let them help him, Jules," she says. "You're safe now and he will be, too."

"I thought he was like... I told him I hated him...but I was just..." None of her sentences finish as she lets Sophie pull her back from River's body.

When his chest is exposed, there's a bullet wound there. I didn't hear a second shot and have no idea who pulled the trigger, but I'm sure as hell going to find out.

"It didn't go all the way through," Maciah says after bending down to quickly inspect the injury. "Call Andie now."

Amersyn has her phone to her ear before he's even finished speaking and steps away.

My gaze flicks to the man with light reddish hair. His eyes are narrowed on my mate, and I move to stand between them, a rumble in my chest. "Is there a problem?"

He blinks but doesn't answer. However, Maciah does while remaining at River's side.

"Kyler, this is Lykem. The dragon you must have seen when we arrived," my boss explains. "His mate is the one who alerted us to the kidnapped supernaturals, and he was looking forward to some time alone with Astor."

Supernaturals? Meaning not just wolves were taken? This is news to me, but not what I'm focusing on right now. While I don't appreciate the dragon's aggression toward my mate, I can sympathize. But only slightly.

"I understand," I say to Lykem, "but my mate was also wronged by him. His death couldn't be avoided."

"Right." His lips barely move as his chest expands. "I'm going to see what I can find outside."

Once the dragon shifter is headed down the stairs, I move toward Jules and Sophie. The former seems to have finally stopped crying, so I decide to figure out if there's something I can do other than stand here.

Sophie might be healing by the second, but that doesn't mean the fury I'd been consumed with when she nearly died doesn't still need a release.

"Did you see who shot him?" I ask Jules as gently as I can.

The young shifter nods against her sister's shoulder, and then her eyes flick toward the stairwell. "He's somewhere down there."

Well, not likely any longer, but maybe there'll be a blood trail to follow if River hurt him first.

I stand, giving Sophie another onceover. *I'll be right back.*

Find that son of a bitch and bring him to me.

That nearly has me smiling, even though there's not a chance in hell of that happening. He's mine if I find him.

There are large areas of smeared blood down the first set of stairs that I head down, and when I turn the corner to go down the second set, there's a body. A man with his heart ripped from his chest. Maybe all that blood covering Jules's hands isn't just from River...

If so, even after having spent more than a decade apart, these two sisters are more alike than either of them probably realizes.

River's going to have his work cut out for him just like I am.

By the time I'm back upstairs, the pink-haired witch named Andie that I've met on occasion before is kneeling over River, likely having quickly teleported in. She already has her glowing palms pressing over the wound as she closes her eyes.

Those gathered around are all quiet, watching her work until she pulls a hand back, revealing a bullet. "There's damage I still need to fix, but the fact that this came out whole is a good sign."

River starts to groan, which has Jules trying to leap for him, but Sophie stops her at the same time Andie presses a thumb over his forehead and he falls still again.

Her sympathetic face turns toward Jules. "He needs to stay calm for me to finish, but I'm going to save him. I promise. He means the world to us as well."

Jules's face falls in defeat, but there's also relief there as Sophie gathers her back into her arms.

I want to go to my mate. The desire to hold her and have physical proof in my hands that she's okay is stronger than I would have ever thought possible. Yet I can't stand the thought of interrupting this moment with her sister.

You came back too quickly, Sophie says without looking at me. *Did you not find the trail of the shooter? I saw blood leading down the stairs.*

No, but he did lose his heart before I found him. I nod at Jules. *Based on the blood on your sister's hands, I think she might know where it is.*

That has my mate smiling. *She turned out pretty amazing, considering who she was left with.*

She did, and she can be even better, I say with sincerity. *We can take her back to East Texas with us if she'll go.*

Finding her mate so young isn't normal, but River's a good man. I'm not worried about him respecting her age and making sure she has the opportunity to grow up before officially becoming his mate. But that's not for us to worry about today.

Andie finally stands and grins widely. "The bleeding has stopped, and his wolf shifter healing has taken over what I started. Whoever knew to put pressure on that wound, keeping everything intact, saved his life."

Jules peeks her head up from Sophie's shoulder and lets out a strangled laugh. "I thought I was hurting him, but I was so fucking scared."

Sophie's mouth drops open. "Language."

That has everyone but me laughing. I'm groaning along with Jules because I know this is just the beginning. The beginning of Sophie stepping in as the parent and not realizing that her sister is no longer the five-year-old she last knew.

River starts to wake up, and this time, nobody stops him. Sophie releases her sister, and we watch, a little uncomfortably, as she launches herself at him.

Jules is only seventeen and River is in his early thirties. That's quite the gap, but when he looks at me and grimaces, I can see the same worries on his face. He's found his mate, but this isn't going to be easy. He's going to have to let her go for a while, and we're going to have to convince the already-traumatized teenager that it's for the best.

Basically, we're asking for hell, but Jules needs to learn healthy relationships before going out into the world, regardless of how much we can trust River. Her "parents" never could show her that, and who the hell knows what Astor has done to her.

It wasn't my intention to share Sophie with anyone anytime soon, but for this, for her sister and my friend, I think I can manage.

With Jules not needing Sophie at the moment, I go to my mate again and wrap an arm around her waist, holding her to my side. My earlier rage is slowly subsiding, especially when I know her body is healing and the threat to her life should be over.

Though, we still haven't heard what else the alpha

Joseph might have to say. He had remained in the room, but I think it's time we found him and got some answers on why he abandoned his people. More than that, how did he know to show back up tonight of all nights?

"Let's go find the alpha," I tell my mate, but it's Maciah who responds first.

"Yes, I have more than a few questions for that man." There's a rumble to the vampire's voice, one I've heard before and am glad is not directed at me.

He and Amersyn start to head back into the room, but Andie grabs the latter's arm. "I'm going to go outside, see if anyone else needs help healing, and then head home. Foster might have yelled at me as I teleported away, and I may have not told him I was leaving for River in my panic."

Maciah shakes his head. "Call that man and put him out of his misery, please."

"But maybe he deserves it a little." Andie smirks and winks at Amersyn. "Fine. I'll call him, check on the others, and then go back to my date night. See you guys next week for Dawsyn's ceremony?"

"We wouldn't miss it for the world," Amersyn says with a sense of pride that I assume is for the soon-to-be Alpha.

I was never part of a big pack, and I've never been close with my parents. In fact, I haven't spoken to them since the day after Cara died when they tried to tell me maybe it was for the best—that I had been too young when I met her anyway—but seeing the connection between Sophie and

Jules, then Maciah, Amersyn, and Andie showing how much they care about River and even Dawsyn... I'm even more ready to quit my job and see what life is like in a pack that has already shown their kindness by taking my mate in.

My hold on Sophie grows tighter as I'm reminded once again that life is short. I won't be wasting another moment of my time. No more living in the past. No more running from my grief.

Sophie tugs at my shirt and pulls me toward her with narrowed eyes. "You're blocking *me* out now."

I completely forgot that I'd done so earlier while I was still shaking on the inside with unfiltered ire, but now that she's said something, I can sense the wall I've created. Without needing to think twice, I let her back in. The amount of warmth I'm filled with proves what idiots we both were for thinking that we didn't need the other at any point tonight.

She pushes up onto her toes and kisses me. "That's better. How about we try not to do that again?"

"I think I can manage that," I tell her, allowing the strength of our bond to remove any lingering fear within me.

Sophie pulls away again, but she doesn't go far. My mate kneels beside River and Jules, who are still on the ground, hugging.

"You saved her before you knew who she was," Sophie says, her tone indifferent, "but we have a lot to discuss."

River's lips form into a thin line before he replies.

"You can trust me. I won't allow any lines to be crossed. She deserves better than that."

I expect Jules to pull away and say something about them discussing her as if she's not present, but the young she-wolf doesn't budge from her position in River's lap as she clings to him.

The trauma of what she's been through, of knowing that her parents are dead, and what might have been if Sophie hadn't killed Astor...I'm sure it's all too much.

If I were her, I'd be blocking out the rest of the world, too.

"Come on," I tell Sophie. "She's fine where she is, and I'd like to know what the hell happened here."

Sophie stands and slips her hand into mine, a slight rumble in her chest. "So would I."

Chapter Thirty-Three

Sophie

My shoulder still burns like a son of a bitch from the bullet wound, but there isn't an injury on my body that is going to keep me from hearing what Joseph has to say.

He left his pack. Left them to Astor.

I know Dawsyn said he was missing, but my brain took that to mean he was dead and the body just hadn't been found yet.

Having him show up when we were already nearly done cleaning up his mess... I have no respect for the man. He's lucky I don't want to cause trouble for Roman and Dawsyn or he'd know it, too.

I mean, him showing up helped save our life so..., my wolf chimes in.

No, it saved the lives of the others Kyler would have continued ripping through to get to me, I reply without a doubt in my mind. *We were already positioned to kill Astor.*

And what a glorious moment that was. The delight in her tone matches that in my chest.

As worried as I am about the other casualties, and as much as I hate that my mother died while finally protecting me, I had let this pack go the moment I decided to come back, even if it took me a while to realize that.

It seems contradictory, but I really only needed closure. Not anything my parents might have offered me had things been different.

I may mourn my mother—definitely not my father— at a later date, but this is the path she chose. I at least don't hate her, and that alone gives me the peace I need to move forward once and for all.

We enter into the blood-soaked room. There are multiple dead shifter bodies beside that of Astor's, and I realize now how lucky Kyler is to have come out mostly unscathed from that fight.

He should have had River as backup, but clearly, the protector hadn't been capable of returning after he left to get Jules to safety.

I shudder a little at the thought of her being mated already, especially to someone so much older, but now that I know River is the same person who saved me all those years ago and from what I've seen with my own eyes, I'm trying to hold back my own teenage trauma.

River isn't Thane and Jules isn't me, even if we seem to be a lot alike without having grown up together.

We'll find a way to make this work, even if my sister hates me for a little while. We're all we have when it comes to family by blood, and I'll do whatever it takes to make sure she has the future she deserves.

Joseph is already standing in front of Maciah and Amersyn when we join them, but it seems we haven't missed much in the conversation.

"After he told me Astor was initiating a coup," Joseph says, "I knew leaving was the best choice."

"How the hell could you think that?" I snap, gaining the attention of the three higher-ranking supernaturals before me and my mate, but that doesn't stop me. "You left them to bow to that psychopath or die. What kind of alpha does that?"

"The kind who knows his job isn't as easy as some people think," the alpha replies. "What you didn't hear before is that I lost my daughter to that bastard. He stole her right out from under me and sold her to humans, who then sent me a picture of her bludgeoned body as a warning not to put my nose where it didn't belong or more would suffer her fate."

Well, shit. Maybe I should have kept listening.

"I had a choice to make," he continues. "I could fight Astor, or I could let him think he'd won, leave men I trusted here, and figure out how to stop him from behind scenes. Yes, I knew some of my people would die, but sometimes a sacrifice has to be made in order to save the whole. But I didn't know how deep this problem with the stolen wolves went, nor who I could trust. Still don't, really, but when I was notified a fight was coming, I began making my way back immediately."

Him and Maciah share a hard stare. The alpha's

inability to trust the protectors is a direct slight to the vampire, but I don't entirely blame Joseph for going out on his own. I can't deny I would have done the same thing.

"And did your men learn what you hoped?" Kyler asks, nodding to Astor's bloody form. "We're not going to get answers from him, and even though he's dead, it doesn't sound like this fight is over."

Especially after hearing about the dragon shifter's mate out in the hallway, there might be a very miniscule part of me that feels bad about killing Astor, but not enough to regret my actions. Others will talk. Eventually.

Joseph nods with a grimace. "Two of the four I left behind are dead, but I believe my plan still worked. They'll be able to give Maciah enough to start pulling at threads, see just how deep this truly goes, and hopefully rescue those who haven't been killed by their captors."

Maciah reaches a hand to the alpha, gripping his shoulder. "You made a hard choice, and your sacrifices won't be in vain. We will find every loose end and stop anyone involved. I won't rest until then."

"Still," Amersyn says sternly, "we're going to need to have a long conversation about how all of this transpired and what could have been done better to lessen the casualties."

I hold back my grin, a little pleased I wasn't the only one thinking along those same lines.

Joseph bows his head. "Yes, we probably should."

Alphas are the leaders of their people, but the protectors have been around long enough to prove their worth, keeping order within all of the supernatural species. They might not technically be in charge, but people don't often cross them and get away with it.

"Now isn't that time, though," Maciah says. "Take care of your people, find who might not be okay with Astor's death, and bring anyone with information to us. We will find a room here in the pack house to stay in until we have what we need."

I grin. There's the Maciah I expected as the protector leader—inviting himself in without asking.

Kyler wraps an arm around me and addresses his boss. "Can we speak privately with you for a moment?"

Joseph takes that as his cue to leave, and once the four of us are left with the dead bodies I'm trying not to notice any longer, Kyler speaks, taking me by surprise.

"I'm officially giving my notice," my mate says. I stare up at him, slack jawed as he continues, "I appreciate the home you've given me these last ten years, but I've found a new one. I'd like to move onto the next part of my life."

Amersyn grins widely and winks at me while Maciah addresses Kyler. "I expected as much once you said she was your mate. Just know that both of you have a place with us anytime, should you wish to return to this life."

My eyes glance toward the hallway. I can't see my sister, but that doesn't mean she's been far from my thoughts. "As fun as that sounds—sincerely—I have a family to put back together and a pack to get to know."

"Dawsyn will be lucky to have the two of you on her side when she takes official control next week," Amersyn says. "You make sure to watch my niece's back. She might have that dragon mate of hers to burn her enemies, but one can never have too many people on their side. Especially when ruling one of the largest packs in the U.S."

"She'll have our loyalty for as long as we're capable of giving it," Kyler replies proudly, and suddenly, I realize that maybe I've been a little selfish.

We've known each other mere days. Mates or not, I haven't asked him what he wants. Yes, he seemed more than eager to quit his job, but officially moving to East Texas, assuming he has no other family that he'd like to be with... Well, that's kind of a bitch move.

Maciah and Amersyn leave, and the moment Kyler and I are alone, I grab both of his hands, turning to face him head on. "What do you want?"

His head cocks to the side, and there's a hint of humor in his voice. "I don't understand the question."

"We don't have to move to Texas," I say, then begin to ramble. "You don't even have to move in with me. I never asked what you wanted. We've only known each other a short time. I just made these assumptions without asking you and—"

Kyler grabs my face and kisses me, shutting me the hell up and pulling me out of my panic. My body melts into his as our bond pulses between us, lighting up with nothing other than pure desire.

Finally, he pulls back until he can look into my eyes. "You are what I want, Sophie. Now and for the rest of this life. If I haven't made that clear, I'm sorry, but I'm saying it now. I want to be where you are. I already told you I love Texas and that I felt at home there whenever I visited for work. There is nothing else in this world that calls to me like you do. We're going to leave this pack, take your sister with us, give her the life you should have had, and never look back. Does that sound okay to you?"

It sounds like I'm one more romantic tangent from falling in love with this man, but who am I kidding? Time means nothing. I've already fallen and gladly so.

"I think I can be okay with all of that," I reply with a grin, holding tightly to his shirt and keeping him close.

"Good, because I really wasn't going to give you a choice," he says, matching my happiness. "Now, let's go break up the mates and hope Jules doesn't murder us in our sleep."

I laugh, but not for long. Jules killed the man who hurt her fated mate, which tells me she's been through more than I wanted to consider before. While I don't think she'll actually try to murder us, I have no doubts that taking her in and trying to remind her that she's young and should enjoy this time with people her age will be difficult, to say the least.

"We'll just have to sleep with one eye open for the next few years," I tell him as we leave the room I hope to never return to.

"You think she'll last that long being separated from her mate?" he asks quietly before we enter the hallway.

"She'll have no choice," I say, hoping River is as good of a man as he's portrayed, because we're going to need his help convincing Jules this is for the best.

Otherwise, Astor won't be the last man I kill, and I'd really prefer him to be.

I'm ready to leave that part of my life behind. Enjoying the simple life, living for the love of my mate, and being part of a pack that doesn't have ill intentions... It all sounds pretty damn awesome and like something that I'm long overdue for.

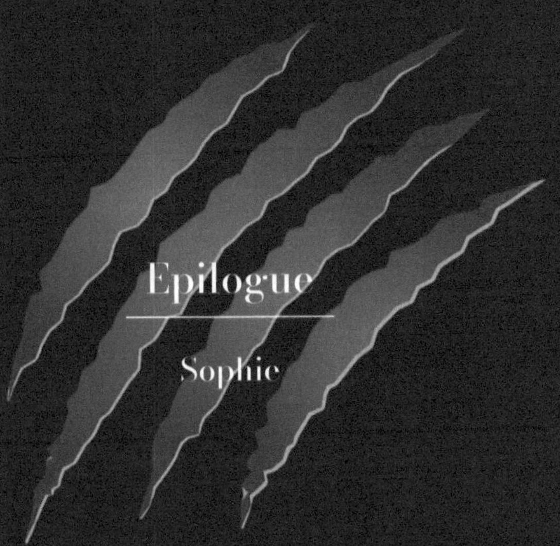

Epilogue

Sophie

This has been the longest week of my life, and that's saying something, considering all the stupid shit I've done.

Jules has said maybe a dozen words to me since she realized what was happening. The only thing that got her to come with us was River explaining he still has a job to do with these missing supernaturals. He did promise to visit and that they could talk by phone, but when he explained to Jules very clearly that they would be friends first, that's when he really won me over.

Still, it's been hell. A hell that I wouldn't trade for anything in the world. Especially as I hear Jules running through the house we've barely moved into and screaming as she opens the door.

The girl hasn't seen her mate in six days, and when I exit the kitchen to see the way she's clinging to him before he's even walked through the threshold, one might assume it's been six months.

Even better, River is grinning widely and keeping his hands above her waist when I walk into the front room. *Good boy.*

"Jules, you're going to suffocate him," I tell her, but she no longer hears me. I'm nothing but the big, bad sister who took away her new favorite toy. She'll thank me one day, after she's lived a little, made her own friends, and stopped looking over her shoulder every other minute.

That's probably the hardest part. She won't tell me what happened with my parents or Astor, but she at least confirmed she was never physically taken advantage of. That, I would have gone on another killing spree for.

I'm doing my best to accept that she's safe now, even if we're not on speaking terms. Yet.

Kyler comes in behind me and goes to River, ignoring the growth wrapped around the other shifter as they shake hands. "We're glad you could make it."

What my mate really means is that he's glad he no longer has to listen to Jules crying at night or wince when we hear something shattering against the wall in her room. At least for the next two days.

Teenage hormones are savage.

"Have you seen Dawsyn yet?" I ask River as he finally moves past the front door, gently guiding Jules away from him.

I expect her to continue clinging to his side, but I'm pleasantly surprised when she chooses to walk next to him, leaving a couple of inches between them as we sit on the couches in the front room—the only two pieces of big furniture that we have so far in the front part of the house.

"No, I stopped here first," River replies. "She's with Cillian and her parents right now. I'll see her soon enough."

Jules grins proudly beside him, as if she knows he came here first just for her sake.

"How are things back in South Carolina?" Kyler asks him since we've chosen to stay out of that mess. Well, mostly.

"Joseph is officially back in charge," River says, though he doesn't seem thrilled about that revelation, based on the crease between his brows. "Maciah and Amersyn have stayed behind and Lykem should be back here by now. Other protectors are keeping post, and we've found two of the locations, but not the one Lykem was most concerned with."

What he's not saying but I can hear in his tone is that the dragon shifter isn't going to be happy until he has his justice. And considering I was the one who killed the man with the most information, I might not be a welcome sight for Lykem until he gets what he wants. At least I have a heads up to give him a wide berth for the foreseeable future, which I can understand from his perspective. He needs to right the wrongs done to his mate, but maybe one day he'll understand I had my own wrongs to settle as well.

"I know we need to be here right now," I say, "but if there's anything we can do from afar, please let us know."

River grins, his gaze moving between Kyler and me.

"Getting bored already with the domesticated lifestyle?" Then, he holds his hands up in defeat as my mate growls at him. "Easy. It was just a joke. Everything is handled for now. We're focusing on the pack for now and using witches to make sure we're getting the truth out of everyone connected to Astor."

Huh. Maybe I need some witchy friends in my life. Then I could force the truth out of Jules.

As soon as the thought enters my mind, I let it go. She'll talk to me when she's ready. I just have to keep reminding myself of that when thoughts of strangling her try to take over.

"Good. Hopefully this will be over before most people even know it was something," Kyler says, the side of his leg brushing against mine.

The mere touch makes me wish we were alone, but I'm not sending River and Jules off together just so I can get laid. I made a choice to take responsibility for my sister, suffering libido be damned.

There will be plenty of people around tonight, my wolf says. *I'm sure they'll be happy to keep an eye on her while we have some fun.*

My wolf and Kyler's have had more alone time than our human halves, but I'm not complaining. Her happiness is at least keeping my bitchiness in check.

River rubs his palms over his jeans. "Agreed. Well, I think I should go find my parents. We have some catching up to do as well."

"I could come with you," Jules says, her voice hopeful and eyes bright.

River shakes his head and offers her a smile. "We talked about this. You'll meet them tonight, though."

Her lower lip juts out, and she falls back onto the couch cushions, proving that we've all made the right choice. Jules is a child. She's been emotionally and physically abused, and while she might be strong and capable as a wolf shifter, she has a lot of growing up to do.

I'm just thankful that River understands that, unlike my first mate.

Jules will have better than I did. At least, moving forward.

———

Dawsyn's party is in full effect, but I've had more than my fair share of peopling for the evening and, thankfully, so has Kyler.

The transfer of power between father and daughter was quick. Roman and Dawsyn were joined by Andie, the pink-haired witch who had healed River. Another elder witch with waist-length grey hair was there as well, but she didn't take part in the actual ceremony, just seemed to be watching over it.

When it was done, Dawsyn turned to her people—eyes bright with the energy she's gained, thanks to the full access she now has to the pack—and told us all to enjoy the night, as we have many things to celebrate and be thankful for.

She's right. For years, I took this life for granted. I'm

more than happy to now have the chance to celebrate the little things.

Like right now.

Stealing my wolf's idea from earlier, I follow Kyler to the middle of the pack forest, finally alone in our human forms for the first time in a week.

Just as I open my mouth to announce that we're probably far enough away from the party, he turns around and pins me to the nearest tree, practically growling. "Not touching you like I want to for the past seven days has been a torture that I know I can't live with long term."

He's not alone in that thought. As much as I love Jules, trying to hide my attraction to Kyler around her isn't going to work. Not that I plan on jumping him in front of her, but abstaining from sex in the house so she doesn't hear... I'll need to ask Dawsyn how she handles that with her kids.

For now, I'll take a good fucking in the middle of the forest to hold me over.

"Show me just how tortured you've been," I tell Kyler with a wicked grin on my face.

He releases me and drops to his knees, his hands pulling at my jeans with an urgency that I'm not sure either of us has ever felt until this moment.

I start kicking off my shoes to help, and he has my lower half naked in record time. My hands go to his shoulders to pull him back up, but he has other plans.

Kyler is slow to rise, first kissing his way up my thighs and then dragging his tongue over my very needy pussy.

My legs part for him without thought, and I pull in a harsh breath as he sucks on my very sensitive nub.

"If your cock isn't between my legs in the next few seconds, I'm going to be...politely angry," I tell him, not sounding nearly as scary as I intend to, thanks to my breathy voice.

"As long as I get to taste you more later, you can have whatever part of me that you want first," he says, finally standing and shoving down his own pants.

I don't even wait for his jeans to get halfway down his thighs before I jump up, wrapping my legs around his waist and holding on to his neck. "I want all of you. Now and always."

He positions his dick at my center and drives into me at the same time he repeats my words, "Now and always."

I know we only have this life together, but that doesn't lessen the intensity of our bond. Kyler is my *now*, and no matter what, he'll forever be a part of my always. Even if we don't remember each other in the next life, having him as mine in this one is something I'll never regret.

Thank you so much for reading Fractured Mates! This is my first full-length standalone in the Mystics and Mayhem world and I'm so happy with how it turned out! Hopefully you agree :) Flip the page for more details on this world and for ways to connect with me!

Mystics and Mayhem

If this is your first trip into the Mystics and Mayhem, welcome! If not, hello again :) For our first timers, the book you've just read—Fractured Mates—is part of the second phase within Mystics and Mayhem and the first standalone within this world!

Check out the list of all the Paranormal Romance stories included in this world below. Ones where you'll always find fierce, yet relatable leading ladies and strong alpha males who sweep them off their feet, along with humor and intrigue that will keep you turning the pages.

While you don't have to read the series in any particular order as there are no spoilers between each one, this is the recommended reading order:

Broken Court (Lucinda and Finn)
Dark Fae Cursed — Dark Fae Freed — Dark Fae
Unrivaled
Boxed Set with Bonus Content

Luna Marked (Cait and Roman—Dawsyn's Parents)
Wolf Kissed — Wolf Taken — Wolf Mated
Boxed Set with Bonus Content
Scorned by Blood (Amersyn and Maciah)
Vampire Heir — Vampire Ash — Vampire Vow
Boxed Set with Bonus Content
Fated to the Wolf (Andie and Foster)
Shifted Magic — Altered Magic — Forged Magic
Boxed Set with Bonus Content
The Hidden Realm (Dawsyn and Cillian)
A Dragon's Wolf — A Dragon's Curse — A Dragon's
Fate
Boxed Set with Bonus Content
Standalones
A Pack Christmas — Fractured Mates

There will likely be at least one more standalone in this world. If you want to stay updated on all the bookish things, or have any questions, join my reader group Heather Renee's Book Warriors on Facebook or send me an email anytime at HeatherReneeAuthor@yahoo.com.

I hope you enjoy this world as much as I have!

Stay in Touch

Find Heather on Facebook:
Reader Group
Want to talk all things books and get updates before anyone else? Come hang with me in my reader group:
Heather Renee's Book Warriors

Author Page
Teaser and big updates are also posted here:
Heather Renee Author

Newsletter:
I send this out sporadically, so don't worry. You won't ever be spammed by me and you get a couple goodies when you sign up!
http://smarturl.it/HeatherReneeNL

Also by Heather Renee

A Christmas weekend in the East Texas Pack filled with ten different POVs, mayhem, laughs, a new mateship, and so much more!

Fractured Mates

A standalone second-chance fated mates novel featuring a food obsessed wolf shifter with trust issues and the protector she never asked for, but can't help falling for.

Individual Series

Raven Point Pack Series

A complete Upper Young Adult Paranormal Romance series featuring wolves, witches, vengeance, and fated mates.

Shadow Veil Academy

A complete Upper Young Adult Urban Fantasy Academy series featuring shifters, elves, witches, and more.

Elite Supernatural Trackers

A complete New Adult Urban Fantasy series featuring witches, demons, a smart-mouthed female lead, alpha males, and a snarky fairy sidekick.

Royal Fae Guardians

A complete Young Adult Urban Fantasy series featuring fae, magic users, a sweet romance, along with snark and humor.

Blood of the Sea Series

A complete Young Adult Paranormal Romance series featuring vampires, open seas adventures, and the occasional pirate.

Standalone Books

Ignite Me - A spicy wolf shifter story featuring a lost heir, the mate who doesn't want her, and the enemies who wish them dead.

Marked Paradox - A Young Adult fae story about a realm divided and one fae to bring them back together.

Contemporary Romance Books with Harper Reed:

The Wicked Duet

A mafia romance with enemies-to-lovers, forced proximity, and a happily-ever-after after more than a bit of unaliving...

Ruthless Truths

Tangled Deceit

The Unexpected Series

A Spicy RomCom trilogy featuring three best friends and their happily-ever-afters!

A Mutually Beneficial Proposal

A Mutually Beneficial Mistake

A Mutually Beneficial Secret

Standalones

A Royal Oops

A Spicy RomCom with royal antics, an epic second chance romance, and a kingdom that needs their new queen.

About the Author

Heather Renee is a USA Today Bestselling author who lives in Oregon. She writes Paranormal Romance and Urban Fantasy novels with a mixture of romance, humor, and sass. Her love of reading eventually led to her passion of writing and giving the gift of escapism.

When Heather's not writing, she's spending time with her loving husband and beautiful daughter, going on their own adventures. She loves to hear from her fans, so visit her website: www.HeatherReneeAuthor.com and check out the Contact Me page for ways to connect.

www.ingramcontent.com/pod-product-compliance
Lightning Source LLC
Chambersburg PA
CBHW050749190726
48285CB00005B/1597